THE GRAVE
GOURMET

THE GRAVE GOURMET

ALEXANDER CAMPION

KENSINGTON BOOKS
www.kensingtonbooks.com

KENSINGTON BOOKS are published by

Kensington Publishing Corp.
119 West 40th Street
New York, NY 10018

All Kensington titles, imprints and distributed lines are available at special quantity discounts for bulk purchases for sales promotion, premiums, fundraising, educational or institutional use.

Special book excerpts or customized printings can also be created to fit specific needs. For details, write or phone the office of the Kensington Special Sales Manager: Attn. Special Sales Department. Kensington Publishing Corp., 119 West 40th Street, New York, NY 10018. Phone: 1-800-221-2647.

Kensington and the K logo Reg. U.S. Pat. & TM Off.

Library of Congress Card Catalogue Number: 2010923996
ISBN-13: 978-0-7582-4669-1
ISBN-10: 0-7582-4669-2

First Hardcover Printing: July 2010

10 9 8 7 6 5 4 3 2 1

Printed in the United States of America

The first one, of course, can only be for T.,
to whom I owe it all.

Acknowledgments

This book would never have seen the light of day without the expertise and tireless efforts of Lyn Hamilton—author of Lara McClintoch mystery series—who indefatigably steered a fledgling writer away from his flights of fancy back onto the straight and narrow. Tragically, just as the book was going to press, at the age of sixty-five, Lyn lost her very private battle with cancer. Her death was a great loss.

I also owe thanks to a dear friend since college, Dr. Tom Santulli, for all his insights into matters medical. And also to my youngest daughter, Charlotte, who, even in the middle of her final exams at nursing school, found the time to respond to the endless prattle of my questions.

Profound thanks also to my agent, Sharon Bowers, and my editor at Kensington, Martin Biro, who were unsparing with their talent and unwavering in their support and understanding. The fact that they both share my love for Capucine is not inconsequential either.

Prologue

With the consummate petulance endemic to opera divas and French chefs, Jean-Basile Labrousse kicked the bag as hard as he could.

It wasn't vegetables. It felt more like meat.

He kicked again, with a vengeance. He could feel the fibers separate just as if he was flattening a scallop.

It really did feel like meat.

He had been sure it was those *potimarrons* he had ordered; the chestnut flavor of the fall squashes would be at its peak for only another week. The farmer must have dropped them off late Friday night and some careless *commis* had tossed the bag negligently into the walk-in refrigerator heedless that they would go soft as he flitted off for the weekend. Nothing enraged Labrousse more than produce being treated with anything short of adulation.

But this was meat. Absolutely. But no meat was supposed to have been delivered on Friday. Something was wrong. He explored the bag with his toe. Something was definitely very wrong. He lurched back out the door and stabbed at the light switch. The neon overhead stuttered into life. It was a man, in a dark suit, lying on his side, curled into a painfully tight ball, palms flat against each other, elbows pressed against his stomach, legs bunched in with knees almost touching chin. Labrousse knelt down and peered intently. The eyes stared fixedly ahead, clouded over like a fish's that would have been quickly rejected at the Rungis market. The man was unquestionably dead. Very dead. Long dead. Labrousse's petulance soared to a new stratum. This was an outrage.

Chapter 1

Capucine Le Tellier rushed into the restaurant. *Late again. I hope he isn't fuming.* She pulled up short at the end of the long zinc bar perpendicular to the front door and scanned the large tobacco-, wine-, and butter-sauce-pungent room for Alexandre. There he was, in the far corner, grinning contentedly as a corpulent waiter in a severe black coat erupted in laughter, shimmying his white floor-length apron as if it were swaying in a breeze.

The covert stares she drew as she walked across the floor sparked a buoyant rush. She preened, straightening, drawing in her tummy, rounding out her buttocks, lifting her breasts against her designer silk blouse. The Sig Sauer automatic holstered at the small of her back nipped into her spine. Her feeling of well-being popped like a soap bubble, drenching her in cold oily dampness.

When she reached Alexandre he rose and swept her in his arms with a stage-whispered whoop. "Absence does indeed make the heart grow fonder," he said, planting an ostentatiously lubricious kiss on her lips.

At the next table—all of two feet away—a shrewish woman in her sixties with blue rinsed hair and a miniature poodle nervously piaffing on the banquette at her side scowled at her husband. "These hussies," she hissed loudly, well within earshot of Alexandre and Capucine. "They think when they cavort with a man twice their age nobody knows what they're after. And him, that bloated old fool, he's as bad as you are, drooling at everything that goes by in a skirt."

At precisely that instant the waiter, who had scuttled away at Capucine's approach, returned, bowed slightly, and handed her a flute of champagne. "*Bonsoir,* Madame l'Inspecteur. You've come just in the nick of time. Monsieur, your husband, his stories are just too good. I can't tear myself away to go to my other tables. They are all getting impatient."

After the waiter left Alexandre winked at his wife affectionately. "My dear, your self-control is admirable. I could see you itching to explain to the poor man that "inspecteurs" have been called "lieutenants" for over a decade and then give him a long lecture on the hierarchical structure of the *Police Judiciaire.*"

Capucine laughed. "*Au contraire.* I'm sure he knows far more about the police than he would like. He hangs on to "inspecteur" because it sounds quaint and inoffensive and fits right in with the opera boulevard libretto restaurant people love so much. Also it sounds far more exalted and he's anxious to please such a revered restaurant critic as you." She crinkled her nose coquettishly.

The woman at the next table leaned toward them, openly eavesdropping.

"And by the way," Capucine said in a clear voice, darting a sideways glance at the woman, "you haven't been twice my age for all of eight years." She smiled sweetly at the woman whose brows had creased in her struggle with the arithmetic. The woman jerked away indignantly.

Alexandre hiked his eyebrows. "Are you harrying the hapless bourgeoisie as a result of insufficient job gratification?" he asked with the barest hint of hopefulness.

"*Pas du tout*. Actually, as it happens, we finally made an arrest on that insider trading case I'm in charge of. I was showered with kudos," Capucine said with an ironic smirk.

Alexandre looked at his wife levelly. "But something's wrong."

Capucine tapped her menu irritably on the glowing whiteness of the tablecloth. "We've been over this a thousand times. I loathe white-collar crime work. Look, I mortified my parents by joining the police so I could be on the streets with real people, dealing with real passions, real crimes. But all I got was endless hours in front of a computer screen. I'm in a trap. I might as well be an accountant with a green eyeshade and my sleeves hitched up with armbands. Believe it or not, most of the people in my department actually leave their guns in the boxes they came in, still wrapped in the original oily paper, and only take them out once every six months to do their mandatory fifteen minutes on the range."

"My love, what an enigma you are. You're on the cutting edge of the police force and all you want to do is pound the pavements like a flatfoot in search of vulgar wife beaters and muggers."

"Don't start. I know your theories about my need to liberate myself from the yoke of my parents' genteel upbringing in order to validate my existence, blah, blah, blah. It's all very nice and well put and all, but the truth of the matter is it makes no sense to pursue a career that bores you comatose."

"That's for dead sure. A job without fervor is like a meal without cheese. Like a kiss without a moustache," Alexandre exclaimed with a raised finger.

"Don't ever think of growing a moustache!" Capucine said with mock alarm.

Alexandre laughed. "Not likely, I was just sympathizing with you. But sooner or later they're bound to respond to all those applications you've made for another section.

Wasn't your *Oncle* Etienne going to pull a string? Since he's Director of the Minister of the Interior's cabinet, his string is bound to be a hawser."

"It backfired. I got the call this afternoon. My request is permanently denied on the grounds that I'm allegedly just too good at what I do. So, my last resort is to take the *commissaire*'s exam and get promoted to senior-grade officer—"

"I knew we wouldn't escape the lecture on the hierarchical structure of the *Police Judiciaire*," Alexandre said interrupting.

"Oh, you're impossible! What I mean is becoming a commissaire is much more than just a promotion. It means joining a whole new hierarchy. It would be like starting all over again. I'd have to do another internship and I'd get to pick the place. You can bet I'd choose a small precinct in a poor neighborhood as far away from the financial brigade as I could get."

"Sounds straightforward enough. Why didn't you think of that months ago?"

"I did, but, as that good woman so tactfully pointed out, I'm just a child. I'm twenty-eight and you have to be thirty to be a commissaire. Unless,"—she paused—"one of the top brass authorizes it." She pursed her lips slightly and pianoed the table with her fingertips. "I'm going to see *Commissaire Principal* Tallon in the *Brigade Criminelle* tomorrow morning and see if he'll do it."

"And if he won't?"

"Well, then I think I may just quit."

Alexandre beamed and beckoned the waiter over. It was not clear to Capucine if the smile was for the waiter or at the idea of her quitting the police.

Chapter 2

Capucine bit the inside of her lip until she could taste the salt of her blood and willed herself not to wither as Commissaire Principal Tallon shook his head in dismay. It was exactly her father's look when she was being taken to task for some adolescent peccadillo.

"Lieutenant, your request is entirely unreasonable," Tallon said, snapping over another page in Capucine's file. "According to this"—he tapped the bundle of papers— "your first year in the fiscal branch has been very successful. Your fitness evaluations are exemplary. I can understand your desire for promotion and I'm sure your *divisonaire* will be happy to endorse your application for the commissaire's exam when you reach the minimum age in—what is it?—two years. Be patient."

"Monsieur le Commissaire Principal, I have spent my entire year in fiscal trying to get out. When I graduated from the academy I requested the Brigade Criminelle but was dumped into the fiscal squad simply because my father is an investment banker. I didn't join the police force to do accounting work. It's not about becoming a commissaire. Every time I apply for a transfer I get turned down. It's clear that the only way I'm going to get into *La Crim* is as a commissaire. Sir, I'd do anything to get away from classroom problems and into real life."

"Real life?" Tallon pursed his lips in the ghost of a smirk, looking her up and down, clearly taking in the black Bill Blass suit she had picked out with such care that morning, convinced that it gave her a tough, street-smart look she was sure would go down well.

The demon of indignation gripped Capucine. She half rose, leaned far over the desk, her weight on the balls of her feet, palms flat on its scarred top. "Commissaire," she said, "I might as well be working at my father's bank. I have yet to arrest anyone who has ever held a gun in his life." She paused. "I've only drawn my own gun on the range. That's just not police work." She felt she was trembling slightly and sat back down with a thump.

Tallon smiled. "I take your point. I'm not very keen on accounting myself. I can't even balance my checkbook." His mood had changed perceptibly. Capucine was not sure if it was her gumption or the view of her breasts she had offered when she leaned over. Either would do. She thanked her lucky stars she had felt omitting a bra was essential to the tough-guy look. But instead of talking on Tallon had plunged back into her file, grunting and occasionally inexpertly poking at his computer keyboard. Capucine fidgeted. The meeting had slipped away from her again.

Just as the silence became unbearable, the phone rang. Tallon glanced at the caller ID screen. His face tightened. He held up his hand. "One moment. I have to take this." He grunted monosyllabically into the telephone in the liquid diphthongs of French virility, occasionally making notes on a scratch pad.

Capucine sneaked a look at Tallon's computer monitor. The screen was one she was all too familiar with, the Police Judiciare data bank on private citizens. She boggled.

The file was headed, "d'Arbeaumont de Huguelet, Alexandre Edouard." Alexandre, her Alexandre.

Tallon was still engrossed in his conversation. Finally he nodded. "Yes, sir. . . . Of course. . . . If you insist. . . . I'll take charge myself. . . . Right. . . . I'll have a team there in half an hour. . . . Yes. . . . Yes. . . . Of course, sir."

He put the phone down and stared contemplatively at Capucine for a few beats. "You know, Lieutenant, the gods just might be smiling at you. That was my boss's boss, the *contrôleur general*. He dumped something in my lap that could get you seconded to the Brigade Criminelle for a week, if you want it. Enough to give you a taste of how things work here and see if you have the stomach for it."

Capucine beamed. "Of course I want it, Commissaire."

"Let me ask you a question, Lieutenant. Do you by any chance happen to know anything about the owner of that fancy restaurant, Diapason, Chef somebody or other?"

"Jean-Basile Labrousse. He's very famous. My husband knows him. Actually my husband knows almost everyone in the restaurant business. He's the restaurant critic for the *Monde*."

"I know," Tallon said, tapping his screen with a fingernail. "I was just reading up on him. Anyway, it seems the *président-directeur général* of Renault has been found dead in the refrigerator of this good Chef Labrousse."

"Good Lord. Poor Jean-Basile. He must be distraught."

"It might make some sense to assign you to this case temporarily. I don't doubt that through your husband you'll have some useful insights into the restaurant business. Anyway I'm over a barrel. I need someone right away and the only lieutenant not up to his eyeballs in work, Lieutenant Rivière, is away on a training course all this week. If you want you can start up the investigation. Examine the crime scene, take the initial depositions, make sure the forensic people are set up, just like they taught you at the academy. You can hand it over to Rivière when he gets back on Monday. The experience might dissuade you from wanting to do this sort of work. You'd have to start right away. If you agree, I'll square it with your boss."

"Commissaire, of course I'll do it. But what happened? People don't just get murdered in three-star restaurants. It's unthinkable."

"Lieutenant, don't get ahead of yourself. It's probably not a murder. So far it's just a dead guy in a refrigerator. If it wasn't for who the dead guy is, the local commissariat would be handling it. But since it's who it is, it came to me. And since you happened to be sitting in my office, and since through your husband you probably know more about the restaurant business than anyone else in this building, and since you're certainly qualified to launch a homicide case, it makes some sense for you to lend a hand."

"Did the inspecteur général supply any details? Do we know what he died of?"

"The guys from the local commissariat are already convinced it's just a case of bad food. It doesn't look all that good for Labrousse. He discovered the body. The local guys seem to think Labrousse panicked and stuffed the body in the refrigerator and took all weekend to find the courage to call us."

"Labrousse would never do anything like that."

"We'll find out, don't worry. You're in charge of the team for the week and you'll report to me. But get two things through your head. This doesn't go beyond one week and you can't fuck up. I want results and I want them fast. Clear?"

"Of course, sir."

"I mean it. Don't think for an instant that this is a permanent reassignment or that it has any bearing on your application for the commissaire's exam whatsoever."

"Oh, yes sir," Capucine said, releasing an insuppressible smile to flutter across the room like a butterfly.

"Go collect Rivière's brigadiers and get out there. Here's the address of the restaurant," he said, needlessly handing her a page from his scratch pad. "The forensic guys are already informed. Make sure you kick the guys from the local commissariat out right away. Don't let them hang around. They get their fingers into everything. Make it clear that you're in charge and check everything out carefully. Report back to me in the afternoon so we can decide what to do next."

Capucine started out the door. "Oh, one last thing, Lieutenant, Rivière's squad has a bit of an—ahh—a reputation. They're good enough, but they need a heavy hand. A very heavy hand. Don't forget that. Now get out there." Tallon smiled at her with a smile that was, just maybe, a bit warmer than one could expect from a commissaire principal. Capucine thanked the guardian angel who had talked her out of the bra when she was choosing her outfit that morning.

Chapter 3

Capucine's little rosy cloud of bubbly anticipation had gradually grown into a huge dark thundercloud of frustration and self-recrimination. After a fruitless half hour of striding up and down the labyrinthine corridors of the legendary Escalier A, Troisième étage—hallowed home of La Crim—trying to locate A-36, the office of Rivière's brigadiers, she was close to tears of frustration. Just as she was about to give up and go back to the ground floor receptionist and ask for directions a third time she heard a deep, throaty female voice. "Sometimes Rivière is just too much. I can see him taking a week off for a real training course, but computers! Give me a fucking break. He has trouble even turning his on. I'll bet he just saw it was in Nice and signed up without bothering to read what it was about. He'll be back with one hell of a tan and we'll have gone stir crazy staring at four walls for a whole fucking week."

A delicate but clearly male voice answered, "Isabelle, your own proclivities should be a better conduit to the understanding of our officer's mind. Those courses are ideal for picking up girls. You should know perfectly well that's Rivière's main interest in life."

"Listen, you creepy little faggot . . ." the reply began, but Capucine had caught sight of a miniscule black plastic tag high up on the door frame—"A-36"—and she peeked cautiously around the doorway. The female voice emanated from a young woman in her middle twenties whose muscular body, straight as the trunk of a small tree, supported a head that would have been handsome had the mousy brown hair not been roughly hacked off, apparently by the owner without benefit of a mirror. Her antagonist was a diametric opposite, lithe and fluid as a ballet dancer, with flowing golden locks of a splendor not equaled in shampoo commercials. There was also a third person in the room, a gargantuan North African who glowered silently at his companions.

"Is this A-36?" Capucine asked. The North African mimed "not a clue" by shrugging, hiking his eyebrows, and puffing out his cheeks. The female looked at him and shook her head in scorn—"It's the office number, you idiot"—and, turning to Capucine, "Yes, madame, it is. Can we help you?"

"So, you must be Brenarouch, Martineau, and Lemercier. I'm Lieutenant Le Tellier. You've been assigned to me for a week. Well, actually, I'm filling in for Lieutenant Rivière for a week and we've all been put on a case and really have to get going right away, but it might be nice to spend a few minutes getting to know each other first," Capucine said in a rush.

The North African, eyeing Capucine's suit, was visibly nonplussed. "Look, uh, Lieutenant, 'scuse me. This is a Crim squad. There must be some sort of mix-up. What is it you do, social work or something like that? You can't be filling in for our lieutenant."

"I'm sorry, m'dam, my partners have no manners," the woman said with exaggerated politeness. "The big one is Brigadier Benarouche, Momo, and the cutie over there is Brigadier Marineau, David, and I'm Brigadier Lemercier,

Isabelle." She stood rigidly at attention. Capucine ignored the cynicism.

How far away from the compulsive discipline and order of the fiscal branch this all was, Capucine thought as she surveyed the tiny office. Papers and files were heaped on two desks pushed together in front of the window, the pile of detritus crowned with a Sig in a holster, a box of ammunition, and three pairs of handcuffs. One wall was adorned with the traditional French clerical office cliché: posters of enormous brightly colored multihulled racing yachts skimming over brilliant tropical waters at breakneck speeds. Incongruously, in the middle of these halcyon images was a small Polaroid of an unusually violent-looking young man apparently suffering a serious seizure. He was fat, sweating, and clearly straining desperately to get at the camera or its operator. His mouth was wide open, caught in the extreme of a scream. He heaved Herculeanly at unseen restraints holding him to the chair. Even trapped in the small, dun Polaroid he was terrifying.

"I see you're admiring Omar," David said chuckling. "He's by far the worst guy we've ever had in here. We hauled him in for some routine background questioning a few months ago. It was like catching the Loch Ness monster when you were fishing for sardines. He went berserk and tried to kill us all. Three guys came in from next door and it took the six of us to get him cuffed to that chair," he said, indicating the twisted chair against the wall. "He destroyed the chair, as you can see, and he got a few solid head butts in on Isabelle. Finally we had to inject him with a sedative. We let him sit in a cell downstairs for the night and threw him out in the morning. A naturally deranged psychotic. A force of nature. I'm sure he's killed someone by now." David smiled happily and Isabelle burst into cheerful laughter.

"Why on earth didn't you arrest him?"

"For what? Everyone tries to punch Isabelle. You probably will too even if you're only here for a week," David said. "Say, is this for real? An actual case? Are we going to get the hell out of here?"

"Oh, yes, absolutely. We have to get going right away. We're already late. A bigwig, the president of Renault, was found dead in Diapason."

"Where?" Momo asked.

"It's a very fancy restaurant in the Seventh. We'll have to take my car. There were none left in the pool. Come on. Off we go."

With the whoops of schoolchildren and knowing glances the three brigadiers collected their guns and hand-cuffs, secreted them in various recesses of their clothing, and shuffled out the door, preceding Capucine.

On the way down the hall Capucine couldn't help over-hearing David whispering angrily to Isabelle. "This beats everything. Rivière sneaks off for a week in the sun and we get stuck with some kooky loser on an asshole case. What next?"

Chapter 4

It was a tight fit for the four of them in Capucine's compact Renault Clio. Momo took the wheel with Capucine next to him while David and Isabelle squeezed uncomfortably into the back. Momo weaved in and out of traffic cursing sotto voce. Normally an aggressive driver, he was greatly affronted by the little car. Clios were notoriously underpowered to begin with and Capucine's had been hamstrung by an automatic transmission.

"*Merde,* Lieutenant, we can't show up at a crime scene in this thing. Some of us have reputations to keep up. Where did you get this piece of crap? At a toy store?" he asked, angrily hammering the accelerator into the floorboard with only minimal effect.

"My husband has pretty much the same reaction. It was a bad choice. I thought it was very cute when I bought it. You should see it with the air-conditioning on. Then it really doesn't move." Capucine laughed cheerfully.

Out of the corner of her eye Capucine caught David and Isabelle silently mouthing the word "cute" and rolling their eyes.

Within a few minutes Momo tired of his inability to accelerate through traffic and indignantly banged the magnetized flashing blue dome light on the roof of the car. "At least you've got one of these things," he said with a cynical sideward glance at Capucine.

"Oh, yes, there's even a siren, but I've never used it."

"Let's not try it now. It would probably stop the car," David said. Isabelle elbowed him in the ribs delightedly.

Traffic evaporated in front of the throbbing blue light and they arrived quickly in the Seventh, the arrondissement of narrow streets, stately ministries, and imposing embassies, where a machine-gun–toting policeman seemed to guard almost every other entrance. Le Diapason, at the apex of a sharply pointed corner, jutted out grandly like the bow of a stately yacht. Two police vehicles, a van and an unmarked sedan, made conspicuous by their oversized jutting antennas, were double-parked on the street.

Inside, a covey of uniformed police from the local commissariat milled around at loose ends. When Capucine strode in purposefully followed by her shambling brigadiers only one or two of the uniformed police gave them even a cursory glance. Taken aback at the lack of reaction, Capucine was at a momentary loss at how to proceed. Irritated at the hesitation, Isabelle snorted and went up to one of the policemen. "*Salut, mon pote*, what's happening?" she said.

"What the hell does it look like? We get to stand around for hours doing fuckall until the P.J. turn up. Then we go back to the commissariat. It's highly motivating. Are you guys here to relieve us?"

"We sure are. Where's your officer?"

The policeman disdainfully nodded at a large eight-top in a back corner where five men sat. "The fat guy," the policeman said. "He's probably hoping they're going to serve him lunch."

A florid man with a protuberant potbelly ballooning

out of a cheap suit had already started to walk over. He came up to Isabelle and stuck out his hand. "Lieutenant Duchamps. Madame, are you in charge?"

"Not even close. Try that one," she replied, jerking her thumb at Capucine.

Suspecting some sort of joke was being played on him, Duchamps walked over to Capucine and stuck out his hand again, "Lieutenant Duchamps of the Seventh Arrondissement West Commissariat. And you are?"

"Lieutenant Le Tellier, Police Judiciare."

"Ah, finally. We've been waiting for you all morning. "I'll give you the grand tour and leave you to it. I have no idea why you people were called in. Looks like a perfectly straightforward case of food poisoning to me. Some restaurant employee panicked and stuffed the stiff in the fridge," Duchamps said peevishly. "If I could get these guys down to the commissariat"—he nodded at the large round table where he had been sitting—"I'd have the answer out of them in no time, but I guess I don't have to teach the P.J. anything about that." He guffawed unpleasantly and glanced disdainfully at Capucine to see if she would share in the joke. She looked at him levelly.

"Anyway, those guys are the head chef, who apparently owns the place, the number two chef, the sommelier, and the maître d'." Capucine recognized them all. Three wore the lugubrious look de rigueur at wakes, but Labrousse was genuinely stricken, staring down at the table, slack mouthed, like a drunk waiting to be taken home after the party is over. Her heart went out to him.

"The head chef says he discovered the body when he came in this morning. The other three showed up right after we got here. There are thirty-two other employees who turned up later. We interviewed them briefly, fingerprinted them, and sent them home. This is a list of their names and the phones where they can be reached for the rest of the day," he said, handing her a sheet of paper.

"The story is the bigwig, Delage, ate here on Friday evening with a pal and then left. No one admits to knowing anything more."

Capucine nodded.

"Anyway, I kept those four here for you guys to have something to bite into," Duchamps said, jabbing the air behind his back with his thumb.

"That's perfect," said Capucine.

"Body's in the kitchen back here," Duchamps said, starting for the back. They pushed through a pair of swinging doors with small glass ports—superfluous precautions intended to prevent waiters from banging into each other—and into a room as sterile as an operating theater in white tile and brushed stainless steel.

"There you go," Duchamps said, pointing at an open metal door in the back wall. "The chef said the door was shut tight when he arrived." The body was just inside the sill, lying on its side, hideously contorted from the pains of death. The victim's expensive flannel suit was twisted around the limbs, and the toes of his shoes were deeply scuffed. A small pool of thin white fluid had congealed on the floor next to the mouth. Close up the odor was overpowering. Behind the body, the walk-in was lined with steel shelves stacked with plastic containers and wooden pallets of fruits, eggs, and vegetables. Given the empty spaces, it was obvious the Monday morning deliveries had been turned away by the police.

It was the first time Capucine had ever seen a dead body. The room spun and she felt her breakfast rise in her throat. She spoke more sharply to Duchamps than she intended. "*Très bien*. We've got it now. No need for your people to remain any longer," and turned on her heel before he could reply. She beckoned to Isabelle. "Brigadier, I have to deal with the restaurant staff out there for a few moments. Make sure nobody touches the body until the forensic people turn up and don't let anyone move or handle anything until I get back."

It was all she could do to get out of the kitchen without throwing up.

In the dining room Labrousse had left the table and was roving aimlessly, straightening chairs and smoothing table pads. He looked even more disoriented than when she had arrived. Capucine walked up to him and touched his arm. Labrousse started.

"Ca . . . Capucine. What are you doing here?" He paused, his mouth partially open. "Of course. You are with the Police Judiciaire. I had forgotten. I always think of you simply as Alexandre's dear wife." He spoke dully with a thick tongue, as if doped. Capucine grasped his arm above the elbow in a motherly gesture and gently led him to a table in a far corner.

He told Capucine his story in a despondent monotone. He had arrived at the restaurant punctually at eight that morning. He always came in early on Mondays to make sure nothing was amiss and to plan out his week. He had gone straight to the walk-in to see if any of the produce had lost its freshness. He had discovered the body. He had recognized it was Delage. He had called the police. That was it.

"I understand Monsieur Delage was here for dinner on Friday. Did you talk to him?" Capucine asked.

"Yes, I came out briefly in the middle of the service to greet the patrons. I almost never do that, but I just could not ignore Jean-Louis. I chatted with him for a few moments. Sadly, that was all the time I could spare." Labrousse paused. "This is a deep wound for me. I've known poor Jean-Louis for nearly thirty-five years. We were friends when we were students." His eyes focused on the middle distance as he lived his memories.

"Do you remember what he ate?"

"No, but a copy of what he ordered will be in my office.

We keep everything until the accountant comes in on Wednesdays. They're on a clipboard on my desk."

Capucine motioned David over and asked him to go to the office and see if he could find the dupe sheets.

In a few minutes he came back with a thick stack of greasy scribbled forms clipped to an aluminum board. He also had a sheet of cream coverstock paper folded into thirds.

"Here you go," he said. "I also found this. I think it's a menu that shows the number codes they use on the dupes." Capucine decided that there was hope for David.

Labrousse thumbed through the pile of forms and held one out to Capucine. "Voilà. Table 8."

After the effort he fell silent again, exhausted. He looked at Capucine with doleful eyes. "I have no idea what to do. I suppose I must do the dinner service. I hope I can find the energy."

At that point the four members of the forensic squad arrived noisily, heading directly for the kitchen pushing a rattling gurney and carrying a seemingly absurd amount of equipment in black bags and shiny aluminum cases.

"Jean-Basile," Capucine continued gently once the racket died down, familiarly using his given name for the first time in her life. "Things may be a little complicated. I don't think the police will let you open for several days. You need to go home now and get some rest. A brigadier will take you and stay there with you. When you've had a chance to recover I'll ask you to come to the prefecture and I'll take your deposition. There's no rush at all." She talked gently to him for a while, shocked at his disarray. When he seemed to have regained some composure she beckoned to David and told him to take Labrousse to his apartment in a cab and stay with him until they were called to the Quai.

When Labrousse left she went over to the eight-top where the three staff members huddled silently. She kept all three at the table and began with the *chef-saucier*. He told his story in the overloud monotone of a man interviewed at the scene of a road accident. He had arrived at nine thirty to find the police from the commissariat already there and had been barred from the kitchen. He had no useful information about Friday night as he had not left the kitchen nor even looked through the windows of the double doors during the entire service. Capucine let him leave.

The maître d' had arrived a few minutes after the *chef-saucier*. He remembered Delage at dinner on Friday quite well. He had eaten with another man, a certain Martin Fleuret, a lawyer, also well known to the restaurant. He had paid the bill with a *Carte Bleue* Visa card. Both had left a little after ten thirty.

"No, no, hold on," he added. "Just as the other man left, Président Delage came back to wash his hands," he said, using the polite euphemism for going to the toilet.

"Did he look at all ill?" Capucine asked.

"Not in the slightest. He actually seemed quite happy. Almost proud of himself. He went to the WC in the front of the restaurant for a few minutes and left right after. I'm sure of it. I wished him good night as he walked through the doors."

"Do you know if he was taken home by his driver?" Capucine asked.

"I wouldn't think he was," the maître d' said. "He didn't like to make his driver wait in the street while he ate and he liked to walk after eating if the weather was fine. He told me that many times."

"And did you see if he came back later? Say, because he had lost something or didn't feel well?"

"No, definitely not. If he had, the coat check girl or the hostess would have alerted me."

Capucine sent the maître d' off, telling him that that he

would be convoked to the Quai des Orfèvres in the next few days to sign a deposition.

Only the sommelier appeared unaffected by the death. Even in jeans and a leather jacket he continued to exude a professional aura of saturnine omniscience. Perhaps it was the tight shiny helmet of brilliantined hair. His lips were pinched in irritation. "Lieutenant, I have been prevented from examining my *cave*. It's vital I determine if any damage has been done. Also, there can be no question of the police traipsing around down there without my supervision. Some of the bottles are irreplaceable and absolutely cannot be disturbed or even touched. Absolutely no one must be allowed in my cellar without me. Is that perfectly clear?"

"Monsieur Rolland, surely you remember me?"

"*Oh là là*. Madame de Huguelet, I'm so sorry. I just didn't recognize you without your husband. Forgive me. You have no idea how upsetting this all is. All I can think of is an army of barbarian flics pulling all my bottles down and shaking them while they dust for fingerprints or whatever. That would be an unconscionable catastrophe."

"Don't give it a second thought. I'll supervise the investigation of the cellar myself. Tell me about Président Delage. How did he behave during dinner?"

"Madame, it was the same as it always was with him. He ordered only one wine, a Forts de Latour 2000, the sort of thing he always drank. Sound, expensive without being extravagant, uninspired. He was never willing to take an adventure with his wine. He and his guest drank sparingly. There was well over a quarter of a bottle remaining when the meal was over. I poured for them myself, but each time I came up he and his guest fell silent. Of course, most people do that. He refused an after-dinner *alcool* and voilà, that was that. Do you think I might run downstairs for a quick look to see if everything is in order?" His eyes darkened in anger when denied and darkened further still when Capucine told him he was to go home.

Abruptly, the gurney returned, pushed at speed by two men, far more quietly this time now that it was laden with the body in a thick black plastic body bag.

Capucine shot up. "What's this? I gave instructions that nothing was to be touched without my authorization."

"Hey," said one of the forensic experts. "We took all the shots we needed, zipped up, and got rolling. Your brigadier back there thought that was just dandy. Anyway, we don't have all day for amateurs to be poking at our stiff. This one's a real stinker and we need to get it in the reefer fast. If you want to play kissy face with it you can come down when we do the autopsy." The two experts pushed the gurney out the door.

Capucine stormed into the kitchen.

"Brigadier Lemercier, what's the meaning of this? I gave you a direct order that the body was not to be disturbed."

From behind her an sepulchral basso profundo intoned, "Now, now missy," almost as if it were the incarnation of her conscience. She wheeled and was startled to find herself facing a man so pallid and desiccated he could have been the victim himself returned to give his deposition before being driven off. But she intuited it was merely one of the forensic experts whose physiognomy had been molded over the years by occupational mimetism. "You have your work to do, and we have ours. At this stage there is nothing noteworthy about the body," he continued in his astonishing voice.

"Besides," said Isabelle, "it was completely icky." She made a stage pantomime of disgust and pinched her nose. "You definitely wouldn't have liked it. This, by the way, is *Ajudant* Dechery from forensics." Capucine danced a mental jig between reaching for her Sig and bursting into tears.

Behind Dechery she could see the door and inside of the walk-in splotched with gray aluminum fingerprint powder. One expert was taking flash pictures with relentless monotony. A second was putting samples of the produce from the walk-in into small plastic containers.

"Also," continued Dechery, "those idiots from the commissariat left the door to the fridge open all morning. Damn body was ancient enough as it was and they had to warm it up for me. That's where all this stench comes from."

Capucine was barely able to speak through the clenched teeth of her rage. "Were you able to estimate the time of death?"

"My dear, the best I can do is guess and say he had been dead at least two days and probably no more than five or six. Obviously we'll know better once we do the autopsy."

"Any idea of what killed him?"

"Well, I'll tell you. It's a good thing I don't have the money for this sort of place. Certainly looks like food poisoning of some kind. Almost sure to be from bad produce. You can't beat good old *Clostridium botulinum* for a painful death. Do you know what he ate?"

"I was just going to figure that out myself," Capucine said, comparing the dupe sheets and menu codes.

"Here you go. He had pheasant *ravioles* in a pheasant consommé to begin with, then sweetbreads grilled on licorice root, and finished with an avocado soufflé. Doesn't sound too bad, does it?"

"There's nothing on there that screams out botulism unless some of it was canned. But that's all idle speculation. We'll know for sure what caused the death in about a week. The bacteriological cultures of the stomach samples take that long to develop. What makes it a bit simpler is that there are no sources of nonbacteriological poisons in anything he apparently ate. You know, mushrooms or oysters or anything like that. Anyway, you won't hear from us until the cultures are done."

With a sinister, deep laugh Duchamps went back to the walk-in. A white painted outline was visible on the floor and the walls were now almost completely covered with fingerprint powder. When the team moved out to start work on the kitchen, Duchamps closed the door with a metallic clang and affixed a large octagonal orange seal across the jamb. It had a distinguished look, almost as if it was the latest honor Diapason had been awarded.

Chapter 5

That night Capucine was unable to sleep. Woken repeatedly by her squirming and noisy plumping up of pillows, Alexandre finally ironically growled an old French proverb, "Sleep is even more perfect when it's shared with a loved one." Capucine jumped out of bed and stalked off to the living room sofa dragging a needlepoint coverlet, pillow under her arm.

The next morning she was still despondent as she arrived at the headquarters building of the fiscal branch; she didn't have the slightest clue what to do next. The approach to white-collar cases always seemed to flow like water from a spring, but now she was utterly stymied.

Even the unintentional cynicism of the fiscal division's address—122, rue Château des Rentiers, the coupon clippers' castle—failed to cheer her up, as it invariably did even in the worst of her moods.

For lack of anything better, her plan for the day was rudimentary, a quick run-through of her office at Rentiers to deal with any departmental effluvia that might have emerged during the night and then down to the Quai des Orfèvres to sic the three brigadiers on the restaurant staff. If in doubt, keep everyone busy.

She was stunned to see a man installed at her desk, a rather attractive man—a very attractive man, actually—his feet on its top carelessly strewing her meticulously ordered stacks of files, poking amateurishly at the keyboard on his lap—her keyboard, actually—lost in childlike concentration. For a brief, wild flash she thought that the room had been reassigned and this was the new tenant waiting impatiently for her to remove her possessions. But that was impossible. This man just couldn't be in the financial brigade. He didn't look at all like an accountant. He looked more like a rock star, or at least a wannabe rock star: designer jeans, Western belt with a large silver buckle, pistol in an American-looking basket weave quick-draw holster, artful stubble, brown eyes smoldering with brooding eroticism.

As Capucine approached the desk, the liquid mahogany pools of those eyes languidly detached themselves from the monitor and lapped over her body. She felt beyond naked; the pools seemed to coalesce in her intimate crevasses.

"Now it makes perfect sense that Tallon put you on my case," the man leered. "I didn't get it before, but I sure get it now." Capucine blushed, simultaneously outraged and seduced.

Unceremoniously, he dumped the keyboard on the desk. It fell upside down. He uncoiled with serpentine grace. He put out his hand. "Jeanloup Rivière, at your service. I fervently hope." His ogle transformed the phatic into a leaden double entendre.

"B . . . But I thought you weren't due back until Monday."

"Little sister, it turned out to be a goddamn computer course. I spent as much of the day on the beach as I could but that got old fast. So I told them I had been called back for a crisis and here I am. Did you miss me?"

"I've never met you."

"You should have. If I'd been here you wouldn't be

scratching around in the dust with nothing to show for your time."

"How do you know what I've been up to?"

"Little sister, little sister. I've been with Tallon since the ass crack of dawn this morning. The hot news is that he's decided to keep you on the case full-time. And he's put me on another case. A real honey. Some citizen did a woman in and left pieces of her body in twenty different metro stops. More my style, Tallon must think. And the best part is that he's asked me to be your guardian angel. You know, show you the ropes, keep an eye on you and all," Rivière said with a leer so exaggerated it looked like farce.

Despite herself Capucine broke into a smile.

"And the good news just keeps on coming. He's even given you my three musketeers for the duration. They seemed happy enough about that. Momo told me you were way more decorative than I am. Anyhow, let's get our delicious asses out of here and get some work done. We've got to jump-start this puppy."

As they arrived at the Quai des Orfèvres Rivière suddenly dropped his cartoon Lothario routine and switched to caricaturing an aloof superior officer.

He peremptorily ordered Capucine to obtain the names and stations of all the police guards of the official buildings and embassies in the vicinity of Diapason for the night of the incident. Capucine looked blank.

"You know, Lieutenant, the *vigies,* those poor sods who are too dumb to make gendarme rank and spend their days stuck out in front of public buildings like sacks of cabbages. Beats the hell out of me why they get automatic weapons. They can hardly hold them, much less shoot them. I'll bet they're not loaded." Capucine had no idea why he wanted the list. But he wanted it within the hour.

Fifty minutes later Capucine was in Rivière's office being undressed by his eyes once again, this time even more thoroughly. He now seemed to know where all the clips and snaps were. Once his inspection was over he ran his eye down the list, circled two names with a fat marker, and shoved it back at her. "Here. Find out where these two guys are right now. They have stuff to tell us. Get back to me in fifteen minutes."

As she rushed off she lashed out at herself. Here was exactly the sort of man she despised most in life: vulgarly macho and arrogantly stupid. And here she was all a-twiddle, rushing around trying to please him. He was attractive, yes, but her reaction was still despicable.

Within the allotted time frame Capucine returned with the addresses the two vigies were currently guarding. Rivière now seemed to be concentrating on her legs. He was clearly a man of eclectic tastes. "That took long enough. Let's get going."

Their first stop was six hundred yards down the rue de Varenne from Diapason at the entrance to a huge eighteenth-century *hôtel particulier.* Rivière clapped the blue dome light on the roof of his car and bounced it up on the sidewalk at speed, screeching to a halt in front of a doltish policeman in an ill-fitting uniform. As if in a blind rage Rivière jumped out and roughly grabbed the man's body armor.

"You Durand?" he sneered.

"Y . . . Y . . . Yessir!"

"You deserted your post on Friday night. I'm going to take you down to the Quai and write you up right now. This isn't going to be some little review board slap on the wrist. Your ass is going to get fired and you're not going to get a centime of pension when I get through with you. Count on it, my friend!" As he spoke he shook the vigie hard enough to rattle his teeth.

"Sir, please, please, I only stepped to the corner to have one cigarette."

"One! You little shits think you've joined a smoking

club. You think we pay you to stand around on street corners chatting with your buddies without giving a good goddamn about the buildings you're supposed to be guarding. Is that it?"

"Sir, please, I only had two or three cigarettes that night."

"Durand, you're truly pathetic. Two or three, my ass. Did anything unusual happen? Your only hope is to tell me something I might want to know, otherwise I'm going to pull you off duty and put you on write-up right now. Better make it good."

"Sir, please, I didn't really see anything. Nothing. Just this one delivery being made."

"Out with it, Durand."

"I was having a smoke on the corner and having a natter with Vigie Clement, who was guarding the Austrian Embassy just across the street."

"You mean the Austrian embassy that's two hundred yards down the street."

"That's the place. So Clement says to me, 'Check this out. Here are a couple of guys actually making a delivery to that fancy restaurant at 2:30 in the morning. These rich dudes don't know the difference between night and day.' He said two guys were carrying a big bag into the restaurant. That's all, sir. Then I went back to my post. But I didn't see it. Clement did."

"And why didn't you report it when the bulletin went out?"

"Well, it didn't seem all that important, it was just a routine delivery, right, and I couldn't very well have said I was off station, now could I have, sir?"

Back in the car Rivière breathed hard through his nose like a bull in an arena, in the grip of his endorphin rush. Capucine felt she should be humiliated at participating in the shameful bullying of a pitiful human being worthy of her every compassion. But she was almost as exhilarated as Rivière. It was like being on a roller coaster. She wanted to shoot her arms up in the air to intensify her giddiness.

Vigie Clement turned out to be considerably lighter than his colleague and was easily lifted off the pavement. He delivered the entirety of his brief testimony with his heels a good two inches clear of the street. He had walked down from his station to the corner opposite Durand's post. From that vantage point he had had a full view of the side entrance to Diapason. At around 2:30 he had seen two men drive up in a car—manufacturer not noted, much less license plate number—and remove a six-foot-long duffel bag from the trunk. With a man holding each end of the bag they carried it into the restaurant straining under the weight. He had not seen them get back into the car since he had had to return to his post quickly. He was keenly sensitive to the responsibility of his duties and couldn't in all conscience stay away from his post for too long no matter how interesting things were. He was sure the lieutenant would be sympathetic to that.

As he got back into the car Rivière put his hand on Capucine's thigh. "Voilà, little sister. That's how it's done. Now we know how the body got back into the restaurant. I did the hard part. All you have to do is find those two guys. Think you can handle that?"

Chapter 6

The next night again proved sleepless for Capucine. At first light a clamor in the kitchen woke her from a fitful half sleep. She found Alexandre at his massive stove resolutely making omelets, his brow crinkled in concentration. The aroma of *cèpes* richly colored the kitchen. Alexandre never looked this determined so early in the morning.

"Poor *bébé*, Alexandre said, bleary-eyed, "you spent most of the night tossing and turning. And when you did get to sleep you kept mumbling about an astrolabe and a missing chart."

"I remember that. I was dreaming that I was on Columbus's ship and we had no charts and were sailing around in circles."

"Tsk, tsk," Alexandre tsked, gently nudging an omelet with a spatula. "This can't go on. It's not just your distress. Any more sleep deprivation and I won't be able to write my name, much less a restaurant review. But fear not. I have the solution! You need a Sancho Panza to point you in the right direction on this case and I, magnanimous as ever, am volunteering."

The natural feminist in Capucine revolted at the idea of

yet another male mentor. Why did men eternally think women were complete incompetents? Not replying, Capucine went to the Pasquini coffee machine that had been her Christmas extravagance for Alexandre and applied herself to the concoction of a large café au lait. As the steam geysered up through the milk her irritation fell away with the suddenness of a damp bathrobe dropping off her shoulders. Alexandre was right, she *was* tilting at windmills. How silly she was being about it all. The idea of Alexandre jiggling along behind her on a trotting mule made her want to giggle. Her accumulated tension erupted into an attack of schoolgirl silliness. She picked up a colander, put it on her head, and said, "So be it. *Alors*, my faithful squire, what are our plans for the day?"

"See, you're getting better already. My noble master, we are going to do the knightly thing. We're going to have a long leisurely lunch at Diapason and see if we can't start some hares."

Capucine sat bolt upright. "We couldn't possibly do that! You'd never get a reservation. Tallon would never let me take the whole afternoon off. It's not even ethical. Would I be there as a flic or as your wife? I'd be abusing your position. We'd be spying on a friend. Everyone would stare at me."

Alexandre laughed cheerfully as he slid the omelets onto their plates. "I've already spoken to Jean-Basile and he'll make room for us. But you'll have to take that utensil off your head or people really will stare at you."

In the end it was Tallon who convinced her. "Lieutenant, a good soldier always capitalizes on the advantages of his terrain. You have the potential to obtain key insider knowledge. You're here to solve a case, not to explore ethics."

Still harboring misgivings, she parked the Clio illegally on the corner opposite the restaurant and rushed in, fifteen minutes late once again. Alexandre was perched on the

edge of the hostesses' desk, peering intently into the décolleté of the striking young blonde. The hostess smiled back
at Alexandre coquettishly.

As Capucine hurried in Alexandre grinned and said,
"Dear, this is Giselle, who just started two months ago. It
seems her predecessor left because—"

Just as Capucine began to clench her teeth the maître d'
floated up so smoothly he might have been on ice skates.
"*Bonjour,* Madame le Lieutenant," Bouteiller said with a
tight but sincere smile. "Will madame follow me? Your
table is ready." Capucine smirked in silent satisfaction at
the reversal of roles. Normally Alexandre, invariably lion-
ized in restaurants, would be the honored guest. She sailed
past him, gloating, and beckoning with a crooked finger.

At the table Capucine couldn't resist chiding Alexandre.
"You're sadly mistaken, my good squire, if you think un-
bridled randiness is integral to the Sancho Panza role."

Alexandre was saved from the need of a retort by the
sacrosanct rogations of ordering food and drink. As he
carried on his dialogue with the maître d', Capucine looked
around the room. There was not an empty seat. But the
sound of American English did seem conspicuous in the
buzz of conversation. For the thousandth time she wondered why it was such a distinctive trait of Americans to
speak in public places as if they were on stage. Also, there
might be more than the usual number of Japanese. Or
maybe she was just being unusually observant.

In due course the appetizers arrived. For Alexandre a
lobster claw reconstructed from pigeon breast and Brittany *homard* and for Capucine Périgord foie gras on a bed
of pureed noix de Saint-Jacques. Alexandre's nostrils quiv-
ered like a hound dog's. For him life never got better than
this.

Halfway through his lobster he sighed and said, "Let's
get to work. Time to compare notes. I'll show you mine
and then you can show me yours.

"From the press's point of view this is now a dead story. Poor Delage was too dull to be newsworthy. And Renault has done the most boring thing they could and put the chief financial officer temporarily in charge. He's even less newsworthy than Delage and he'll just sit as still as possible trying very hard not to rock the boat until the board appoints a full-time president after an eternal deliberation.

"On the other hand, the rumor mill of well-heeled Paris is cranking full strength. They've decided it's definitely a case of food poisoning. If a bigwig wants to impress a colleague by inviting him here, he's laughed at. 'Are you trying to poison me? What have I done to you?' Overnight poor Jean-Basile has become a laughingstock. It's his worst nightmare."

"But the place is packed," Capucine said.

"You're right, but they're all tourists. Not a member of the establishment in sight," Alexandre said with obvious exaggeration. "If this keeps up Jean-Basile might as well put up a souvenir stand in the front. With that delicious creature up there he'd make a killing selling little Eiffel Towers with thermometers in them."

"The irony of that," Capucine said, "is that the forensic people have now decided it wasn't food poisoning after all. Of course they hem and haw and say nothing will be definite until the cultures are ready in another week, but since the death was from respiratory failure it could only have been the result of a chemical poison, botulism, or bad oysters. Since there were no preserves or oysters on the menu, logically it had to be a chemical poison of some sort. Mind you, they're a little put out that none of the classic poisons showed up in the autopsy, but they're doing another round of tests and hoping for something totally obscure."

Alexandre harrumphed. "And I'm sure they will come up with something. There hasn't been a case of food poisoning in a three-star restaurant in the entire history of France."

Just then the maître d' returned with two *aide-serveurs* bearing tiny silver cups on transparent crystal dishes.

"Madame le Lieutenant, monsieur," Bouteiller said, "this is a little surprise to clear your pallets between courses. Oyster sorbet with a mousse of sweet Melissa, lemon-scent geranium, and verveine," he announced proudly.

"The plot thickens," Alexandre said with a frown.

"I beg your pardon!" the maître d' said with concern.

The meal marched on with its stately cadence. Main courses of rack of lamb raised to inconceivable heights with lemon and coriander for Alexandre and a dish of carrots, kohlrabi, turnips, and radishes brilliantly seasoned with an intricate mixture of Indian spices for Capucine. Then the cheeses, incomparably better than elsewhere, presumably because they were conditioned in a sixteenth-century cellar by a master *affineur*, one of Labrousse's cronies. After, the desserts, strawberries in an undeconstructable sauce that had the aroma of hibiscus but none of the taste for Capucine and a soufflé of pistachios, pralines, and black chocolate for Alexandre. Finally, coffee and a plate of sweet macaroons made with vegetables from Labrousse's own country garden, tilled by horse alone where no chemical had ever penetrated.

Capucine's almost postcoital afterglow was blown away by Labrousse's appearance. He shambled down the aisle between the tables smiling with only the bottom of his face at the few remaining patrons and made his way as directly as he could to Alexandre and Capucine's table. Despite his seemingly insuperable talent in the kitchen he was decidedly more haggard than when Capucine had seen him on Monday. An aide-serveur rushed up with a chair and Labrousse sat down with a thud. *"C'était?"* Labrousse asked with the brutal understatement French chefs use when speaking of food. "Was it as expected?"

Alexandre smiled warmly at him. "*Rien à dire.*" In a country where everyone was a food critic and felt no meal should pass without a retort, *rien à dire*, nothing to complain about, was the highest possible accolade. Labrousse beamed.

"It was exceptional, even for you," Capucine added. "I particularly loved the oyster sorbet. It tasted more oystery than oysters in the shell."

"That's the whole idea," Labrousse said. "It's all the rage, this molecular gastronomy. You extract the essence of the produce and reconstitute it with a few tricks from the laboratory and it becomes something entirely new with heightened flavor."

"But," Capucine went on, "we didn't see any oysters in the kitchen on Monday."

"Ah, my dear, always the police officer. Of course you didn't. It's a tradition that goes back to the Revolution. Good restaurants never serve seafood of any kind on Monday. The patrons would think it had been sitting in warm kitchens all day Sunday, and that just wouldn't do."

Labrousse brightened up slightly. "Let's drink a little sip of something." He arched an eyebrow at a waiter who was removing tablecloths and whispered to him when he scurried over. "It's a very old *alcool de framboise* that I get from a friend in the Midi."

When the waiter had gone, Labrousse deflated as the exhilaration of the afternoon's stint at the stove wore off. "Did you really think it was up to standard? I nearly thought I'd lost it with all this business. You have no idea how the police have affected me."

He flushed and grabbed Capucine's hand. "My dear, I certainly didn't mean you. Without you there I don't know what I'd have done!"

The crystal decanter of framboise arrived, nestled in a

silver tureen of crushed ice, and was poured out into tiny, tulip-shaped crystal glasses. The chemical bite of freezingly pure alcohol with barely the faintest hint of raspberry slashed through the lingering taste of lunch that was just beginning to go stale in the mouth.

"Let me tell you," Labrousse continued, "the situation is impossible. The tension in the kitchen is strong enough to separate the sauces. The slightest incident becomes a serious dispute. But that's not the worst of it. My patrons are abandoning me. Did you see who was here today? There were so many cancellations that I had to let in some of the backlog of Americans and Japanese. If I do too much of that I won't have a French client left."

He took another sip of his framboise.

"The situation is *grave*."

When it was finally time to go, Alexandre walked Capucine across the street to her car and held the door open for her. "As your Sancho, my advice is to focus on Renault. If your lab boys wind up deciding it's murder after all, as they undoubtedly will, it's almost inevitable the solution will be there."

As her car proceeded off at its leisurely pace Capucine thought about it. He was right, of course, but she still had the distinct feeling that the entire outing had been well engineered as the sort of maneuver a mama fox attempts when trying to draw the hounds away from her cubs.

Chapter 7

The Renault headquarters building was lavishly decked out in the bland opulence so dear to the heart of French big business: affluence without ostentation. Capucine, in a cream Inès de la Fressange suit, dutifully trotted after Rivière, his tough flic outfit enhanced by a scruffy leather jacket and well-worn cowboy boots. Crossing the deep pile prairie of the reception area, she was torn between relief at finding herself back in her environment and revulsion at the world she longed to escape.

Eight almost identical blond receptionists, resembling each other so closely they could well have been clones, dressed in flight attendant–style uniforms complete with large corporate logo brooches, were at a thirty-foot-long white marble counter. Their seats were on a recess a foot and a half below floor level so that their eyes just skimmed the surface of the counter and their computer screens were hidden from view.

Rivière sprawled over the countertop and goggled down at one of the receptionists as frankly as if he were a roué in a nightclub about to order a drink from a topless bartender. He was visibly disconcerted when she stared back at him dispassionately. Abashed, he announced almost timidly that they had an appointment with Monsieur d'Arbaumont. The receptionist stroked her keyboard, murmured inaudibly into a miniscule mouthpiece attached to a headset buried in her hair, and, almost without pause, smilingly turned to Capucine and announced that they were to go to the fifteenth floor, where they would be met at the elevator. Rivière gritted his teeth.

A matronly secretary greeted them warmly. In the center of the wall opposite the elevator a large chrome sign laid claim to the floor for the *"Direction Financière."* It was clear that, either to emphasize the interim character of his appointment or even possibly out of respect for his late boss, the acting president had opted to remain in his own office rather than move into Delage's.

As Capucine had expected, Thiebaud d'Arbaumont turned out to be an archetypal senior executive of the old school. The tiny navy blue rosette of the Order of Merit and the miniscule blood red ribbon of the Legion of Honor established his rank to the cognoscenti and his impeccably tailored Savile Row suit to all others. He welcomed the police officers with the buckram affability of a funeral director, intending to lubricate the start of the interview with the traditional well-polished patter of senior executives. Just as he began to relish the sonority of his alexandrines, Rivière interrupted him rudely.

"Look, pal, this is an investigation of a possible murder. Let's cut the cackle and just get down to it, okay?"

D'Arbaumont's affability crumbled like spun sugar. It was not clear to Capucine if it was the affront to this meter or if he was shocked at the notion of murder occurring in his world.

"Surely that can't be. Why on earth would anyone want to murder Président Delage?"

"That was exactly what I was going to ask you," Capucine said with a soothing smile.

"I have no idea. No idea at all. Président Delage's entire

life was the company. He had virtually no outside interests. When his wife passed away seven or eight years ago, just after he became president, he threw himself into his position body and soul."

"Does he have any close friends in the company?" Capucine asked.

"Not that I know of. Naturally, he spent a good deal of time with his five direct reports, but I doubt any of us saw him socially." D'Arbaumont paused. "Actually, now that I think about it, in the last week or so he may have spent a bit more time than usual with Florian Guyon, who's in charge of R & D. That was unusual, particularly since—"

Visibly exasperated, Rivière jumped in impatiently. "Hey, can the office gossip. We don't have all day here. Cut to the chase, my friend, and give us something useful. Did he have his hand in the till? Was one of his mistresses pissed off at him? What was going on with the guy? Get specific."

D'Arbaumont pursed his lips. "I'm afraid I really have nothing more to add," he said stiffly. "I wonder if you could excuse me. My schedule really is rather fraught this morning."

Rivière turned on his heel and strode out. Capucine could almost hear him growl. He stopped short in the hallway. "Look, little sister, this is your case, remember. I'm just here to give you a hand if you need it. If you want to spend all week here gabbing about 'direct reports' and 'R & D' and whatever other bullshit these fat-cat faggots come up with, suit yourself. Me, I'm going back to the Quai where I have a real case on the boil."

Heaving a deep sigh of relief, Capucine sought out Clotilde Lancrey-Javal, Delage's secretary, a comely brunette in her early forties, clearly grieved by the death of her boss. She sat in a tiny room adjacent to the ominously closed door of the president's office. She, too, was clearly eager to be helpful, but as she chatted with Capucine her eyes flicked incessantly at her computer screen.

She smiled in apology. "I'm sorry. You can't imagine what it's been like since the président's death. I'm inundated. Monsieur d'Arbaumont has made it very clear to everyone that his role is only titular and he wants everything directed to the office of the president to be handled here."

"You must be swamped. I won't be long. I promise. Just a few questions about Président Delage. How well did you know him?"

"Not at all, really. I've only been here for six months and he was very stiff and formal and not at all chatty. Of course, I handled his agenda and made his reservations and calls and all that, so I know what he did, but he never gossiped about his life in the least."

"Did you make the reservation for his dinner at Diapason?"

"Of course. It had been set up for a week. He ate with Maître Fleuret, his lawyer, who was also a personal friend. They met over dinner about once a month or so. But you must know that already."

"Did you notice anything out of the ordinary in the weeks before he died?"

"No, nothing really. Of course the Paris Automobile Salon is a month away and he was focused on getting speeches written and organizing dinners and meetings. Oh, yes. Maybe there's one thing, but I'm not sure if it's important. The Wednesday before he died he asked me to call Olivier Ménard. You know, the chef de cabinet for the président. The président of the Republic, that is," she said grandly.

"They were friends since they were students at university. Every now and then Président Delage would be invited to Monsieur Ménard's for dinner. But this didn't seem social, somehow. It was almost as if there was some urgent reason for the meeting. Président Delage seemed upset when the call wasn't returned within an hour and he asked me to call again the same day, which was unusual. You know, pushy. Thank God Ménard's secretary called very early Thursday morning and we scheduled a phone conversation for that afternoon. Président Delage seemed very relieved. After they spoke Président Delage told me he was going to have lunch at Monsieur Ménard's house on Saturday. I'm sure it can't have anything to do with his death, obviously, but it did strike me as unusual at the time."

They chatted on for a few more minutes, Clotilde's eyes jolting to her screen with increasing intensity. When Capucine asked her if she could make an appointment with Monsieur Guyon she beamed in obvious relief that the interview was over. She was genuinely apologetic that Monsieur Guyon would not be available until the end of the week when he returned from a trip to Lyon.

Back at the Quai Capucine looked up the number for the Elysée Palace in the interministerial telephone directory and found herself speaking to a crusty switchboard operator.

"Monsieur Ménard, *s'il vous plait.*"

After an interminable wait a supercilious male voice came on the line and asked the nature of the caller's business with Monsieur Ménard.

"This is the Police Judiciare. We require an official interview with Monsieur Ménard."

"In that case, madame, someone from the Ministry of the Interior must contact the Elysée directly. Such an appointment cannot be made at your level."

The tone was such a burlesque of disdain that Capucine was unable to get mad. Laughing, she thanked the man and rang off. The best part, she reminded herself, was that Ménard would undoubtedly fall over himself getting to the phone if Alexandre, or any other well-known journalist for that matter, wanted to see him.

Happily, Capucine could count on dear, doting Oncle Norbert, who would do anything for her, particularly after the wet firecracker of his attempt to lubricate Capucine's transfer. Two hours after her call to him, an entirely different man—this one politely brisk and purposeful—rang from the Elysée. "Madame de Huguelet?" Capucine recalled that Oncle Norbert disapproved of her not using her married name at the police. "Can I ask you to please hold for the chef de cabinet?"

Ménard's love of blather and bon mots did not entirely mask his hawklike senior civil servant acuteness. His two-beat pauses as he deliberately measured his words unnerved Capucine.

"Ah, Président Delage, *quelle tragédie*, but as the scriptures tell us, we know neither the day nor the hour.

"I understand you had invited him to lunch for the Saturday after he died."

". . . Yes . . . I had . . . You are correct."

"Was it a social occasion or was the luncheon prompted by anything specific?"

". . . Social, of course. He was going to come to my home to eat en famille, as it were. . . . Although I have to say the lunch was his . . . initiative.

"How do you mean?"

"He called me during the week wanting to ask my advice about something. He sounded a bit . . . agitated . . . It was apparently a matter of some . . . urgency."

"Did he give you any indication of what it was about?"

"No. He said he had a problem that might require the intervention of the DGSE or one of the other government security agencies and he wanted my advice on how to proceed. But since he never came to lunch, I have no idea what it was all about. Now we'll never know."

Despite the boilerplate of a highly skilled player, Capucine had the distinct feeling he was holding something back.

Chapter 8

Capucine hesitated, her finger poised on the elevator button in the lobby of the "swimming pool," the DGSE's drab headquarters in the even more drab Twentieth Arrondissement. This was folly. If Tallon ever found out he'd sling her off the case and blot her file with a reprimand nasty enough to cripple her career forever. Of course, Jacques was like a brother. She had grown up with him. Even so, for Tallon it would still be the high treason of parading police secrets in another ministry. But you can't make an omelet without breaking at least some eggs and this particular omelet just had to be made.

"Cousin, I've come to you for help," Capucine said to a young man of about her age who was far too well dressed to be employed anywhere, much less as a functionary in a government agency. "I'm working on a case that may involve the DGSE. I need your advice."

"Advice? How sweet of you. After all the big-sistering you've done for me over the years I'm touched." Jacques made a moue and brought his eyebrows together in exaggerated humility. "But don't forget that even though I'm on the director's staff, I'm just a junior underling around here. I have no stripes on my uniform at all. In fact, I don't even have a uniform."

"That's not what I hear. I understand you've become quite the evil Machiavellian potentate. You have everyone's ear and are a master manipulator of ministerial politics."

Jacques grinned a childish grin and carefully adjusted the silk square in his breast pocket. "Cousine, flattery will get you everywhere. *Alors*, Catullus said to Claudia, 'Take the panties off your thoughts and we'll give them a good spanking.' "

Capucine launched into a summary of the case. When she reached Rivière's interrogation of the two vigies Jacques guffawed loudly.

"Ah ha! I saw that expression. Looks like you have the hots for this delectable flic. I told you that geriatric foodie of yours was too stodgy to keep you interested for long!" He whooped with laughter.

"Jacques, will you shut up. This case is very important to me. And I'm still every bit as much in love with Alexandre as I ever was. And . . . well, you know . . . just as interested, and all that. More so, even."

Jacques whooped again and poked his cousin in the ribs. "Gotcha!"

"Jacques, please! Let me get to the end of the story. It seems that Delage had made a date to have lunch at the house of Olivier Ménard for the Saturday after he died. Oncle Norbert bullied Ménard into speaking to me and it turns out that Delage wanted to consult him about alerting the DGSE—or maybe another government security agency—about an undisclosed matter. Ménard told me that was the end of the story, but I had a strong feeling he was hiding something."

"Slow talking Oli . . . vi . . . er Mé . . . nard? He just always sounds like he's . . . what is the right word? . . . ah,

yes . . . *concealing* something. He's the most secretive man
in the government. He won't eat in a restaurant because he
can't bring himself to reveal to the waiter what he wants.
Probably thinks it's a . . . state . . . secret." Jacques erupted
in a shriek of laughter.

"You're in luck, though. The silly old fool actually did
call my boss, the director, who was quite irritated. He dic-
tated the file note to me. Ménard had a vague story. He
wanted us to send an agent to see a man called Guyon
who is in charge of R & D at Renault. Apparently some
development project or other at Renault had been leaked.
Hardly the sort of thing we'd be interested in. The director
sent him packing. Told him to take it to the DST. After all,
they do domestic spooking and we do the foreign stuff.
That's presumably what Ménard would have told Delage
if he had seen him."

"Sounds rather underwhelming," Capucine said, crestfallen.

"Cheer up, cousine chérie, you can still stick white-hot
needles under the toenails of this man Guyon. Maybe it'll
turn out to be a sinister plot." Jacques shrieked his high-
pitched laugh. "I'll call the liaison guy at the DST for you.
Maybe they got a call. They're supposed to keep us informed about all their actions, but with them you never
know. And if we hear anything here I'll call you instanter."

"You won't forget?"

"Forget my favorite cousin? The one who taught me
to . . ." He paused and then put a finger to his lips, rolled
his eyes, and said theatrically, "Shush, these offices are all
bugged."

"Jacques, you're impossible!"

As he showed her out, he put his arm around her waist
and fondled her rib cage. "Who'd have ever thought that
my hottest cousin would wind up getting her rocks off
with a big Pooh Bear?" Capucine slapped his cheek hard

and walked down the hall. Two secretaries gave her very quizzical looks as she waited for the elevator.

In the elevator she felt the same vague unease as after the call with Ménard. Had Jacques been just a little too glib with his facts or was that just part of his international spy persona?

Chapter 9

By the time she'd spent forty minutes waiting to see Florian Guyon, Jacques' idea of inserting hot needles under his toenails had acquired a definite appeal. For the first fifteen minutes of the wait Guyon's secretary had been sympathetic, apologizing repeatedly for the delay, attempting to ply her with coffee and cold drinks, insisting she wouldn't be waiting more than a minute or two more. But as time wore on the secretary seemed to find the awkwardness of the situation contagious and averted her eyes whenever Capucine's gaze met hers. Just as Capucine was about to stalk out and have the Quai order him down for an interview, the secretary's phone buzzed and she sighed a little sigh. "He's ready to see you now."

As she sat down in a stiff leather chair across from Guyon's desk it was obvious that, like many moneyed Frenchmen, he held the police in considerable disdain. What surprised her was his obvious nervousness.

"How can I help you, mademoiselle?" Guyon asked, with undisguised condescension.

Capucine stared at him levelly for an instant. "I understand that Président Delage had expressed an interest in having the DGSE investigate a leak from your department just before his death. Can you comment on that?"

Guyon paled slightly and his breathing became more rapid. "I don't know who told you what, but it sounds like a complete exaggeration. I attended a meeting of R & D executives in Korea a few weeks ago and had the impression that a few too many people were conversant with some of our development projects. Nothing more than that. I brought it up in an update session with Président Delage and we discussed the possibility of tightening our security systems."

Capucine stared at him for a moment. "Nothing more than that?"

"No. Not really."

"So Président Delage just might have wanted to consult the DGSE in a general way about improving security. Is that it?"

"Probably," Guyon said with a smirk, relaxing a little.

"But I have it on good authority that the request was very specific. That it concerned a specific project."

Guyon became even more pale, breathing very quickly through his mouth. "Look, let me be clear: I have no idea even if it was a leak, but, yes, there were rumors floating around Seoul that were distressingly close to some of the work we are doing here."

"Can you be more specific?"

"Mademoiselle, there is no point to this conversation. The Seoul conference was about improvements to engine efficiency. I'm sure you can understand that with the current gasoline crisis that is the top concern of all the manufacturers. We have a number of engine projects ongoing. As it happens, the DGSE is already looking into the situation. Just yesterday an agent visited one of our test sites to ascertain if it was possible for any data to have been stolen." At the sound of his own blather Guyon visibly re-laxed, leaning back in his chair.

"Well," Capucine said with her best schoolgirl smile. "Can you be a little more specific about the project or projects that the DGSE are investigating?"

"Mademoiselle, you have to understand that these things are very technical. To be honest with you, most development projects are really just vectors for the marketing department. Something to build ads around. Sales gimmicks, really." Guyon smiled and looked at Capucine to see if the explanation had satisfied her. She stared back at him without expression.

"I'm going to insist you give me some details."

"Look, mademoiselle," he said, fully intending the title to be disdainful. Then thinking better of it and glancing at her left hand he corrected himself. "Oh, do forgive me, madame," he said ironically. "This is not a police matter. The police have no rights here. I've answered your questions. I'm certainly not going to give you privileged information. If you want anything more, you can always try your luck with a juge d'instruction and see how far you get. As far as I'm concerned this interview is over." He swiveled slightly in his chair puffing out his chest, making the thin blue ribbon of the Chevalier of the Order of Merit—his establishment badge—all the more conspicuous.

Capucine smiled thinly and got up. "Thank you for your consideration, monsieur. I'm sure we'll meet again in the very near future." She felt betrayed. *Why had Jacques not told her about a DGSE investigation?*

Chapter 10

That evening Capucine dragged herself through the apartment doorway at ten o'clock, utterly exhausted and in a perfectly foul mood. Hearing Alexandre in the kitchen she went straight to him. They lived in what had been Alexandre's bachelor flat, a rambling, disjointed series of rooms deep in the Marais, in an area that was only just showing the first tentative signs of becoming fashionable.

Capucine's redecoration had been far-reaching, but it had been made perfectly clear that the kitchen was Alexandre's sanctum and not to be meddled with. The largest room in the apartment, it was filled with deeply scarred, oversized antiques purloined from the attic of Alexandre's parents' country house decades before. Two large oak armoires housed a vast hodgepodge of pots, pans, small appliances, and kitchen impedimenta. A once elegant mahogany glass-fronted display cabinet contained a haphazard collection of bottles and jars: herbs, spices, vinegars, oils, mysterious liquids and powders. The walls were festooned with hanging garlands of garlic and peppers, magnetic racks of knives, cleavers, and unidentifiable metallic instruments. A collection of herbs grew in Italian clay pots—most cracked or chipped—in the south-facing window. High up on the top of an armoire, a collection of Alexandre's empty bottles of memorable wines collected dust. Capucine itched to throw them out.

The epicenter of the room was Alexandre's pride and joy, a brand-new La Cornue range, imposing in its black enamel and polished brass trim, built around a central cooking plaque just like a professional kitchen's *piano*. The plaque was about two-and-a-half feet in diameter, ferociously hot in the middle, the heat diminishing gradually toward the edge; rather than fiddle with minute adjustments to a flame, the cook simply moved his pot closer or farther away from the middle of the plaque.

As Capucine clumped in, Alexandre was in a rapture, correcting the seasoning of an apparently finished stock while preparing to start another. Two chairs had been pulled from the table and their backs were draped with hanging ribbons of pasta hung out to dry. Alexandre was having a culinary extravaganza. She felt a stab of irritation as she saw his bliss with his own world while she floundered in hers. Here he was, happily planning on staying up until three or four in the morning when all she wanted to do was collapse into bed. Life was so unfair.

She kicked off her shoes angrily, unclipped the heavy pistol from her belt, and clunked it down on the enormous farm table that filled the room.

Alexandre swept her up in a bear hug. "Poor bébé. Tough flics don't cry."

"The hell they don't." Capucine kicked him in the shin with her stockinged foot, only half playfully.

"Baby," Alexandre crooned on, "what are those appalling Gestapo types doing to you? You must quit that dreadful job immediately and take up a life of writing endlessly boring monographs on the sociopsychology of crime. That way you can spend your whole day at home eating with me and become hugely fat and twice as lovable. I would offer you anything in my kingdom if you did that."

She smiled up at him and stroked the slight gibbosity of his stomach gently.

"Anything at all? Really anything? How about something of no value? What if I just asked for those dusty bottles up there?"

"Ah, my dear, there you ask for too much. You ask for the irreplaceable." He moved over to the shelf, selected two bottles, blew off some of the dust, and held them high in the air like a banderillero about to place his darts. "Château Pétrus 1961 and Château d'Yquem 1945. Both downed in this very room. Today, if you could find them at all, either one would be a steal at ten thousand euros, which would make them literally more costly than gold. You see, these things are now dinosaurs of the past. Even if one had the money it would be immoral to drink something so expensive. These empty bottles are archaeological relics."

"So I'm condemned to be a flic. Damn! I was ready for a life of leisurely intellectual pursuit."

"Your day was that bad?"

"Worse. Filled with humiliation and obfuscation."

"I have the perfect antidote for both." Alexandre twisted the cork out of a squat bottle of Dom Pérignon so dexterously it made little more than the most discrete whisper of a sigh, poured two flutes halfway to the top, and handed one to his wife. "Start with the humiliation part."

"I saw an extraordinarily pompous man at Renault who had the presumption to treat me like a streetwalker simply because I was a cop. Worse, he tried to give me a runaround. Delage seems to have wanted to contact the DGSE about some sort of leak in this man's department. The man in question tried as hard as he could to get me to believe that it was really just about improving Renault's security. The sad part is that he half convinced me." She caught herself before mentioning Jacques. Entirely unreasonably, Alexandre actually seemed to be jealous of her sweet little cousin.

"What about the obfuscation?"

"Forensics finally came out of the closet and announced that it's murder by poisoning."

"How wonderful to be so confident of the obvious."

"Actually it's a bit complicated. At first the lab thought it was the oysters used in the sorbet that did Delage in. They supposed the oysters might have been contaminated by red-tide algae. The symptoms were perfectly consistent. You know, it's that algae that builds up every now and then on the Atlantic coast and produces something called saxitoxin. The oysters eat it and become yummy poison capsules."

"Of course. Two elderly people died from oysters in Arcachon last year. There was a big to-do." Alexandre said.

"Exactly. The lab tests showed that Delage had saxitoxin in his blood. So it really looked like the restaurant might have been sold bad oysters."

"But then why didn't everyone in the restaurant get it? The sorbet was served to all the patrons." Alexandre asked.

"Excellent question but it turns out to be completely irrelevant. It's perfectly clear that the poison didn't come from oysters."

As her enthusiasm filled the sails of Capucine's tale, Alexandre began dinner. He picked up one of the long sheets of pasta from the back of a chair, dusted some flour on the table, threw the pasta down with élan, and dotted it with triangles of foie gras. Then he produced a large black truffle from a jar in the refrigerator and shaved it carefully with a sinister-looking long-bladed knife with a carved handle. Finally he placed another sheet of pasta on top, pressed down around each of the pieces of foie gras, and cut out oversized ravioles with his brigand's knife.

"How can they know?" Alexandre asked.

"It took forensics a while to get around to making up their minds about how much of the toxin Delage had actually ingested. Apparently the calculation is pretty tricky, but it turns out he would have had to eat the equivalent of seventy-eight oysters."

"And if oysters really are aphrodisiac, and he had eaten that many, and if all of them had worked, what a night he would have had," Alexandre murmured.

"Smart-ass. Do you want to hear this or not? If you're not going to take it seriously I'm just going to go to bed."

Alexandre smiled at her, ladled a good portion of the completed stock into a copper saucepot, and turned on the heat. "Go on, my love. Don't let me distract you."

"Even if the oysters were pureed and reduced to make the sorbet, the amount in Delage's blood was so high it would have had to come from a concentrate made in a chemical laboratory. Forensics said there was no question about that."

"Isn't that pushing this new molecular gastronomy to excessive lengths?"

"Keep this up and I really am going to bed, dinner or no dinner. The next thing forensics did was to go over the body with an even finer-tooth comb than they had used the first time around. They found a miniscule hole in the neck going into the jugular vein. Under the microscope it turned out to have been made by a hypodermic needle. Is dinner ever going to be ready? All of a sudden I'm starving."

"Patience, my intrepid policewoman, only a moment or two more. So now all is clear. Delage was injected by a waiter with an expert knowledge of anatomy and poisons because he was upset over his tip, is that it?"

"Don't be such an ass. It had to be outside the restaurant or in the WC when he went there just before he left."

On the stove the liquid was boiling, making cheerful plopping sounds. Alexandre dropped in the ravioles with a small handful of julienned truffle slices and a healthy slosh from a bottle taken from the refrigerator. In less than four minutes the ravioles were ready.

"Interesting. So it wasn't the food and most likely didn't happen at the restaurant," Alexandre said, gently lifting the ravioles with a slotted spoon and placing them in large rustic soup bowls. Then he ladled some of the broth into the bowls and brought them to the table.

"Voilà," he said, bringing the bowls to the table. "*Ravioles de foie gras truffés* in a pheasant and Monbazillac broth. And the best part is that we get to finish the Monbazillac with it."

The ravioles were glorious. Alexandre's joie de vivre leeched into Capucine's spirits and lifted them. "You know, my dear," she said, "your oyster thing, that's just an old wives' tale. Oysters aren't really aphrodisiacs. And to think each one would work individually—"

"Don't be too sure, my pet. You know the story about the Saint-Germain cutie who was lunching with her pal complaining about her beau's declining ardor. She's in tears and says, 'That thing you told me to do, you know, feeding him oysters; well, it's just not that great. He ate a dozen at dinner and only five of them worked!' "

Capucine didn't crack a smile.

"As a matter of fact, I had a dozen for lunch myself. If you want to keep count you'll have to take one of your socks off before you go to bed."

Somehow, as they finished the ravioles and then the bottle of wine, Capucine never got around to telling Alexandre what she had planned for the next day.

"Enough of this," she said with a giggle. "Let's go to bed. It's going to feel funny with only one sock on."

Chapter 11

Capucine was on the phone at 8:30 the next morning crisply convoking Diapason's three senior employees to the Quai with all the insouciance she imagined in Rivière. Well, perhaps not quite, since she chose the times carefully to avoid any conflict with their jobs. One of the last things she wanted to do was to make life even more difficult for Jean-Basile Labrousse.

The first on the list was the chef saucier, Silvestre Perrault, who arrived at 10:00. With his bald head, thick tortoiseshell glasses, tweed jacket, gray flannel trousers, and professorial serenity he seemed anything but the number-two chef of a major restaurant. Capucine knew that one of Labrousse's many eccentricities was his refusal to have a sous-chef whose only function was to act as second in command. The number-two spot was reserved for the most senior of the chefs de partie, the chef saucier, who not only had his own complex dishes to prepare but had to be ready to manage the kitchen if the need arose. Perrault had little to add to his initial statement except for a comment that at one point in the service Labrousse had unexpectedly donned a fresh jacket and neck cloth to make one of his rare tours of the dining room. "He couldn't have picked a worse moment. One of the line chefs had got himself *dans le jus*, as we say, and was a good three minutes behind his colleagues, who were doing the entrées for a four-top. Just as I was bailing him out and falling behind at my own station, Chef dumped the supervision of the whole kitchen on me. I'm used to him being a little absentminded, but I thought that was definitely over the top." Perrault laughed. When Capucine told him about the two men who had been seen dragging a bag into the kitchen in the middle of the night, he was visibly shocked and alarmed that keys to the side door might be in circulation. He asked Capucine if he could be authorized to change the lock. Forty-five minutes after he arrived he was gone, presumably on the way to the locksmith's.

Jean-Jacques Bouteiller, the maître d', was next, arriving at 4:00, after the luncheon service had wound down. He came with an ingenuously complicitous smile. It was a bit unsettling to see him out of his severe blue suit and in a worn plaid sweater a size too large. He proved decidedly chatty when out from under Labrousse's eagle eye. Surprisingly, he turned out to be an avid reader of the gossip press and a doting fan of his celebrity clients. Contrary to all appearances he paid a great deal of attention to the patrons' deportment. He had volumes to say about Delage's dinner. It seemed that at the beginning of the meal the atmosphere at the table had been tense to the point of acrimony but then improved considerably as the evening went on. By the time coffee was served both men were jovial. When Bouteiller had spoken to Delage after he left the men's room after dinner he was positively beaming. But Bouteiller regretted that, try as he might, he had overheard none of the conversation and didn't have a clue what the substance of the tension might have been.

He was less taken aback than Perrault by the 2:30 A.M. delivery. He knew little about what went on in the kitchen but was aware of a large number of small deliveries of produce as Labrousse was supplied by a multitude of local artisans. These deliveries were a famous example of Labrousse's eccentricity. Some of them came at surprising times, but 2:30 in the morning did seem exceptional. He was also astounded that anyone might have been given the key.

The last was Grégoire Rolland, the sommelier, who arrived at 5:00. He, too, seemed to metamorphose when away from the restaurant. Sycophantic servility had replaced sommelier severity. He fawned over Capucine and poured syrupy adulation on Alexandre. Despite herself, Capucine's irritation made her brusque. Offended, Rolland shrouded himself in the cloak of professional reticence that seemed the earmark of Diapason's employees. It took several minutes of wide-eyed girlish curiosity about Rolland's noble métier before peace was restored enough to allow him to be prodded toward the subject of the dinner. But once the sluice gates were opened an unstoppable flow of disdain rippled down the channel.

"Président Delage's taste in wine was insipid, hardly in keeping with a man of his position. That night he ordered a Forts de Latour, a second growth of the most noble of the Pauillacs for sure, but still a complete banality. The big name makes the wine safe. A man who orders a second growth is like a man who settles for the ugly sister because he is afraid to risk the reproach of the beautiful sibling, and once he is married he basks in the glory of his sister-in-law," he said with a sneer.

"I had no idea you were so demanding of your patrons," Capucine said.

"Of course I am. That's why I'm at Diapason: it meets my standards. In order to work properly I need a certain level of cuisine and a certain level of clientele." Rolland smirked. "Diapason has both." He winked at Capucine.

"You wouldn't think so, but finding the necessary culinary level is the hard part. Anyone can charge high prices, but Diapason is one of the few places where the cuisine is up to my cellar." Capucine arched her eyebrows in distaste at his arrogance, a gesture he mistook for disbelief. "Think about it. Let's say someone orders a bottle of 1945 Château Haut-Brion—of which I have an entire case still in the original box, by the way—I have to be confident the meal will live up to the greatness of the wine before I serve it."

"There are actually people who order wine that's that expensive?"

"Oh, dear yes. In fact, my problem is to restrain them. Some of these Americans would happily get plastered on ten-thousand-euro wines. Obviously I'd never serve it to them, of course."

"I'm sure you've already heard of the mysterious 2:30 A.M. delivery. What do you make of it?"

"Doesn't surprise me at all. Chef Labrousse is famous for being devoted to any number of tiny regional producers. They deliver at any hour of the day or night."

"But doesn't 2:30 in the morning seem excessive even for a regional farmer?"

Rolland smiled an offensively oily smile. "Lieutenant, you don't mean to tell me that with that husband of yours you haven't figured it out already? You're making sport of me."

"Rolland, it's never a good idea to be coy with the police. What are you talking about?"

"You know, of course, that in the past few decades many of our most traditional delicacies have been declared illegal. Absinthe, beque-figues, ortolans are all gone. Apparently, foie gras will be next on the list. Can you imagine? Naturally, a number of people consider these so-called illegalities an absurdity. Like Prohibition was in the United

States." He put his finger to his lips dramatically and said, "I'm sworn to secrecy, naturally. I mustn't lead you to believe that anything illegal could ever transpire at Diapason's. Never!" He raised his hands palms outward in mock horror. "But such meals are available in many a three-star restaurant. If you were interested in, say, a meal of ortolans, I could make the suggestion of a most excellent place and even advise you of the proper wines to go with it. But, I'm sure you understand, that is absolutely as far as I can go. My lips are sealed."

By seven Capucine was home impatiently snapping through the pages of *Vogue* and *Marie Claire*, ears straining for Alexandre's footfall. He eventually turned up a little before eight.

"Finally!" she said, jumping up to greet him.

"Ahh, yearning for me, I see. How lovely. I'm moved to the very core of my being. But is it really me, or are your days in that beastly place becoming too long? Give it up! Stay with me all day. Then our joy will be boundless."

"Alexandre, be serious. I need your professional advice."

"With pleasure: throw open the prison doors; release all the prisoners; feed them exquisitely; the country will be entirely free of crime."

"Please, I really do need your help. What's an ortolan?"

Alexandre burst into laughter. When he recovered he said, "I need something to drink, and apparently so do you." Still chuckling, he twisted open a bottle of champagne and poured them both flutes. "What's this all about?"

"No, you first. Tell me and then I'll fill you in."

"Well, chérie, an ortolan is a tiny little bird. A very yummy tiny little bird that with great sagacity summers in northern Europe and flies south to winter in North Africa, as we all should. Sadly for them but happily for us along the way they are netted in great quantities in the Landes and eaten with enormous appreciation."

"Is that legal?"

"Sadly not. Apparently they appear to be an endangered species so hunting them is forbidden. But that certainly doesn't prevent the Landais from catching about a hundred thousand of the little darlings each year. And who could blame them since they sell them for about a hundred and fifty euros each."

"So that's it? We're talking about poaching?"

"There's a bit more. A number of delicate souls are shocked at the way the birds are prepared. The process is a bit barbaric. First they are caught by being driven into nets by beaters. And then they are blinded with a hot poker." Capucine grimaced. "The dark is supposed to be restful for the little things and give them an appetite. They are fed on a special diet, usually millet, grapes, and figs, until they are four times their original size. As you can imagine, there is great controversy about the perfect diet. At that point their cute little beaks are forced open and a single drop of aged Armagnac—nothing else will do—is popped down their gullets. They die in a paroxysm of delight. Then, and only then, are they ready to eat."

"So it's about birds that are poached and then tortured to death?"

"Actually, it's even a bit more complicated. They have to be eaten in a certain way. Obviously, there are any number of recipes. But no matter how they're cooked, the diner puts his napkin over his head like a little tent, picks up the steaming bird by the beak, puts the whole thing in his mouth, and lets it cool while the delicious fat trickles slowly down his throat. Then he eats it bit by bit, everything but the beak. The napkin is supposed to intensify the aroma of the bird, but it is often said that it's really to hide the spectacle from God's view."

"You're making this up, you overstuffed old dipsomaniac! That's the most ridiculous story I've ever heard. It sounds vile and gross."

"I most certainly am not making it up. Ortolan is held to be the epitome of French cuisine. A dish you absolutely must eat before you die. So much so that when Mitterrand finally knew he was only days away from the end, he had himself carted to a restaurant, trussed up in blankets at the table with a dozen friends, and consumed a Pantagruelian meal of oysters, foie gras, capons, and ortolans. The whole thing found its way into the press, pictures of benapkined heads and all, and so the public knew not only that he was about to expire but also exactly to what extent he thought the laws of France applied to him personally. In his case the napkin kept much more than the ingestion of a hapless bird from God's sight."

"Jean-Louis Rolland—you know, Jean-Basile's sommelier—hinted that the mysterious midnight delivery might have been ortolans for some sinister secret meal that Jean-Basile was planning."

Alexandre burst into laughter again. "He was pulling your leg. He's a funny one, Rolland. I've never been able to figure him out. This whole ortolan thing really is very much ado about very little. The general public likes to think of it as some sort of highly secret black mass of the obscenely rich. But in fact in the Landes any number of restaurants serve ortolan more or less openly. They don't actually put them on the menu, of course, and they're certainly not cheap, but they're easy enough to get if you ask. And they don't really do that funny business with the napkins except at frou-frou dinners. Anyway, no one is going to bother sneaking ortolans into Diapason in the middle of the night." He paused. "Also, when you think about it, since those boys with the 2:30 A.M. bag were staggering under the load, there would have been enough birds to feed an army if that's what it was filled with. I hardly see Jean-Basile wholesaling endangered game on the side."

Capucine pouted. "So that damned man was just having his little joke at the expense of a foolish girl wannabe flic, is that it? What do you need to do to be taken seriously in this business?" As Alexandre attempted to hug her she slipped out from under his embrace and stalked off to the bedroom.

Chapter 12

When she arrived at the Quai the next morning, an angry red lozenge throbbed on Capucine's screen: an urgent e-mail convoking her to a meeting with Tallon that had been scheduled for fifteen minutes earlier. Rushing into his office, she was dismayed to find Rivière already there. At first she thought she was the latecomer at some sort of early-morning male-bonding session. But no, Rivière was slumped dejectedly in his chair while Tallon leaned on the sill of his open window moodily meditating on the scene below. The room was damp with defeat and unfulfilled expectation.

The last few days' newspapers were heaped in an unruly pile on the corner of Tallon's desk. They had not been kind to the Police Judiciaire. The press had lost interest in Delage for three days, but a lull in domestic and international news had incited a number of editors to inflate the case into a minor cause célèbre. The police were accused of indifference and incompetence, and an outrage had been fabricated from whole cloth describing a quasi-government employee dining at the public's expense in a restaurant where a meal for four cost more than the monthly minimum wage. In actual fact Renault had been privatized for over a decade and Delage had paid out of his own pocket. Tallon must be under considerable pressure from his superiors to produce results or, at the very least, some newsworthy bones to throw the press.

As Capucine stood at the desk waiting to be invited to sit, three brigadiers in the courtyard below were in the process of extracting two Arab men from a police van. The detainees' hands were cuffed behind their backs and they had difficulty getting out. One lost his balance and stopped to steady himself. A brigadier slapped the back of his head to get him moving, hard enough for the crack to be heard in the room. Tallon shook his head in disappointment. It was not clear if the disappointment was with the brigadiers in the courtyard or the situation in general. He spun his chair and focused on Capucine.

"Lieutenant, if you remain in the Brigade Criminelle you will discover that these cases usually go one of two ways. Sometimes the right lead pops up immediately. Then everyone is happy. The press becomes like a litter of fawning puppy dogs licking our photogenic officers, like Lieutenant Rivière here, as they pose for pictures and gloat about their victories. Or, sometimes, nothing comes up and we have to do the work of real flics."

He paused. Capucine waited for the other shoe to fall. Eventually he resumed, "And that's what we have to start to do now: cast our net very wide and draw it in very slowly and very carefully. Invariably, and I mean invariably, there will be one little lump of evidence in the sludge we drag back that will produce the murderer. But while we do our monotonous work the press will mock us and most of our police officers will get so bored they will be driven to do things like run off to the South of France to take computer courses."

Rivière bridled. "Sir, that's unfair. The very morning I got back from that course I found out how the body had been introduced into the restaurant."

"I wasn't talking about you. But since you bring it up, Lieutenant, all you did was conclude the obvious: in a street that has a higher number of vigies guarding buildings than most streets have pedestrians, one of those vigies would have noticed something. Brilliant police work." Rivière sagged like a balloon the morning after a birthday party.

"By the way," Tallon said, looking at Capucine. "I asked Lieutenant Rivière, who is in the blissful state of having a very solid lead in his dismemberment case, to sit in with us this morning so we could benefit from his profound insights. We've just spent the morning going over the file."

"Yeah," said Rivière. "And I've got a bunch of questions. Like, you didn't say if Delage's secretary was hot. I'll bet she was. These corporate bigwigs all have pinups for secretaries."

Capucine snorted and sat down.

"The question is not entirely without foundation," Tallon said. "Did you come across anything that led you to believe Delage might have had any romantic entanglements with anyone?"

"As a matter of fact, it seems he did have a very short liaison with a woman called Karine Bergeron ten years ago. He was in charge of strategic planning at Renault at the time."

Tallon shuffled through the pages in the file. "I didn't see any mention of that."

"It seemed extraneous to the case," Capucine said. "In fact it's really a complete accident we know about it at all. Delage was tagged as 'sensitive' ever since the May '68 uprising for writing a letter to the *Monde* that someone thought was overly leftist. His phone had been tapped episodically ever since. He had a coup de foudre for this Bergeron woman. They had a few evenings together and went off to Normandy for one weekend. Then he ended it. It's rather charming, really."

Tallon and Rivière shot each other knowing looks.

"With that one exception Delage was particularly devoted to his wife. She died eight years ago, two years after this incident, and he threw himself into his work and became practically a recluse. There is no evidence whatsoever that he's had any other relationships."

"Lieutenant," Tallon said, "in the future please avoid omissions in your reports. All the details must be included, even if—"

The phone rang. "Merde, here we go again," he muttered as he looked at the caller ID screen. Tallon lifted his hand, palm toward them, demanding silence.

After a few "Yeses," and "I sees," one "You don't say," two "the DGSE, eh?" and a few grunts, he concluded with, "Trés bien. I'll send a lieutenant right over." When she heard the first "DGSE" Capucine started, sat bolt upright, and felt the blood rush to her cheeks.

"All right," Tallon said, "we'll have to finish this meeting later. That was the divisionnaire. His department just received a call from the DGSE. Seems someone from Renault called them trying to reach a nonexistent *agent*. The call was from someone in Renault's R & D division. I'm surprised the DGSE made the link to us." Capucine felt her blush deepen. "They must be more zealous readers of the national press than I thought." Tallon ripped a sheet off his pad. "Lieutenant Le Tellier, this is the name of the DGSE officer who called. Get over there and find out what it's all about. It's hard to worm anything out of the DGSE but see if there's any link at all with Delage."

Chapter 13

It took Capucine nearly an hour to drive to the "Pool," but once there her meeting had been very brief. There was no love lost between the Police Judiciaire and the DGSE. The officer who had taken the call for the nonexistent agent succinctly summarized the situation: a certain Lionel Vaillant had called asking for Agent Arnaud Etienne. This Vaillant was a researcher in Renault's R & D department and based in the headquarters building in Billancourt. There was no Arnaud Etienne at the DGSE nor had there ever been. Also, the DGSE had no current interest in Renault and had no open dossiers involving the company at that time. Relaxing a little, the officer said he was sure it was a case of fraudulent impersonation of a government agent, which was a police matter, not a national security concern. Capucine signed a form certifying that the case was now the responsibility of the Police Judiciaire and that a follow-up report would in due course be furnished to the DGSE. The meeting was over in less than ten minutes. On her way out she was sorely tempted to make a surprise visit to Jacques. The two incidents involving Renault's R & D department and the DGSE just couldn't be a coincidence. She needed to talk to Jacques. It really did seem like something was being held back. But she was a good hour from Renault and wanted to interview the caller while the episode was still fresh, particularly before he had a chance to mull it over during lunch. Jacques would just have to wait.

She drove directly to the Renault headquarters on the assumption that Vaillant was highly likely to have the sort of job that would keep him in the office all day. When called by one of the eight matched receptionists he announced he would be right down.

When he arrived Capucine led him over to an ensemble of uncomfortable-looking steel-and-leather Bauhaus furniture at the farthest corner of the reception area, well out of earshot of the receptionists. She produced her identity wallet—badge on one side, ID card on the other. Vaillant recoiled, galvanized as if electrodes had been applied to his temples. He looked around wildly.

"Is this about parking tickets?" he asked, at the edge of panic. "I don't have all that many unpaid ones, really."

Capucine smiled at him gently. "No, no. I'm Lieutenant Le Tellier from the Police Judiciaire. We don't deal with parking tickets. I never pay mine, either."

"Then what's going on?" Vaillant's eyes searched the room in his nervousness, unappeased by her little joke.

"Well, it seems that you called the DGSE this morning, trying to reach a certain Arnaud Etienne. Is that right?"

"Yes. Yes, I did. I gave Agent Etienne a tour of one of our installations last week. I had some additional information I wanted to give him, but the only number on his card was his cell phone. I didn't want to presume to use that so I looked up the office number. Surely there's nothing wrong in doing that. Is there? Is it some kind of breach of security? Should I have used the cell phone number?"

Capucine gave him a toned-down version of her little-girl smile and said nothing.

After a pause she asked, "And how was it that Agent Etienne was given a tour of your installation?"

"Well, he's the agent in charge of our security, of course. Monsieur Guyon—he's the *directeur* in charge of all of R & D—asked me to take him out to this test site and show him around the test vehicles. Monsieur Guyon called me himself," he said with a show of pride, as if a direct call from on high not only established his status but was also full validation of any possible action on his part.

"It seemed reasonable that the agent responsible for security on Project Typhon would need to be fully au courant of the project's advancement."

"And Project Typhon is one of your development projects, is that right?" Capucine asked smoothly.

Lionel checked, staring at her with a crafty look that was slowly replaced by one of alarm. "You must know all about Project Typhon. Don't you?"

Capucine was aware she had blundered. "I'm not here to question you on your projects. I'm here to talk about this so called Agent Etienne," she said sharply.

Lionel became as sullen as an adolescent caught in a fib. "There's really not all that much more to tell. Monsieur Guyon called and gave me instructions to take someone on a tour of a site. Which I did. The gentleman asked some questions I couldn't answer during the visit. Once I had the answers I tried to call him. Voilà. I'm not sure I have anything more to add."

Capucine's friendly girl-next-door manner vanished. "Look, Lionel," she said, using his given name for the first time. "Either you cooperate here or you'll cooperate at the Quai des Orfèvres. Keep this up and I'll march you out of here to my car. Show the slightest signs of resistance and I'll be happy to cuff you in front of these charming ladies," she said, inclining her head at the battery of receptionists, most of who were now bobbing up and down to peer at them over the top of the counter like ducks in a fun-fair shooting gallery.

"I'm sorry," Lionel said, deflated. "I don't know why I'm being blamed for anything. What I told you is the truth. Monsieur Guyon did call me himself to tell me to take a DGSE agent around the site. So why shouldn't I have done it?"

"And why would an automobile development project possibly be of any interest to the DGSE?" Capucine asked.

"You really don't know about Project Typhon, do you?" Lionel shook his head in amazement.

"And are you in charge of it?"

"Good Lord, no. Of course not. I just run a small sub-project."

"And did this Etienne actually tell you he was a DGSE agent?"

"You mean he wasn't? Of course he was. Monsieur Guyon himself told me an agent was coming." Lionel paused. "He gave me his card. Look, it says so right on it." Lionel dug in his pockets and finally found a card with a stylized French flag over the words MINISTÈRE DE LA DÉFENSE—DIRECTION GÉNÉRAL DE LA SÉCURITÉ EXTÉRIEUR. The card looked perfectly authentic except for the single phone number listed. The prefix "06" was used for cell phones throughout France, and no agent would put that on his card.

"I'll keep this, if you don't mind," she said.

Lionel nodded meekly.

"So why did Guyon ask you to show a DGSE agent around? Why didn't he take him himself?"

"I have no idea. At the time I thought it might be because Monsieur Guyon thought I was good at public relations. I took it as a pat on the back. Now I guess it just makes me look dumb." He paused. "Look, I have no idea what's going on here, but whatever it is I really have nothing to do with it. Nothing."

Chapter 14

A s Vaillant disappeared into the elevator Capucine went to one of the receptionists and asked to be connected to Monsieur Guyon on the house phone.

She asked his secretary if Guyon was available. After a pause his secretary came back on the line and said, "I'm sorry. Monsieur Guyon won't be able to see you today. He's tied up in meetings. He suggested you call tomorrow or the day after and perhaps he could find an opening next week."

"Oh," Capucine replied sweetly, "please tell him he doesn't have to bother. I'll be sending a squad car this afternoon to have him brought down to the Quai des Orfèvres."

"Just a minute, please."

"Madame, monsieur asks if it would be convenient for you to come up now. It seems a meeting has just been cancelled."

Guyon met her at the door to his office, his expression flipping back and forth between disdain and fear like an old-style neon sign. "Well, Lieutenant, what is urgent enough to warrant your barging in like this?"

Capucine stared at him levelly for an instant. "It would appear, monsieur, that you ordered one of your staff to show an individual around one of your installations claiming that that individual was an agent of the DGSE. The individual had nothing to do with the DGSE. What do you have to say about that?"

Guyon's face drained of color. "I understood you were with the Police Judiciaire," he stammered. "What does the police have to do with this?"

"Just answer the question."

"Well, an agent phoned . . . Agent Etienne phoned me and asked for an appointment. He had been assigned to take charge of security on Project Typhon and quite naturally wanted to meet me. So, I met with him here and briefed him on the latest developments. Then I suggested he look at the current prototype in a test car. A physical demonstration would make it easier for him to understand." Guyon paused, the sound of his voice giving him confidence.

"But you see, Monsieur Guyon, this man Etienne was not employed by the DGSE at all."

"That's impossible. What makes you think that?"

"It's quite simple. One of your staff, a certain Lionel Vaillant, attempted to call this Agent Etienne to give him additional information. Vaillant called the DGSE directly, not his cell phone, which was listed on his card, and since the DGSE had never heard of Etienne they called us."

"That's ridiculous. Agent Etienne's direct line is on its card as well as his cell phone. Bound to be. Here." Guyon opened the central drawer of his desk, rooted around, came up with a card identical to the one Vaillant had given her, and looked at it carefully. "You're right. There's just a cell phone number," he said with dismay.

"I'll take that," Capucine said, holding out her hand.

"Are you quite sure Etienne was a fake? Maybe he was just using a made-up name for security reasons. You know, a nom de guerre? That's possible, isn't it?"

"I'm sorry, he was clearly a fraud. What is less clear is why you were so ready to give him the keys to the establishment without any confirmation at all. Let's talk about that part, shall we?"

Guyon went pale again. His brow became visibly damp. "Are you accusing me of negligence? Are you accusing me of a crime?"

"Hardly." Much as she enjoyed the man's discomfiture, Capucine was well aware she would get further by loosening up a little. "But you must admit it's curious that a man of your obvious circumspection would be so trusting."

Guyon seemed close to a state of panic. His breathing had become shallow and his blink rate had slowed perceptibly.

"Well," Capucine said, trotting out her ever-effective schoolgirl smile. "Why don't you tell me a little about the project. I know a little about Typhon, but I'd like to know more. It sounds fascinating." She realized too late it was once again exactly the wrong thing to have said.

"Typhon?" Guyon almost screeched. "Who told you about that? That fool Vaillant, I'll bet. It's just one of our development projects. Almost all of them are of concern to the DGSE. My guess was that Etienne was just starting with Typhon to warm up before getting on with the serious stuff." Guyon laughed nervously.

He looked at Capucine to see if the explanation had satisfied her. She stared back without expression.

"Look, if you are all that curious about our development work, I'd be happy to have someone give you an overview presentation. Someone more competent than that imbecile Vaillant, of course. I could schedule it for tomorrow morning, or whenever is convenient for you. We have some wonderful new colors for the coming model year. We have a brand-new fabric coating that is absolutely stainproof. I'm sure that would interest you, no?"

"Monsieur, I'd rather we stick to Project Typhon."

Underneath the pallor, Guyon's face became rigid. "Madame, I've answered all your questions. As far as I'm concerned this interview is over."

As he got up to shake her hand, Guyon swayed visibly.

Chapter 15

At seven that night Capucine was in her new office at the Quai completing her daily activity report when she received a call.

"Lieutenant? I was hoping I'd catch you before you left. Do you have a moment?" She recognized the voice immediately.

"Of course, Monsieur Vaillant. I was just filling out paperwork. What's up?"

"I had a really bad afternoon. I mean like really bad. Monsieur Guyon called me to his office. He was totally pissed off. I've no idea why. Anyway, he's taken me off Project Typhon and assigned me to something ridiculous about color indicators for brake-pad wear. Man, he was so mad I'm sure he would have fired me on the spot if he could've."

"Well, then be thankful for living in a socialized state where the law guarantees your job. It doesn't surprise me, though. Monsieur Guyon did look a little out of sorts when I saw him, that's for sure."

"Well, I'm dead meat here; he's definitely after my ass. I'm going to have to look elsewhere, no doubt about that." Lionel paused. "Listen, I realize I wasn't all that helpful when we met this afternoon."

"And you think the PJ is going to make trouble for you when you look for another job, is that it?" Capucine laughed.

"No, no, of course not. It's just that I felt . . . well, you know . . . Look, if you'd like, I'd be happy to tell you everything I know about the project."

"And get a gold star for good conduct, is that it?" Capucine said with a smile in her voice. "Okay, come in tomorrow morning and I'll take a formal deposition. Say at eight. That way you won't be too late for work. Come to the main entrance and just ask for me."

She hadn't bothered to give him the address. Who in Paris didn't know where to find the Police Judiciaire?

Lionel inched down the corridor timidly peering into doors. When he finally found Capucine's tiny office he went in smiling meekly and said, "They just told me to come up here and look for you. I got a bit lost in the corridors. I . . . uh . . . thought security would be tighter."

Capucine laughed. "We're not all that worried that the bad guys will try to force their way in. Sit right here," she said, indicating the standard-issue dented metal office chair with one bent leg. "Welcome to the Police Judiciaire. Make yourself at home." Normally compulsively neat, since she moved into her new office Capucine had reluctantly taken to strewing her desk with pistol, ammunition clips, handcuffs, and the other accoutrements of the métier in order to seem more like a flic. Even she found the result unconvincing. Lionel looked around, eyes wide.

"Want some coffee? There's still half a pot left in the office next door."

"Thanks. That would be great."

"*Alors,*" Capucine said when she returned, making an

adjustment in the angle of her computer monitor and carefully aligning the keyboard to the edge of the desk. "Shall we start on that deposition?"

"I'm all set."

"First, your identity papers."

Lionel handed her his national identity card.

"Name, last, first, middle," she asked while looking at his ID, which contained precisely those data.

For the next ten minutes Capucine painstakingly typed in a long list of biographical details, specific enough to include items such as the dates and department of birth of his parents. Only when this was done did she ask him to provide a more complete version of his statement of the previous day, which she typed as a succinct three-paragraph summary, printed it out, and handed it to Lionel.

"Here, read this and tell me if it's okay. I'm going to get you to sign the whole thing when it's done."

Lionel announced it was perfect.

"Okay," she said, pushing the keyboard away and sliding the printout into a file folder. "Now tell me about Project Typhon."

"It's totally awesome. It's this device that shoots a mix of catalysts into the cylinder head and makes engines three times more powerful."

"So they go faster?" Capucine asked.

"That's not the idea. What it does is make any given car, with just a few modifications, use only a third as much gas. With gas prices the way they are, it's a totally major breakthrough. Jesus, it'll revolutionize the industry."

"But why is Guyon so secretive about it?" Capucine asked. "If it's done the patents must have been applied for so security leaks won't be an issue."

"That's just it. There's still an important thing left to do. We've figured out the right chemical composition for the catalysts—there are three of them—and all about the quantity and timing of the injection, and a whole ton of other technical stuff. But the nozzle is far from ready. See, the brilliant thing about Project Typhon is that the catalysts, which start out life as unstable liquids, are transformed into hard lozenges so they're safe. Then an electric current is run through them to produce a tiny puff of gas, which is injected into the cylinder head. It's brilliant, the way it's going to work. Once the nozzle is done, we're good to go. But we're not quite there yet."

"So what did you show that phony agent at the test track?"

Vaillant looked at Capucine with admiration. "You sure catch on fast. We have a bunch of vans rigged up with the catalysts in gaseous form in tanks. There are computers in the vans that inject the gases into the engine. The vans are used for practical testing of the catalysts at different speeds and loads and all that stuff. Let me tell you, when we took that lumpy van from zero to sixty in three seconds, burning the rubber off the tires, that agent was one impressed dude! When he got out of the car he had to make a trip to the john. I bet he nearly wet his pants." Vaillant laughed uproariously.

"You have no problem with adding all this to your deposition, I hope."

"Hey, that's what I came down here for. To be as helpful as possible."

Capucine typed up the addendum and printed out a draft. Lionel wrote in a few changes. Capucine typed in the corrections but did not print the document out.

"Okay," Capucine said, "now tell me about this 'Agent Etienne.' "

"Gee, there's not that much to tell. Like I told you yesterday, I got this call from Guyon, who says I have to go up to our installation at Courcelles-lès-Gisors and show this DGSE agent around the place and give him a ride in one of the test cars. So I did all that and even did one better and took the guy to lunch. We went to this two-star

restaurant in the village. He lapped it up, let me tell you."
Vaillant suddenly looked crestfallen. "You know, I'll bet
you that bastard Guyon is not going to approve my expense account for that lunch since he didn't actually ask
me to do it. It was goddamn expensive, too."

"You poor thing. What did this agent look like?"

"Not much to tell. A business-type guy. Fortyish. You
know. Suit. The sort of guy you'd find in any business.
Nothing to tell he was an agent. I guess spooks are supposed to look like that."

Capucine leaned toward Lionel. "Come on, you can do
better than that. Think. Close your eyes. Picture the man.
What was distinctive about him?"

"Just like I said, your basic business guy." Lionel's brow
furrowed in concentration. "Wait. There is something. He
spoke like a Belgian. Well, not exactly like a Belgian, but
there was something in the way he spoke that was odd.
Like he was a foreigner, but the kind of foreigner who
grew up speaking French. Does that help?"

"Anything helps at this stage."

Later, after Vaillant had left and Capucine had reread
his deposition, the enormous potential of the Renault invention hit her. She had the unsettling feeling of having
wandered into the wrong set for the film she was supposed
to be making.

Chapter 16

That afternoon another e-mail from Tallon's secretary summoned Capucine to finish the update session. She buzzed with the satisfaction of having something significant to report—at last. But when she arrived she was again irked to find Rivière already there, this time apparently well ensconced, chortling gutturally with Tallon. The strength of the male cabal was just too much. Hoping that she would eventually come to believe it, she had repeatedly told herself that Tallon's desire for Rivière to act as her mentor was reasonable enough given her inexperience in homicide cases. But the combination of his Casanova routine and his flagrant lack of interest in her work was just too much for her not to conclude that Rivière's only possible added value was his gender.

Despite her dismay Capucine launched into Vaillant's description of Project Typhon with élan. When she finished Rivière flapped his open hand like a flag and whistled, "*Pas mal.* I'm going to have to get one of those gadgets when they come out. I'd love to see my car do a wheelie like a motorcycle."

"Jeanloup, you're missing the point. It's not a hot rod

item. If it really can cut gas consumption by three-quarters it would revolutionize the automobile industry. Just think, it would even transform the oil industry and have a major impact on the world's economy."

Rivière shrugged and blew air out of his mouth in the classic gesture of Gallic indifference. Tallon said nothing and looked at her, stone-faced. "What else?" he asked. When Capucine forged ahead with Vaillant's description of the fraudulent agent's foreign accent, Tallon relaxed slightly, making a noise that sounded like the executive summary of a contented Labrador stretching out in front of a fireplace. "Good. That's something that could be followed up. What else?"

"The brigadiers ran down the cell phone number of the phony DGSE agent. The number was part of a large block that was sold by Bouygues to a company in Paris. It seems that many of these phone companies sell large bundles of SIM cards—"

Tallon raised a hand. "Lieutenant, spare me the technobabble. What the hell are you talking about? Get to the point."

As Capucine smarted from the rebuff, Rivière jumped in, the sage who would pour oil—no doubt because it was soon to be a debased commodity—on troubled waters. "Commissaire, let me explain. You're on the other side of the generation gap from cell phones." He grinned with satisfaction despite Tallon's frown. "Those little chip things you slide in the slot under the battery in cell phones are called 'SIM cards.' You can move your number from one phone to another by taking the chip out and putting it in another phone."

"I didn't know that," Tallon said without interest.

"Well, what Le Tellier is trying to explain is that all the big phone companies sell these cards in blocks to large corporations. These are prepaid accounts, not billed monthly, so there's no expense account stuff. The guy just gets his phone and that's that."

"Ruuuff," Tallon grunted as if clearing his throat, his enthusiasm visibly declining. He looked away from Rivière and focused on Capucine. "Lieutenant Le Tellier, what does this have to do with the case?" he asked irritably.

"The phone number is not traceable back to an individual, but we do know it was in a block of cards sold to a small data recovery company called Ibas, based in Paris," Capucine said.

"Good," Tallon said. "Go over there and shake up a couple of people and see if you can trace the number to somebody. Shouldn't be too hard in a small operation."

"There could be a complication. I checked them out on the Ministry of Finance database. The tax people have just finished a great new listing that tags any French company with a strong enough financial link to a foreign company to make it possible for them to move profits out before they are taxed here. This Ibas came up. They are a subsidiary of a subsidiary of an American company. It could be that some of the phones were used for visiting staff."

"What's the parent company called?"

"Trag, Inc."

Tallon squinched. "Trag, eh," he said slowly. "Well, at least things begin to make a little more sense. But it puts a whole new complexion on the case." He stared out the window lost in thought for a few seconds and then pursed his lips at the two lieutenants' blank looks. "And neither of you have any idea who that is, right?"

Capucine shook her head. Rivière shrank into his seat like a schoolboy trying to make himself invisible because he didn't know the answer to the teacher's question.

"Trag is something only the Americans could dream up. It's a private DGSE. Any private citizen with a big enough bank account can use to do whatever he wants. Trag doesn't

care. Imagine the consequences of a fully equipped merce-
nary espionage agency with 15,000 employees completely
on the loose."

The two lieutenants stared at him, perplexed.

"In theory Trag does only legitimate corporate work,"
Tallon continued. "Things like investigating companies
for acquisitions or guarding against industrial espionage
or even retrieving hostages. Much as a policeman hates a
private detective, you have to admit there's need for that
sort of stuff in today's world. But the problem with Trag is
that they don't hesitate to cross the line. Just last year the
Brazilian police raided them and found Trag had been
guilty of sabotaging a major corporate acquisition and
even spying on their president."

"Excuse me, Commissaire," Rivière said. "I don't get it.
Cool dudes for sure, but why do we care?"

"Simple. The thing they're best at is industrial espionage. Not only will they protect your company from
spies but they'll spy on your competitors for you if that's
what you want." He paused to let this sink in.

"Big fucking deal," Rivière said. "They get caught, they
get caught."

"It's a bit more tricky than that. Trag seems to be so
hand in glove with the CIA that nobody knows where one
ends and the other begins."

"So are these guys foreign agents or not?" Rivière
asked. Subtlety irritated him.

"They're private citizens with no official diplomatic immunity. If they're up to industrial espionage in France, or
if they're involved in Delage's death in any way, they're
definitely eligible to be long-term guests of the nation."

"With respect, Commissaire, what's the problem here?
Let's just go get them," Rivière said.

"I think I understand." Capucine said. "If it becomes
known that Trag is involved the case will be taken away
from us and handed over to the DST, is that it?"

"Precisely," Tallon said in the tone of grade-school teacher awarding a pupil a gold star. "Handed over to the DST with kid gloves made from the finest Alpine goats so the DST can dither and do nothing until the press has forgotten about it."

"Sir," Capucine asked. "Have you ever come across Trag before?"

"About ten years ago the minister of the interior, a very emotional gentleman from Provence, got it through his head that there were more CIA agents in France than there were rats in the Paris metro. He got a number of them sent home, but the big fish just signed on with Trag and slipped through the net. The minister ordered the DST to bug Trag like no company has ever been bugged before. There was a mike behind every picture, in every lightbulb, in every phone. They even went after Trag's clients. Of course, it wasn't the DST who did the actual work, it was the PJ. Before we really found out anything there was a very sharp protest from the American government. We were seriously damaging Franco-American relations. They made it sound like we were bugging the U.S. Embassy. Our government went belly-up and blamed it on 'rogue elements' in the PJ and DST. A number of wrists were slapped, some of them badly."

From his tone, Capucine had the impression Tallon's wrist was one of the ones that had stung the most.

"How does this affect the case?" Capucine asked.

He gave her a sly look. "We're going to let our juge d'instruction worry about it. It's her call, after all. I'll try and get us in tomorrow morning." He smiled at Rivière with complicity and said, "It's not a *juge* we know. The ministry, with its infinite wisdom, has handed this case to one who deals with commercial cases, I guess because the functionary stopped reading the file when he got to the word 'Renault.' "

Rivière guffawed. "Don't worry, Commissaire, I'll watch my language."

"By the way, Lieutenant Le Tellier," Tallon continued. "I see that you've worked with this juge once already. A certain Madame d'Agremont. I'm sure with you around she won't be too unsettled by our uncouth ways." Rivière's guffaw sounded almost like a belch.

Chapter 17

The businesslike white stone building that housed the juges d'instruction who dealt with corporate matters had figured as a large part of Capucine's past in the fiscal squad. She had spent far more time reporting on her work to its denizens than to her superiors in the police. As inquisitorial magistrates, the juges were responsible for bringing cases to court and were in charge of the police the way a bombardier takes command of the plane when it is over target. It had never failed to amaze Capucine that the building was so heavily guarded but she assumed it was only because the authorities equated the potential danger to the sums involved.

As the three officers walked through the familiar glass door of the building a metal detector, invisible in the door frame, triggered a discreet flashing red light at the receiving guardian's desk. A jovial stocky man in his middle sixties, undoubtedly retired from the police, rose beaming. "Step over here and check your artillery with me. Don't be shy."

Capucine and Rivière handed over their Sigs in exchange for a numbered plastic tag. Tallon remained behind, pacing in the hall, apparently lost in thought.

"You too, Monsieur le Commissaire," the guardian boomed cheerfully.

"Commissaire Principal!" Rivière hissed at him.

"I don't care if he's the goddamned president of the Republic. No one goes in to see a juge wearing a piece."

At the commotion, two uniformed gendarmes had started to move forward, their hands on their holstered pistols. The man at the desk waved them back.

Tallon came over, smiling easily.

"That's okay," the receiving officer said. "I know what a commissaire looks like even without seeing his tricolor card."

"Sorry, my mind was elsewhere. Here you go." He slid a big .357 Magnum Manurhin F1—made even clunkier by the addition of a Trausch rubber butt—from a well-worn leather shoulder holster and handed it grip first to the receptionist. It was the old-model police sidearm, no longer authorized since the Sig had been introduced, altered in a way particularly favored by the Police Judiciaire.

"That's what I carry, too," the guardian said, pulling his jacket open to reveal a similar revolver. "It's worth it even if it can get you reprimanded. I don't trust these new-fangled things. They look like they're made of plastic. Who needs fifteen shots? Six is plenty if you can shoot straight and shoot a real bullet. Right, Monsieur le Commissaire Principal?" he said, emphasizing the word "principal" and darting a sarcastic look at Rivière.

Tallon smiled at the receiving officer. "Regulations sometimes do need to be put into perspective just a bit."

Madame le Juge d'Agremont was in her early fifties, incongruously a bit vain, her black suit showing more cleavage than Capucine would have dared on the job. Surprisingly, the décolletage reinforced her look of a woman who would brook no nonsense whatsoever. Madame le Juge was a very powerful woman indeed and knew it.

D'Agremont greeted Capucine like a favorite niece. "Ma petite Capucine, so you've moved into the Brigade Criminelle. How courageous of you!" Capucine was unable to suppress a blush. Rivière guffawed and was shushed by Tallon. The world of the juges never failed to surprise Capucine. It was the only environment where the police lost all their privileges, where they became almost the suspects. She was struck by Tallon's overt subservience. He was a different man. Of course, it really wasn't all that surprising; after all, she was the boss. Only Rivière, openly ogling d'Agremont's décolleté, stayed completely in character.

Tallon summarized the week's work, deferring to the lieutenants occasionally to amplify a piece of data. D'Agremont never interrupted but held up her index finger every now and then, as if she were hitting a PAUSE button, to make a note with a gold Waterman fountain pen.

When the summary was over she looked at Tallon severely. "There's not much here, is there, Monsieur le Commissaire Principal?"

Tallon shook his head. "No, there isn't, Madame le Juge."

"In a nutshell, a murder has been committed. But there is no apparent motive. Nor are there any credible suspects. You know, of course, that I need a suspect in order to send the dossier to the public prosecutor. You also know that your job is to present me with that suspect."

Tallon said nothing.

"Now," she continued, "we have an anomalous situation with this Project Typhon. There's no demonstrated, or even logical, connection. It's just an anomalous situation.

"We also have a second anomalous situation with this impersonation of a DGSE agent and a thin link—a very tenuous link—between that impersonation and Trag, Inc. Two anomalies. Interesting. Suggestive. But nothing that even comes close to incriminating Trag.

"Do you agree, Monsieur le Commissaire Principal?"

"Of course, Madame le Juge."

"So we are faced with a potential ambush here. The minute a possible suspect, as defined in French law, is known to be acting on Trag's behalf this case could well be removed from our jurisdiction." She paused. "That is abundantly obvious after the last fuckup with Trag."

The three detectives, even though obscenities were part of their natural vocabularies, were profoundly shocked, as much by the depth of emotion as by the word itself in such an austere mouth.

"Monsieur le Commissaire Principal, I want you to continue investigating the crime according to routine. And I also want you to investigate around Trag. Around, not directly. Keep a safe distance. A very safe distance. I'm not going to authorize wiretapping or bugging of any kind and I'm not going to authorize what the law terms 'close surveillance.' "

The three detectives nodded.

"Having said that, I've used this language in the purely legal sense. I know the officer's exam requires a very thorough understanding of the legal niceties of these terms, so I won't waste your time with definitions. Get back to work and let me know when something breaks."

Chapter 18

By Saturday afternoon Capucine was stale, irritable, and moody. She convinced herself a break would improve things. Nothing much had happened after the meeting with the juge d'instruction. She had spent the rest of the day interviewing a series of social acquaintances Delage saw infrequently, all of them dead ends. It seemed like pointless make-work. She decided to take the rest of the day off and keep away from the Quai until Monday.

She was at home by three in the afternoon and spent the rest of the day in an afghan on the sofa reading and then dining with Alexandre at the bistro around the corner. After, they had found their way to bed quite early but had gone to sleep very late.

The next morning Alexandre woke in high spirits, keen on trying out a seafood restaurant that had just opened near the Bastille. "Think red-checked tablecloths; think mountains of oysters: *Speciales, Bélons, Fines de Claires*; think *oursins, langoustines, moules, bulots* you prize out of their shells with little pins; think the whole lot washed down with gallons of very dry Sancerre. You'll love it! Just what you need to get you out of your funk."

At the word "oyster" Capucine's face had clouded.

The restaurant proved to be everything Alexandre promised, a caricature of a classic Parisian seafood bistro, but a successful one nonetheless. The oak paneling and white square ceramic floor tiles, at most a few days old, had been skillfully distressed by the decorators and looked almost authentic enough for the diner to feel the place might really have been around while the Bastille was still standing. A green stand outside was staffed by rotund rubicund men in Breton fishing outfits to give the impression that the seafood was actually supplied by independent Breton artisans who journeyed out to Loctudy at the crack of dawn each morning to select the best from their family boats. The waiters, dressed in immemorial black jackets over ankle-length aprons starched and bleached to an unnatural whiteness, bustled with a hospitable arrogance that seemed to have been polished by the centuries.

As always Alexandre had reserved in his own name and the maître d' had clearly been on the lookout for him. He and Capucine were ushered to a quiet table in a corner with the deference normally reserved for rock stars. Over the inevitable flute of complimentary champagne Alexandre was treated to a detailed recitative of the trials and tribulations of the restaurant's opening, which he received with ill-disguised impatience. Cutting the tale short, Alexandre ordered the largest of the *plateaux de fruits de mer* and a bottle of Sancerre that was little known but, in his opinion, particularly excellent. The restaurant was packed with prosperous-looking Parisians happily set on an extended Sunday lunch, creating a din that was somehow pleasing despite the uproar.

Capucine smiled at him. "In my world you have to beat people up to find out anything. In yours the more you scowl the more they chatter away. And they offer you free champagne to boot. Maybe you're right and I am in the wrong business."

The seafood arrived rapidly. The waiter first set a steel

frame about a foot high on the table, then placed several little dishes with butter, brown bread, lemon sections, and sauce Mignonette—made from red wine vinegar and shallots—in the middle of the frame and finally returned with a huge metal plateau heaped with crushed ice and a profligate display of every possible variety of seafood arrayed with an engineer's precision in meticulously concentric circles.

For the first fifteen minutes the concentration required to dismember langoustines and suck oysters from their half shells without wasting any of the precious juice precluded anything more than monosyllabic conversation.

Alexander looked over at his wife affectionately. "Makes you feel better about the world, eh?"

"Absolutely, but I'm still dreading going back to work tomorrow. I have absolutely no idea what to do next."

"Tell me about it."

"We had a very curious session with the juge d'instruction on Friday. Actually, I worked with her once before and she was very direct and easy to get along with. But yesterday she was entirely cryptic. Her instructions were riddles, worse than the Delphic oracle."

"Who was it?"

"A rather imposing woman called Marie-Hélène d'Agremont."

"Ah, *la brave* Marie-Hélène! I know her quite well. Or at least I used to. We were students together."

Capucine laughed. "You know everyone! What was she like?"

"Very bright, very zealous, and very political. I wouldn't say she was exactly consumed with ambition, but she definitely knew what she wanted. And she was very . . ." Alexandre paused. "Well, let's say she was calculating, Machiavellian, really, in her way of getting it. How'd the session go?"

For the space of a heartbeat Capucine was tempted to

press Alexandre about his history with Marie-Hélène d'A-
gremont but decided to stick with the case. Anyway, lunch
was never a good time to pry into Alexandre's past.

"Well, for openers she seemed as disconcerted as Commissaire Tallon that Trag might be involved, and—"

"Hold on," Alexandre interjected, "you never told me
that. What's this about Trag?"

"It's not all that much, really. I discovered the phony
DGSE agent's cell phone had originally been issued to a
subsidiary of this Trag."

"Well, then they're in it up to their ears. That can't be
an accident. Tallon must have had conniptions."

"How did you know?" Capucine asked.

"Well, I'm sure you know all about that CIA hare that
the Minister of the Interior started way back when."

Capucine nodded. "Tallon told us all about it."

"Well, it was my paper that originally published the list
of spies to be deported. I was just a cub reporter in those
days. Did he tell you about what happened?" Capucine
nodded. "I was assigned to the story and stayed with it
until the end. I'll bet Tallon didn't tell you that he was one
of the flics who was involved in harassing Trag's French
clients, did he? When the wind shifted he was one of those
severely reprimanded. He was lucky he didn't get exiled to
the boondocks or worse."

"No wonder he reacted so strongly when he heard
about Trag."

"Marie-Hélène must have leaped like a gaffed salmon,
too," Alexandre said with a smile.

"Why would it be a problem for her?"

"Simple. She wants you people to complete a beautiful
little case, so she can package it up all tied in string and
red sealing wax and hand it to the public prosecutor, who
will tell her she's brilliant. That's what floats her boat. If it
becomes a Trag thing, it'll get lifted out of her hands and
given to the DST. In fact, because of the impersonation,

the DGSE might be able to grab it. That would mean that you guys and your juge would be kicked out. That would drive Marie-Hélène wild. Coitus interruptus was never her thing," Alexandre bubbled with an irritatingly secret little chuckle.

"I'm not going to go there," Capucine said with a pretty moue. "But it was definitely odd. Normally these juges are overly directive. They think they can do better police work than the flics. But she wasn't. She just told us she wouldn't sign an authorization for any kind of investigative work on Trag and told us to get on with it. Tallon just sat there saying, 'Yes, ma'am, three bags full.' "

"That doesn't surprise me."

"Well, we're stuck. There are no leads at all except Trag. They're the gateway to the solution. And we can't go near them. Tallon will never let us."

"What did Tallon say after the meeting?"

"He didn't say anything. He just did his *roman noir* scowl and said he'd see me on Monday."

"Well, he's weighing the risks of Marie-Hélène's dare."

"What dare? What are you talking about?" Capucine asked, annoyed.

"Simple. I'm sure she put on a holier-than-thou school-marm expression when she told you she wasn't going to sign any papers of any kind on Trag, right?"

"You really do know her. She was infuriating."

"My guess is that she was goading you to do something on your own. I'll also bet that Tallon understood that."

"But there's absolutely nothing we can do. Or at least nothing I can think of." Capucine began making meticulous piles of bivalve shells on her plate, separating them painstakingly by species. "Now's the perfect time for your little speech on how silly I'm being and all I have to do is quit the force and life will be perfect and wonderful and all."

"On the contrary," Alexandre answered carelessly, rooting earnestly through the crushed ice in search of a stray clam. "Not only do you seem to be getting the hang of it, but I'm beginning to find this case quite challenging. Definitely far more interesting than those insider trading sagas where you could never understand who was on the inside and who was on the outside."

Alexandre squinted and pursed his lips in an attempt at representing fathomless Asian wisdom but only managing to look like he had gas. In a stentorian voice he said, "As great Lao Tzu say, 'When deprived of own tactics, must use those of enemy.' "

Chapter 19

By ten on Monday morning Capucine knew exactly what she was going to do. She closed the door to her office, took a deep breath, and extracted the cell phone from her bag. She dialed the number on "Agent Etienne's" card. It rang for so long she thought it would kick into voice mail, but at the last instant someone picked up. A male voice answered with a curt, "*Oui?*"

Capucine attempted the trepidation of a timid office worker. "Hello? Is this Agent Etienne?" she asked, hoping her assumed lack of self-assurance was convincing.

"Yes," replied the voice, still short.

"I'm calling at the request of Lionel Vaillant."

"Oh, yes, of course," came the reply, the speaker clearly relaxing.

"Monsieur Vaillant has been reassigned to a new project. I'm on his team. I mean, I . . . uh . . . I was. I used to work for him. Before he got reassigned. And . . . uh . . . he had prepared a package with the data he thought you would find helpful. And he asked me to call to see how we could get it to you."

"That was very considerate of him. Would you like me to come and collect it?"

"Gosh, that would be perfect. I was afraid you were going to want me to come to Paris. Would it be too much trouble to come to the headquarters building? That would be so kind of you."

"No problem at all. How about this afternoon? Around three? Would that be okay?"

"Fine. Just ask for Marie Mercier at the desk. Thanks. I really appreciate your coming all the way out here. See you later."

Capucine pushed the red NO button on her phone. So far, so good. It was truly amazing how gullible some normally quick-witted people could be.

Even Tallon had liked the plan. "I was going to try something else along the same lines, but this might be even more effective," he had said.

Capucine arrived in Billancourt at two thirty with the three brigadiers squeezed into the Clio. She left them outside and went up to the long marble reception desk carrying a bulky manila envelope. There was no one else in the lobby. She held up her identity wallet with her police card on one side and badge on the other. The eight receptionists gathered in a gaggle and stared at it, fascinated, mute. The words "Police Judiciaire" always produced emotion.

"Listen carefully. A dangerous suspect will be coming here in a few minutes. He will ask to see a Marie Mercier. Send him to me. I will be in that corner over there. Is that clear?"

All eight nodded and murmured something that could be understood as "Oui, madame."

Capucine retreated to her corner and looked out the plate-glass window, searching for the brigadiers. She couldn't see them but knew that they would be keyed up, glued to their two-way radios.

At exactly three o'clock a man walked in, went up to

the desk, and asked a question of the middle receptionist. She half stood up and pointed to Capucine in the corner.

The man walked over to her, smiling.

"Mademoiselle Mercier?"

"Monsieur Etienne?"

Etienne nodded.

"Please sit down," Capucine said, making a show of holding the envelope awkwardly. Her plan was to get the phony agent seated, explain who she was, and arrest him quietly. It was a police truism that people who were already seated were less likely to bolt, and Capucine was keen on avoiding a scandal at Renault, particularly under the circumstances.

Etienne was all charm. "What happened to my friend Lionel?"

"Oh, he was assigned to a new project. Actually, it was a bit of a promotion."

"Still on Typhon, though?"

"Oh," Capucine giggled. "I can't talk about that. It's secret."

Etienne smiled wryly. Capucine was aware she had said something to alert him, but had no clue as to what it might have been. He glanced nervously right and left and then looked at Capucine with contrived flirtatiousness. "I didn't see you at the test track. I certainly would have noticed a girl as pretty as you."

"Oh, I don't work at Courcelles. I work upstairs here," Capucine replied with a coquettish smile.

Etienne's smile thinned a little. "I'm sure you're going to make me sign for that envelope and verify my identification. But would you mind if I just went to the washroom for a second first? I've been on the road since lunchtime."

Without waiting for an answer he got up and walked rapidly toward a glass door at the end of the hall.

Capucine was on her feet in a second, radio in hand,

alerting the brigadiers. "Suspect on the move. Heading toward the north side. David and Isabelle, cover that part of the building. Momo, take the car up to the door at the north end. I'm going after him."

Past the lobby doors, Etienne broke into a jog. Suddenly he turned a sharp right down a hallway. Capucine was no more than fifty feet behind him. When she rounded the corner the hallway was deserted and completely quiet. She stopped, listening intently, all her senses alive, and then moved ahead at a quick walk, as quietly as she could. She was sure he had sprinted, once out of sight, and had run down one of the hallways that branched out in front.

She advanced for a long minute or two, looking right and left down the intersecting hallways, seeing and hearing nothing. Suddenly she heard the distant *click* of the reception area door shutting behind her. She turned and ran, punching the walkie-talkie into life. "God damn it! I lost him. He doubled around and went for the main entrance. Start the car. I'll be right there. If he gets away it'll be over my fucking dead body." The good news, she told herself, was that she was finally beginning to sound like a flic.

Chapter 20

B y the time she got to the front door the car was right in front of it, Momo's screeching stop punctuated by dark tread marks on the driveway. Capucine jumped into the front passenger seat and Momo floored the gas pedal. The Clio eased forward at its stately pace. "What happened?" Momo asked.

"He's a smart cookie. He faked a trip to the john, hid in an office, and doubled back once I passed him."

"Well," said Momo, "he's in a navy BMW 525 no more than twenty seconds ahead of us. We'll see him once we reach the road."

Capucine nodded vigorously, talking excitedly into the microphone of the car radio, announcing to the PJ radio-control desk that they were giving chase to a suspect and that they would probably need the help of the Billancourt roadblock, but it would take a few minutes before she could announce the location.

They raced down the long Renault driveway, Momo rhythmically pumping the accelerator and swearing enthusiastically in the vain hope of getting the sluggish car to move faster. At the avenue du Général Leclerc he turned a hard left almost at full speed, tires complaining loudly, forcing an oncoming car to brake hard. The driver leaned out his window and was heard to yell something about "dirty Arab immigrants who steal French jobs and who should be driven back across the Mediterranean with whips." Momo leaned out of the window, smiled sweetly at him, jerked his fist sharply upward, middle finger raised, and then banged the blue light loudly on the roof. He flicked a switch on the dash. The light began its arterial pulsing. He angrily flicked another switch. The car was filled with the deafening two-tone braying *pan pon pan pon* of the French police.

"Do you see him?" Capucine yelled over the din.

"Yeah. He's about two hundred yards ahead of us."

The avenue Leclerc ran dead straight for about two miles until it reached the boulevard Périphérique, Paris's ring road. A mile ahead it went through an underpass that had been dug under a town square made up of the intersection of six streets. A perfect site for a roadblock. Capucine cupped her hand around the microphone against the wail of the siren and gave instructions that the Billancourt police were to put up a roadblock in the middle of the underpass.

They raced on, the BMW weaving skillfully in and out of traffic while the Renault labored to keep up. The Clio's speedometer read eighty-three miles an hour, ten miles less than promised in the sales brochure, but the brochure hadn't envisaged the car stuffed full of police officers. The BMW, of course, could go considerably faster than that, but it was hampered by traffic, no deterrent for the Clio since cars evaporated at the sound of the siren. It looked like a safe bet that they would be right behind when Etienne hit the roadblock.

Suddenly the BMW disappeared as it dropped down the ramp. When they arrived only seconds after, they could see the BMW already rocketing up the ramp on the far side of the underpass while the Billancourt gendarmes struggled

awkwardly to extract a bulky roll of spike tape from a police van. All four shouted out a spontaneous "Merde!" as
they shot by.

In under a minute Etienne would reach the Périphérique
and be faced with a key tactical choice. He could get on
the Périphérique, a six-lane highway, and attempt to capi-
talize on his speed advantage, or he could go straight into
Paris's Sixteenth Arrondissement and hope to lose the police in side streets, or he could turn into the Bois de Boulogne and probably make even better speed than on the
Périphérique, while keeping open the option of quickly
turning off into the city.

He chose the Bois.

Momo nodded in approval. "That's what I would have
done, too. You can get a lot of speed in the Bois. The Sixteenth Arrondissement runs its length so he can disappear
in there whenever he wants. And in the Bois we won't be
able to tell where he's going to go so we won't be able to
set up roadblocks. He knows what he's doing. That's for
sure."

They raced north, skidding to the left around the hippo-
drome and into the stately woods of the Bois. The prostitutes were already out. The officers could see them ahead,
prancing by the roadside, some bare breasted, some completely naked except for stiletto heels. By the time the police car came up they had vanished into the trees as if they
had never existed. Capucine had a feeling that if the perp
had had just thirty seconds more lead time, he would have
tried a ruse with the hookers. But he didn't have a thirty-
second lead.

They reached the long, dead-straight allée de Long-
champ. Etienne stepped on the gas, accelerating to a hundred miles an hour, and shot away from the Clio. Within
seconds he reached the Porte Maillot roundabout. It was
obvious he hoped to leave the police far enough behind so
he could disappear into the streets of the Seventeenth Ar-

rondissement. But Capucine had called ahead and there were four Paris gendarmes on hand to note exactly where he went.

Etienne barreled up the avenue de La Grande Armée toward the Etoile roundabout and the Champs-Elysées. People stopped and heads turned as they roared by. "At least we're pleasing the tourists. Lord knows that's important," Isabelle commented. "Maybe next time we can get Momo to wear a beret and tuck a baguette under his arm."

Instead of heading down the Champs-Elysées, Etienne turned down the avenue Marceau toward the Seine. At the bottom of the hill he rocketed onto the voie sur berge, the four-lane thoroughfare that parallels the Seine almost at water level.

Mistake. They had him. There was no way he could get off the voie before the police could set up a roadblock. Capucine got busy on the radio.

They reached the denouement in the Fourth Arrondissement, four miles away. Etienne had increased his lead gradually, gaining nearly a quarter of a mile on the Clio. At the Hôtel de Ville—Paris's town hall—Etienne made his move and soared up the exit ramp. Ironically it was the same exit he would have taken if he had been going directly to the Police Judiciaire's headquarters.

From the Clio Capucine could see the two navy blue police vans parked on either side of the top of the ramp. She imagined she heard the shark's teeth of wickedly curved spurs burst and shred the tires. The BMW skidded across the avenue out of control on its steel wheels in a fireworks of sparks until it hit the far curb, hard.

Etienne leaped out and ran. Two gendarmes on the street yelled. Momo squeaked the tiny Clio through the opening as the tape was pulled back and shot diagonally across the avenue, catching up to Etienne at the steel fence around the plaza in front of the town hall. Capucine jumped out, pulled her Sig out from the small of her back, held it high over her head, and fired all fifteen shots into the air as fast as she could pull the trigger. The staccato was so tight it sounded a single shearing noise like a huge sheet being torn in two. Etienne froze, bent at the waist, his arms stretched out horizontally. The crowd in front of the Hôtel de Ville dispersed in a confused run like a flock of alarmed pigeons. Capucine continued to hold her pistol in the air, tripped the extractor lever, caught the empty magazine as it fell, slammed in a new one, and snicked the slide back in place. Momo stared at her with admiration.

Chapter 21

A bove all else the French police love of a show of force. Less than a minute after Etienne surrendered, three additional vans arrived discharging over forty uniformed police officers. Some of these concerned themselves with controlling the steadily increasing crowd and blocking traffic in front of the Hôtel de Ville, but most just milled around looking officious. There was much shaking of hands and expressions of camaraderie between units. At the epicenter Etienne stood silent, his hands handcuffed behind his back, waiting patiently, surrounded by Capucine and her three brigadiers, who had all holstered their guns. No one spoke. All five were catching their breath after the chase.

After a short pause Etienne looked down at Capucine, smiled boyishly, and said, "Well, I guess you caught me." Capucine looked at him evenly, not answering.

A large navy blue Peugeot 407 pulled up. Two burly plainclothesmen got out, took Etienne firmly but gently by the upper arms, and eased him into the backseat of the car. The two plainclothesmen slid into the front seats while Capucine pushed into the vacant back next to Etienne. They drove the two blocks to the Quai des Orfèvres with the erratic sharp bursts of acceleration characteristic of police drivers, the car's siren wailing its deafening complaint and the blue light pulsing like the throb of a migraine.

At the Quai des Orfèvres Etienne was taken directly to the second-level basement, through a studded steel door with a judas window, and into a large, damp room well below the water level of the Seine. The room was shockingly silent after the commotion on the street. Ancient green paint flaked humidly from the walls. In the exact center of the room was a scarred oak table with a metal chair at either side. A single light hung from the ceiling, its dented dome lighting casting a tight spot of light onto the table. Save for the hypnotic swaying of the shadows, waving back and forth like seaweed on an ocean bed as the lamp pendulated in the breeze from the open door, Capucine thought the scene would have been perfect as a set for a third degree in a low-budget film.

Etienne's pockets had been emptied and the contents examined closely and laid out on the table: an American passport in the name of Guy Thomas with an unusual number of airport entry stamps, a cell phone, a few coins, and a brand-new wallet containing only two credit cards, three of the Etienne DGSE business cards, a few euro notes, and a laminated plastic New York State driver's license, also in the name of Guy Thomas. Nothing else.

The prisoner's hands were held by two pairs of handcuffs, each clipped to the crossbar between the legs of the chair. He had enough freedom of movement to lean forward but not enough to rise from the chair.

In the room were six police officers, including Capucine, anonymous in the shadows.

An amiable round man in his shirtsleeves, straight out of a thirties detective film, an old-style Manurhin revolver sagging in a sweat-blackened leather holster in his armpit, began the questioning. Given the threatening mood of the scene, he was unnaturally polite and cheerful as he paced around the prisoner with a pronounced limp. Capucine had never seen him before.

"So," he said in a calm, reassuring voice, like a pediatrician encouraging a frightened child to tell where it hurt. "Why don't you start out by telling us who you are."

The prisoner smiled easily. "Of course. My name is Guy Thomas and I'm an American here on a week's vacation." When he had been chatting with Capucine in front of the Hôtel de Ville his fluent French would have passed him as a native. Now he spoke with a strong American accent in elementary pidgin French.

The officer smiled. "Of course you are. But let's start with the basics: age, address, employer, address in Paris."

The prisoner explained confidently, wearing a patient smile, that he worked for a software company in New York; was on vacation in Paris, where he liked to come as often as he could; and was staying at the apartment of a friend who happened to be out of town.

"Excellent," said the detective with an encouraging smile. "Now comes the interesting part. Please explain what you were doing at Renault that resulted in your attempting to escape from the police at high speed for over eight miles."

"Yes," the prisoner replied in halting French. "I have to say I'm a bit annoyed about that. I went to Renault to inquire about buying a car and having it sent home. They're very difficult to come by in the States, you know. While I was there a woman started yelling at me. I didn't really understand what she said, but she chased me down the hall. I made it to my car, but she kept after me. I had no idea she was a policewoman. I'm guessing she thought I was someone else, but I still think I may have to complain to the embassy. I'm also going to have to insist you release me immediately."

A young squint-eyed detective loomed up from the

shadows behind the prisoner. "Listen, asshole," he said through clenched teeth, "you're not going anywhere. We have the right to keep you for seventy-two hours and I can promise you you're not going to leave this room for a single one of them. And by then, fuckface, we're going to know all there is to know about you. Then you're going to go to another room down the hall just like this one and that will be your first step on a journey that will keep you behind bars for the rest of your life. You'd better believe it. And you're not going to be feeling all that healthy on that journey." He laughed menacingly.

The angry detective retreated back into the gloom like a moray eel slithering back into its hole in the rock. It was all very much like a stage play. Throughout the tirade the older detective had continued to gaze at the prisoner placidly. "Tell me again." He smiled almost apologetically. "So you come to Paris frequently on vacation and one day decided it would be fun to buy a car—"

The prisoner was made to repeat his story again, and again, and once again. The hours clumped on leadenly. People came and went in the room, held whispered conversations in the corners, came and went again. The prisoner seemed hardly to tire and told his silly story over and over with his patient little smile as if he were talking to children or maybe even the illiterate officials of a barbarous Third World country. The older detective remained unassailably affable, and the younger one undulated out episodically to spit his venom in brief spurts.

In the course of those long hours Capucine remained almost invisible in the penumbra, saying nothing but occasionally receiving whispered reports. It seemed that one of the numerous airport stamps corresponded to the date the prisoner claimed he had arrived in France the last time, and he was actually staying at the address he gave, an apartment rented by an individual who had not yet been located. They had not had confirmation of his New York

employment but would call at three A.M. Paris time when
New York offices opened.

After several hours of this the steel door opened with a
grating shriek and Tallon strode in. The ambiance changed
as palpably as if a battery of lights had been switched on.
Tallon approached the desk and stared hard at the prisoner for a few heartbeats. "Why don't you cut the crap?
It's not getting you anywhere," he said.

Etienne widened his eyes in a pantomime of surprise.
"What you mean?" he asked. His French, which had been
improving gradually as the interrogation went on, reverted
to its initial beginner's level.

"You're a Trag operative. You've been impersonating a
DGSE agent, a crime punishable by fifteen years' imprisonment. You've attempted to escape arresting officers,
provoking an incident endangering innocent citizens, another crime punishable by imprisonment. You're also the
prime suspect in a capital crime. In the blink of an eye I
can send you up for over twenty years. Start talking!"

The prisoner tirelessly resumed his litany. "Monsieur, I
don't know if your colleagues have told you, but I am an
American on vacation in Paris. I went to Renault to buy a
car and that woman started chasing me."

Tallon started to walk around the table in angry gyres.

"I work for the Brianfield Office Systems Company in
New York. I'm an American citizen. That woma—"

The impact was deafening in the small room. From behind Tallon had hit the prisoner on the top of the head
with a thick book. Etienne uttered not a sound. Drops of
blood appeared in his ears. Gently he put his head down
on the table, his face turned sideways, breathing shallowly,
his eyes open, unseeing.

The young officer who had been playing the bad-cop
role picked Etienne's head up by the hair and slapped him
twice on his left cheek, using the inside of his hand so he
wouldn't leave marks.

"Don't go to sleep on us now, you little cunt." He shook the prisoner by the hair until his eyes snapped into focus.

"Again," ordered Tallon.

"I'm an American citizen. I came to Paris for a week's va—"

The impact was just as loud, just as shocking the second time. The blood was now oozing from his ears and trickling down his neck onto his collar.

The process continued for some time. At each iteration the prisoner became increasingly oblivious, repeating his story in a mumble that became decreasingly audible. His face progressively turned a pasty cadaverous white. Finally he sank onto the table for good. The bad cop was unable to rouse him.

Tallon looked disgusted. "Pfuuuf," as if to say, "Look what they send us nowadays." He beckoned Capucine with his finger and said brusquely, "Call the duty doctor. Have him checked every fifteen minutes. No stimulants. No painkillers. Call me if his blood pressure goes below 70/50 or if he wakes up. I'll be in my office."

Tallon marched out, followed by the other officers, leaving Capucine alone with her prisoner.

The doctor came. He cleaned the blood out of the prisoner's ears, took his blood pressure, snorted, said it was hardly worth checking every fifteen minutes. But he did peer through the judas every now and then. The prisoner lay immobile, head on the table, breathing in flat little breaths. His color was bad. The hours continued to trudge on oppressively.

Deep into the night the prisoner woke slowly and fell backward in the chair. He started to shake his head to clear it but stopped suddenly as if in sharp pain. He pivoted his body for a cautious look around the room and saw that it was empty except for Capucine. "Can I have some water . . . please," he bleated in perfect French.

Expressionless, Capucine pressed a small button inset into the door frame. A uniformed policeman appeared. "Bring a small tin of juice," she ordered.

When it came she held the three-inch aluminum can to the prisoner's lips and let him sip slowly. A bit of his color returned along with a hint of sparkle to his eyes.

"You're being a fool, you know," she said with a slight smile. "I'll have to call the commissaire principal back down here in a minute. He really doesn't like you. He'll go on beating you until you talk sensibly or you collapse for good. If that happens, there'll be a good chance you'll have a subdural hematoma. That would not be good for you since you'd be parked in a normal detention cell upstairs waiting for a deportation order, which would come topped up with a writ of *interdiction du territoire* that would keep you out of France forever, and then, in the fullness of time, they'd put you on a flight to New York. You'd have a blood leak in your brain for at least a week before you could see a real doctor. You know what the consequence of that might be?"

The prisoner thought for a moment. "You might have a point there," he said with a sheepish smile. "Stop him from hitting me with that goddamn phone book and I'll tell you my tale."

"It's not a phone book anymore. We stopped using them when they made them smaller. It's the directory of French lawyers. Heavier and far more appropriate, don't you think?"

The prisoner's mirth emerged as the feeblest of snorts. But Capucine suspected it might be the first real laughter that room had heard in a good many years.

"Well, okay," he began. "I have no idea how you found out, but you're right. I am a Trag operative."

Capucine left the Quai des Orfèvres at 6:30 in the morning. Guy Thomas, which apparently was his real name, had given his statement. Given it again. And would give it a third time before it was printed out for him to sign. He would remain handcuffed to the chair in the damp room far below river level until he was taken to the juge d'instruction. Tallon definitely did not like him.

Driving home she made a small detour to the bakery that made the particularly good croissants, bought six *pur beurres*, and then went home. Alexandre was sound asleep on his back, his stomach a gentle and endearing convexity in the bedclothes. He snored quietly, a deeply reassuring sound to Capucine.

She took a long shower using a new bar of Hermès soap, part of a basket someone had given her for her birthday. The smell was cloying but the soap succeeded in eradicating the interrogation-cell stench of sweat and fear and dissipating a good part of the wretchedness of the evening.

Alexandre awoke clear-eyed and smiling and came into the bathroom to brush his teeth. "Most men would be alarmed if their gorgeous wives dragged themselves in at the crack of dawn, but I'm confident your rashest peccancy was biffing evildoers."

"Biffing is not the sort of word the Police Judiciaire use. That's because the reality is far too inhuman to joke about."

"Angel, I know all about it, trust me. All journalists do," he said, taking her in his arms. "Don't quote me, but I suppose it has to be done."

Capucine pulled away and said brightly, "Come on, I brought croissants. Let's have breakfast. I'll tell you what happened."

Capucine edged Alexandre away from the Pasquini, deftly produced two frothy cups of café au lait, and consumed one of the croissants with appetite. She was licking the butter off her fingers and contemplating a second croissant when Alexandre became impatient.

"So what *did* happen?"

"Well, my little plan worked. We caught the guy. Not without a little running around, of course. We chased him from Billancourt to nearly the front door of the prefecture. It was a car chase right out of an American movie . . . Well, almost."

"In your Clio? He must be a very accommodating man."

"Momo was driving. The next part was far less pleasant. It took all night for us to crack the poor man. Or rather, for Tallon to crack him. With a directory on the head. His story was simple. He's a Trag guy, all right. They'd been sniffing around like Labradors after a downed pheasant, certain that sooner or later some company would make a gas catalyst that really worked. Our boy was assigned to Renault. When the président died he thought he finally might have found a way in and called on Renault's head of R & D with the DGSE scam that Guyon fell for. So his bet paid off and he obtained a fair amount of data."

"Was Tallon able to worm his client's name out of him?"

"He claimed they were just trolling the field and if they came up with something they'd know what to do with it. He couldn't be shaken on that."

"That might even be true," Alexandre said. "What did he know about the président's death?"

"Nothing, it seems. He was pretty convincing about that. We went over it again and again. He just read about it in the papers. Figured Renault would be in a tizzy and ripe for someone to buy a shaggy-dog story. It was a long shot with no downside risk. If it hadn't been for that carelessness with the cell phone—which probably wasn't even his fault—no one would have ever traced anything back to Trag and they would have all the information they'd hoped for."

"And you're convinced he wasn't connected with the murder."

"Totally. We know he was out of the country that Friday and even Tallon agrees that it's highly unlikely Trag would engineer a Machiavellian plot to assassinate the president of Renault."

"So what happens now?"

"You tell me. What do you think your precious Marie-Hélène's going to do to our Trag agent?"

"Oh, that's easy. She'll let him go. She'll never get any mileage out of the impersonation of an agent business in court and the worst she could do with the car chase is revoke his license if he had a French one, which I'm sure he doesn't. In fact, if she moved to take him to court for any reason at all the DGSE would probably pull the whole case out from under her before she had a crack at tagging the murderer and that's the last thing she wants."

"We're back to square one," Capucine sighed. Her eyes filled with tears and she deflated as Alexandre took her in his arms.

Chapter 22

The next morning, after the luxury of a twelve-hour night, Capucine arrived cotton-headed at the Quai and was jarred awake by the winking ruby eye of an "urgent" intradepartmental e-mail on her screen. She was wanted immediately by Tallon.

Capucine had not seen Tallon since his theatrical appearance in the interrogation room. Once again she was dismayed to see Rivière already sitting in front of Tallon's desk, this time stretched out indolently in a tipped-back wooden chair, cigarette dangling from his lips, a posture he no doubt imagined made him look like James Dean. Did Rivière spend the entire day closeted with Tallon?

In contrast Tallon sat jauntily at his desk, smirking the smug smirk adults reserve for children they perceive to have done something clever or naughty but which is entirely beyond their comprehension. Capucine was reminded of an emotionally charged afternoon in her childhood when a precocious seven-year-old cousin had arrived in the salon of her aunt's château just as tea was about to be served to the entire family, happily announcing that she had just discovered something wonderful to do with a spoon and was ecstatic at the idea of showing it off to the assembled company. Tallon's expression reminded her of her uncles' barely repressed grins. She had had no idea if she would be praised or criticized, but one way or the other it was beyond irritating.

"Sit down, sit down, Lieutenant," Tallon said with his knowing grin. "Last week was refreshing. A good healthy emetic for the case. I enjoyed hearing about you running around shooting your gun off in all directions like a Western movie. And it also did me good to see that smug *Amerloque* get his just deserts, a great deal of good. Cleared the air. Didn't get us anywhere, but it definitely cleared the air. That's for sure." His smile broadened. "Don't get me wrong, Lieutenant. Actually, you did quite well. Very well indeed."

Rivière looked puzzled. He set his chair upright with a bang and looked anxiously back and forth at Tallon and Capucine like an excited spaniel hoping to get a treat.

Capucine was irritated. This was a new and not entirely likeable Tallon. She had a limited capacity for being mocked. Her only satisfaction was Rivière's obvious mystification.

"Madame le Juge d'Agremont called me late last night. She released that Trag insect. She had had him carted over to her office for an interview, what she called a 'private' interview with only a shorthand stenographer present. She felt sorry for him. She found his condition, and I quote, 'piteous.' So she gave him a good dressing-down, threatened him with a writ barring him from the French territory if he ever gets so much as a parking ticket here, and had someone over there throw him into a taxi. Voilà. The last of Trag." Despite herself, Capucine was impressed that Alexandre's augury had been right on the money.

"But after all that fun we still have the case to solve," Tallon continued. "So we're going to take a new approach. No more speeding around chasing people and shooting at everything in sight. We're going to be delicate

and subtle and insightful. And that brings me to Lieutenant Rivière here. Judging by your recent zeal, he's done
a beautiful job of tutoring you in homicide techniques.
We're both in his debt. However, as he has just been explaining to me, he's been neglecting his current case. He
has a suspect he thinks is ready to take the fall, but he hasn't
had the time to exhaust an embarrassment of riches of
other leads." He smiled cynically at Rivière. "I need you to
pull out all the stops. I want to go to court with a bullet-
proof dossier. I'm giving you two weeks to put a case together that would give even the stupidest prosecutor an
easy conviction. So, no more"—Tallon paused slightly for
emphasis—"flirting with the Delage case. Now, get out of
here and get to work." Rivière looked like a chastened
schoolboy as he murmured, "Oui, Monsieur le Commissaire," and shuffled out of the room. If she hadn't felt the
reproach was really aimed at her, Capucine might have almost felt sorry for him.

"He's a very solid man. Very solid," Tallon said, once
Rivière had left. "However, he has his own particular approach to things that certainly doesn't include sensitivity
to nuance." Tallon gave a deep-throated bark that might
have been a laugh. "*Bref*, you don't need him anymore
and he'd just get in your way. I want you to proceed delicately. Patiently. With your ears open to catch anything. If
you feel you're out of your depth, come to me directly. No
need to consult Lieutenant Rivière unless it suits you. Is
that clear?"

Capucine nodded.

"Très bien. We're going to take a new tack, paying more
attention to the psychological aspects of the case. That's
more up your alley, *non?*"

"Oui, Monsieur le Commissaire." Capucine had no
idea where this was going.

"So let's get down to it. I want you to start with this
woman, Karine Bergeron."

"Delage's old girlfriend? Rivière's already seen her."

Tallon waved a file folder in the air, apparently Rivière's report on the interview. "So he has. He asked straightforward questions and got straightforward answers. I want something more subtle."

"Do you really think Delage's two-week affair over a decade ago could have anything to do with his murder?"

"Lieutenant, you will find, if you are successful in permanently reorienting your career in the direction that you seem to want it to take, that crimes of passion are more subtle than these crimes of accounting you specialize in. They are possibly less intricate, but they are definitely more subtle. If a man takes your money, it's obvious what he wants. But a man with a woman, well, who knows?"

Capucine smarted at the rebuff while realizing that none had been intended.

"Spend some time with this woman. Get on her wavelength. Understand what was happening in Delage's life at that point. See if you can pick up any threads that might turn out to be long ones. Then come back and we'll move on to the next item."

Thinking about it in her Clio, Capucine had been unsure if being freed of Rivière was good or bad. One thing was sure: if word got out that his work was being redone by a rookie, Rivière was going to resign his membership in her fan club.

Chapter 23

Since delicacy was the order of day, Capucine had suggested the interview with Karine Bergeron take place on Saturday afternoon at her Seventeenth Arrondissement apartment, hoping that five o'clock would be a relaxed moment between afternoon shopping and whatever plans she might have for the evening. Despite Parisian snobbery, which wrote off the Seventeenth as the poor man's Sixteenth—"*très Dix-septième*" was the chic set's ultimate damnation—Capucine thought it was one of the most pleasant neighborhoods in Paris, filled with spacious apartments overlooking broad, tree-lined avenues.

The apartment turned out to be well lighted and spacious, with a view of the grassed-over rail bed of the abandoned little train that had puffed around Paris's perimeter in the days prior to World War II. The flat was filled with sleek inexpensive Ikea furniture contrasted by the occasional heavily ornate Louis Philippe piece, testimony to Karine's share of an inheritance from previous generations of prosperous bourgeois that had undoubtedly consisted more of manners and taste than hard assets.

Karine was in her late forties, unselfconsciously rejoicing in her svelte figure, carefully dressed in a pencil skirt and a striking, flowered silk blouse. Genuinely curious, Capucine asked her where she had purchased it. Karine served them pale Oolong tea in exquisite pale blue Sevres china. They discovered they had a distant cousin in common. The afternoon wore on serenely. Police work seemed very far away.

Much later Karine said, "You don't seem like a police officer at all. Certainly very different from the man who came to see me before. He was straight out of a Luc Besson movie."

"I hope he wasn't rude."

"No, no, not at all," she said apologetically. "Just very brusque. Very in character. Also, I'm afraid I wasn't very communicative. I was still in a state of shock over dear Jean-Louis's death. The whole subject is still very painful."

"Yes," said Capucine, "it must have been totally unexpected." She put two fingers on the back of Karine's wrist. "I wonder if we could talk about your entente with President Delage?"

"That's a much more elegant way of putting it than that lieutenant did. He was offensively ribald," Karine said.

"What is there to say? We were very much in love. It was blissful. But he decided he just couldn't leave Nadine, his wife, and didn't want to cheat on her behind her back. So we ended the affair. Of course, we never stopped being wonderfully close friends."

"What do you mean? You continued the relationship?"

"Certainly not. That would have been impossible. I became a friend of the family. You know, regularly at their house for dinner parties. That sort of thing. I became quite fond of poor Nadine as well. Of course, the dear never had any idea that anything had happened between Jean-Louis and me."

Capucine sipped her tea. It was almost colorless, its flavor ethereal and slightly acid.

"The situation must have been a torment for you," Capucine said.

"Yes and no. You see, I had another gentleman friend. Martin Fleuret."

"Do you mean the man who was with Delage for his last dinner?" Capucine wanted to bite her tongue at the tactlessness of the phrase.

"Yes, he was one of Jean-Louis's closest friends, as well as his personal lawyer."

"Wasn't the situation rather uncomfortable?" Capucine asked.

"No, not really. It was all so sudden. You see, in those days I worked at Renault as a secretary. One day Jean-Louis's assistant fell sick and I was asked to fill in for her. It was love at first sight. But as I told you, he broke it off after two weeks. I only told Martin about it much later."

"And you continued your relationship with Monsieur Fleuret?"

"Yes. Somehow, my love for Jean-Louis seemed to have nothing to do with what I felt—feel—for Martin. They were such different sorts of relationships. Nothing had changed between us."

"I doubt Monsieur Fleuret saw it that way."

"Men are so linear about these things, as I'm sure you know. Anyway, Martin swallowed his pride about the whole episode. He wanted us to get married. He's been after me to get married ever since."

"Oh, I know how little men can understand. I really do. So you've refused to marry Monsieur Fleuret?"

"Well, for a long while I did. Somehow it didn't seem fair to Jean-Louis. I suppose I always hoped he still loved me. I thought things might change when Nadine passed away, but they didn't. I never knew what to do."

"And now?" Capucine asked gently.

"Well, I think I might just marry Martin after all. Neither of us is getting any younger, and it will make him so happy. I just might."

Chapter 24

Capucine took a strong dislike to Martin Fleuret even before she met him. She found his office rankling. It was located in an overstuffed and pretentious neighborhood near the Parc Monceau, jammed with overstuffed and pretentious Louis Philippe velvet furniture artfully chosen to give an impression of stolidity and propriety.

Fleuret received her somewhat breathlessly, attempting to convey the impression that he had stepped out of a desperately important meeting to receive her and was counting the seconds until he could get back to it.

Despite Capucine's near certainty that she might have met Fleuret at a dinner party or two, his condescension was as complete as if she were a menial subordinate he was forced to talk to at an office Christmas party.

"You know, of course, that I have already seen your Lieutenant Rivière," Fleuret began. "It was necessary to disabuse him of a ridiculous notion that I had had an altercation with Président Delage over dinner. I can't imagine where he acquired such an idea. I hope you don't intend to persist in that vein."

"Maître, I think we know all we need to know about

your dinner with Président Delage. For the time being, at least. No, I'm here today to talk about Karine Bergeron."

Fleuret recoiled as if he had been slapped. "Mademoiselle Bergeron has nothing to do with the matter. Nothing whatsoever." His lips stretched into a tight thin colorless line and his eyes darkened around a pinpoint of pupil.

"Maître Fleuret," Capucine said soothingly, "I'm sure you can understand that in a case of this sort the investigation is unusually thorough. It often involves aspects that are apparently irrelevant."

"I know only one thing, that a competent police force would have had it solved long ago. You are just meddling with innocent people because you don't have a clue how to proceed." He rose, walked in a tight, nervous circle, and sat down again. "All right. I suppose I can't stop you. What do you want to know?"

"I understand that you have had a romantic attachment to Karine Bergeron for some time."

"What of it? Neither of us is married. We're both adults. What business is it of yours?"

"I also understand that you had been pressing her to get married and she had refused due to her attachment to the late Président Delage."

"Ridiculous. Utterly ridiculous. It's true that we have discussed marriage on and off over the years. The timing has never been appropriate. We both, let me repeat that, we *both* have agreed the timing was not appropriate."

"And do you feel it is more 'appropriate' now that Président Delage is no longer with us?"

"Madame, that question is blatantly offensive. It is the sort of comment that will oblige me to make a complaint to your superiors."

"Very well, then, let me try another approach. What did you do after your dinner with Président Delage?"

"I went home, Lieutenant. I went home like a man who

had a great deal of work to do the next morning, even if it was a Saturday."

"I see. Since you've been so helpful, I'll be frank with you. We now believe that the death of the président was a murder, not an accidental poisoning. And that the murder was committed during the night following your dinner. But we couldn't seem to come up with anyone who has a motive. That is, we couldn't until today. It would seem that things are going to get a lot better for you with Président Delage out of the way."

"Madame, your offensiveness really has no limits. I really am going to make a complaint. Jean-Louis Delage was one of my closest friends. His death was a great personal loss to me. However, as it happens, I have what you in your sordid little milieu call an alibi. After the dinner I went to the apartment of Mademoiselle Bergeron and I remained there until the following morning. So my whereabouts are fully accounted for."

Chapter 25

"**M**onkey brains! You actually ate monkey brains?" the pretty blonde shrieked, open-mouthed. The table erupted in laughter. Alexandre beamed.

"You're too adorable," the hostess said. "You're so engrossed in your fiancé you don't listen to dinner conversation anymore. Alexandre was just telling us about the worst cocktails he's ever had. It seems Monkey Brains are made with Sambuca, Bailey's, and Campari. The Bailey's congeals to look like squashed brains and the Campari makes it look like it's all covered in blood."

"Sounds thoroughly delightful," the fiancé said. "You see, my pet, the world would be a very dangerous place indeed without restaurant critics. Intrepidly, they forge ahead, swinging their knives and forks fearlessly, clearing a safe path for us timid souls. Let's drink to their courage!"

It was a dinner party for eight at the apartment of one of Capucine's university classmates. Now a management consultant, she lived with her boyfriend in a small but masterfully decorated flat on the rue des Francs-Bourgeois near the place des Vosges, in the pricey heart of the Marais. Despite the crushing hours of her job she nurtured her social life with the intensity of an intern caring for a patient on life support. She made a point of having at least two carefully orchestrated dinners every month, each complete with eucalyptus branches artfully laid over starched linen napkins and exotic aspics prepared by the gourmet food shop around the corner. Like most Paris *diners en ville,* the guests rarely arrived until after nine and usually remained at the table until one or two in the morning exchanging meticulously crafted epigrams.

The longer Capucine spent with the Police Judiciaire the more she detested such evenings. Her inability to make droll small talk about her job set her apart—fiscal fraud hardly made for witty conversation in bourgeois circles—and she found the slavish attention to social nuances increasingly irritating. Still, she felt a loyalty to her classmates and would have hated to lose them from sight. Alexandre, on the other hand, adored evenings with Capucine's friends, relishing their youthful adulation of his wit.

That night Capucine's stock of patience was depleted. Using the telepathy particular to identical twins and married couples she shot a look at Alexandre instructing him in no uncertain terms to implement an immediate retreat. As self-consciously as an untalented stage actor rushing his exit line before he is booed, Alexandre rose, muttered something about having still to file his next morning's piece—which, in fact, he had e-mailed at one in the afternoon following a leisurely breakfast—and escorted Capucine out after the requisite air kisses and shoulder-thumping embraces.

"That was precipitous," he said in the elevator. "Are you exhausted?"

"On the contrary. I'm too keyed up for that sort of thing. I need to vent about the case. Anyway, my patience with those inanities is wearing thinner and thinner. Let's go get a drink somewhere. Let's go get several drinks."

* * *

They wound up at Pershing Hall. Originally built by charitable subscriptions from the United States as a hospital for recuperating American soldiers in the closing days of World War I, it had been recently transformed into one of the most posh hotels in Paris. At that hour the bar was populated with impossibly anorexic adorables in impossibly brief couturier dresses sipping impossibly colored mixed drinks. A disc jockey ardently played techno rock at a level so low as to be audible only to the barely adolescent. For all others the impact was no more than an unsettling throb in the seat of the pants, not too dissimilar from the sensation of a ship's engine during a trans-Atlantic crossing.

A waiter materialized like a congealing mist, deposited a malt whiskey for Alexandre and a vodka on the rocks with a twist of lemon peel for Capucine, and dematerialized just as wordlessly. Alexandre regarded Capucine tenderly. "Case getting you down?"

"I don't know why, but it is. We seem to be making progress, but I just have this feeling that nothing we've got so far will pan out."

"A good rant will make you feel better. What's going on?"

"Tallon's changed the approach. He wants me to redo all of Rivière's initial background interviews so my legendary nose for subtlety will sniff out something that Rivière missed."

"At least Tallon's figured out where the talent is. I'm a great fan of that nose myself. What's it produced so far?"

"A two-week fling Delage had twelve years ago has paid off in a small way. Turns out she's been seeing the guy Delage had dinner with the fatal night and the guy in question is extremely keen on marrying her. But the bad news for him is that she continued to have a soft spot for Delage and refused to even think of getting married in the hopes she might get Delage back one day. So now we have some-

THE GRAVE GOURMET   131

one who was at the scene of the crime that night and who also has a motive."

"You don't sound too convinced."

"Of course I'm not. For openers, he claims he left the restaurant and went straight to the woman's place and spent the night there. Not the most solid alibi on earth, but an alibi nonetheless. On top of that, it's hard to figure out how he could have known about the oysters. It's not absolutely impossible, of course. He must know tons of people who eat at Diapason regularly and one of them might have mentioned it, but it's a stretch. The real deal breaker is that it would seem impossible that he could have got his hands on weapons-grade saxitoxin."

"So it's weapons grade now, is it?"

"That was a given from the moment we knew it was saxitoxin poisoning. Making a saxitoxin poison is not something you can just do in your kitchen like reducing a duck sauce. It requires a whole bunch of specialized lab equipment and a lot of technical know-how to make it work. And it just so happens the stuff is ideal for chemical warfare. The victims become partially paralyzed almost immediately, all calm and peaceful while remaining fully conscious, and then progressively get more and more paralyzed until they eventually die of asphyxiation. In the bad old days it was on the official NATO weapons roster as Agent TZ. I'm sure any number of countries still stockpile it on the sly."

"And one assumes this poor chap had no access to an arsenal, is that it?"

"Exactly, he's a family lawyer, and a very stuffy one at that."

"So what happens next?"

"Tallon was so pleased that we had a new suspect he wants me to keep on redoing Rivière's interviews. He's a motive freak. As our hostess of the evening would say, the Police Judiciaire methodology is entirely 'motive driven.'

That may be effective in ninety percent of the cases, but it's not going to work this time. Our scarce commodity is suspects who have any access to means, not suspects who have a motive."

"So what would you do differently?"

"Focus on the restaurant, of course. That's where the means lie."

"You could well be right about that," Alexandre said. Capucine looked at him carefully to see if he was tipsy.

"My problem," Capucine said, "is I don't know how to make restaurant people talk. When I interviewed the three top guys down at the Quai they either said nothing or made fun of me in that supercilious restaurant way they have."

"That's because you were trying too hard. Believe me, getting restaurant people to run off at the mouth is the easiest thing on earth. And to make it even easier for you, every day they'll present you with a device that is even better than one of those Agatha Christie scenes—you know, where all the characters gather in the study falling over each other to blab their secrets to the detective."

"What are you talking about?"

"The staff meal, of course. All restaurants have one. It's one of the grand traditions of the business: all employees receive free food twice a day. Sometimes it's wonderful, sometimes not. The theory is that before each service a junior chef is appointed to cook up something with leftovers, scraps, and rejected produce. The young chef reveals his budding genius and the staff bonds over an enchanting repast. In practice it sometimes works out that way but a good deal of the time the staff is served what should have gone into the garbage bin. But one way or the other in every restaurant in Paris you can bet the entire crew is sitting down lapping up whatever is put in front of them. All you have to do is sit down with them."

"But I can't just waltz in. You forget how leery people are of flics."

"But not flics with your level of . . . um . . . pulchritude. You have a trump card. Good time to play it. They'll welcome you with open arms and drool all over you. I know kitchen staffs. Trust me on that one."

Chapter 26

It wasn't Alexandre's love of playing the oracle that irritated Capucine; it was the fact that his prophesies invariably proved correct. At five in the afternoon she had found Diapason's door unlocked and the dining room deserted. Hearing the sounds of an animated gathering in the kitchen she had peered through one of the glass peepholes. As Alexandre had predicted, the entire staff was gathered around steel prep tables, noisily gobbling up a meal. She was seized by a déjà vu flash of an afternoon when, having just started at a new school, she had been dragged off by her mother to a birthday party where she didn't know a soul. The irrational feeling of shame and humiliation was the same. Her ears burned. She blushed. Delage was absent but Bouteiller, avuncular in his baggy tweed jacket, sat at the head of the farthest table. She resolutely decided to make for him and pushed through the green leather doors.

Surprised by the intrusion of a stranger, the group fell silent, but once they recognized Capucine they resumed eating with gusto; their looks softened and there were even a few scattered smiles and greetings. Bouteiller came up to her, very much the executive officer in charge.

"I apologize, Lieutenant, I wasn't informed of your visit. How can I help you? Is there anyone in particular you wish to interview?" he asked.

"Actually, Monsieur Bouteiller, I don't have a specific agenda. I thought I'd sit in on your staff meal and see how things were going in the restaurant."

A distressingly pretty adolescent, who must have been an intern *aide-chef*, jumped up, "Please sit here. We're having a pot-au-feu. I made it myself, and in all modesty it's exquisite. It's just some beef cheeks and veal shanks we couldn't use and a few carrots, leeks, and potatoes, and, of course, my secret spices." The extent of his pride in what was probably the first meal they had let him make all by himself was beyond charming.

The table erupted in laughter. "Secret spices, my ass! How secret is a bay leaf, a bunch of thyme, and a pinch of pepper?" said the next man at the table. "Mind you"—he winked conspiratorially at Capucine—"if you could talk him out of one of the marrow bones he stuck in there and spread the marrow on a baguette dipped in the broth, you'd have a dish fit for Chef himself!"

It was a motley but boisterously cheerful group. The prep cooks, the armpit sweat stains just meeting in the back of their ragged smocks, were perking up after the exhaustion of a long day of chopping and dicing. The cook staff, refreshed from their post-lunch break, were already in baggy striped uniform pants but still in T-shirts. The blazing white smocks, neckerchiefs, and caps would not be donned until just before the evening service started. The front of the house staff were relaxed, still in street clothes, hours away from needing their uniforms. Even the delectable Giselle was in jeans, although to Capucine's informed eye the designer version couldn't have cost less than five hundred euros and were beautifully set off by a pair of Chanel mules.

Sommelier Rolland was striding around with a proprietary air, dotting the table with bottles of cheap labelless *vin ordinaire*. After a momentary disappearance he oozed up to Capucine proffering the inevitable flute of champagne with a simpery welcome. The unctuousness he had displayed at the Quai was apparently still fully operative. Capucine wondered if it was his normal off-duty persona. "How nice of you to join us. What serendipity. Do sit down. Alfonse will be mortally offended if you don't try his pot-au-feu. You know how chefs can be, even very young ones."

With much scraping of stools, the staff scooted around to make room for Capucine at the middle of the table. A small man with dark sweat-stringy hair, olive skin, a heavily stained smock—Lebanese, perhaps—undoubtedly one of the afternoon prep cooks who chopped produce at blinding speed for hours on end without a break, smiled a broken-toothed smile at her and said, "Lieutenant, how considerate of you to come by and share our little meal. Some of us were a little afraid we would be called down to the Quai. You never know what will happen down there when you can't produce an immigration card."

Just as she was struggling for a suitable reply, Rolland—suddenly reverted to his inscrutable sommelier persona—returned with a bottle and one of the crystal wineglasses used in the front of the house. "Réserve de la Comtesse, 2000," he said, enunciating as carefully as if he were explaining electricity to a Congolese tribesman. "As you may know, it's the second wine of Pichon-Longueville-Comtesse de Lalande. It's the exception to the rule I was propounding the other day. I'm sure you'll find it particularly delicate." The bottle was almost exactly half full. Capucine wondered if Rolland had opened it for the seniors at the staff meal or if it was a perquisite left over from lunch. Yet another thing to ask Alexandre.

Either the wine or Rolland's insufferableness broke her

timidity. She made a little speech. "It's very kind of you all to receive me like this," she said, looking around the table. "I need your help and it seemed more reasonable for me to come here than to have you all down to the Quai. Here's what I need. At 2:30 in the morning the night Président Delage died two men were seen dragging a very heavy duffel bag in through the kitchen door. Do any of you know anything about that?"

The cohesiveness of the table fragmented into a multitude of separate whispered conversations. After a long pause one of the prep cooks—a Turk—spoke up. "Madame, I have worked in many restaurants in your beautiful country, but I have never been in one that has so many deliveries. It is as if each type of produce comes from a different place. Potatoes from here. Mushrooms from there. Many of these suppliers are small local farmers. It is a big problem for the prep staff. Very often things come in late. We have to rush through the prep work. But Chef will do it his way even if it makes our life very difficult. You would think it would have been one of these suppliers who came in the middle of the night. But how could it have been? How would he have gotten in? None of us has a key!"

There were nods of agreement around the table. "He's quite right," Bouteiller said. "I have a key, of course, as does Perrault, and I believe there is an extra in the drawer of the hostess's desk, but no one else has one. Nor would Chef, or anyone else, give one to a supplier. I locked up for the night on Friday and can affirm no one was left to wait for anything. I'm sorry we can't be more helpful."

It was frustrating. Capucine had the distinct impression there was more to be gleaned, but being aggressive certainly wouldn't make anyone speak. She changed tack. "There's one other thing. I know this is a little delicate, but I understand that Président Delage and his guest, Martin Fleuret, had some sort of argument during dinner. Does anyone know anything about that?" There was an awkward silence; everyone conspicuously avoided looking at her.

"Obviously," Capucine went on, "no one here is going to gossip about what patrons speak about during their meals." She gave a little smile she hoped conveyed her complicity. "But a valued client of the restaurant has been murdered and we need all of you to help bring the culprit to justice. It's the responsible thing to do."

The table again fractured into shards of animated private conversation. Only two boys, teenagers in jeans, who looked like they might be aide-serveurs, sat rigidly, staring straight ahead silently, lips squeezed tight as an extra precaution against betraying their secret. Making them even more conspicuous, Bouteiller peppered them with warning glances.

"Monsieur Bouteiller," Capucine said, "if those boys know anything, let them speak. The discretion of a restaurateur is one thing, obstruction of justice is a whole other kettle of fish."

Bouteiller scowled, shrugged, and jerked his head toward the boys, "Très bien, out with it."

"Well, madame," began one of the boys, "at the beginning of the meal, Arsène—he's the *serveur* who's our boss—served Président Delage the *Coquetier au liqueur d'érable acidulé*. You know, it's a signature dish: softboiled eggs with a vinegar and maple syrup sauce. The eggs are delivered just before dinner. Can you believe it, they are actually laid that morning," he said with adolescent wonder. "Anyway, Président Delage said he wanted some more of the sauce on the side because there was never enough." A man in his early thirties sitting a few seats down the table, whom Capucine assumed was the Arsène in question, nodded vigorously. "So," the boy continued, "Arsène went back to the kitchen to get it and left us standing there. We did what we were supposed to and backed five paces away from the table and stood at attention and all while we were waiting, but we could still hear the conversation pretty well."

"Good," said Capucine, her excitement rising despite herself. "What did they say?"

"Well," the other boy jumped in, "Président Delage's friend seemed really pissed off. He said something like, 'How can you ask me to give it up? This is the best thing I've ever done!' "

Once they were into the story the boys weren't to be stopped. The first one elbowed his pal aside. "Yeah, so Delage gives him this big sneer and says something like, 'If this is the best thing you've ever done I feel sorry for you.' Then they just stared at each other, you know, like in the Westerns, the big face-off, like one of them was going to draw a Colt Peacemaker and start blasting away."

"So then what?" asked Capucine.

"So then nothing. Arsène came up with the sauce and we all went back to the waiter's area." The boys were so delighted with having penetrated the lives of exalted patrons they didn't notice the anticlimax.

Capucine was at a loss. They so obviously had nothing more to say. Perrault saved the day. He stood up like a sergeant major and ordered, *"Au travail!"* The staff dinner was suddenly over. Capucine felt as if she had been left on the dock as the stately liner eased off to sea.

Chapter 27

Three days later Alexandre had one of his caprices and insisted on taking Capucine to a late dinner at Hand, the latest hot spot for *le tout Paris*.

"I thought you hated this place," Capucine said when they arrived.

"I absolutely loathe it. Its überchef Armand Duval's latest attempt to squeeze a few more euros out of the world of haute cuisine."

"So why are we here? Although you have to admit the decor is kind of cute." Capucine sat on a banquette strewn with Bargello needlepoint throw pillows while Alexandre reclined in an enormous wicker throne. The tableware consisted of lacquered Japanese bento boxes equipped with ergonomically designed cutlery as well as expensive-looking ebony chopsticks.

" 'Know thine enemy,' as has so often been said," Alexandre said with a smirk. Capucine was almost disappointed she was not treated to his Asian Sage face. "And Duval is definitely the enemy despite his unquestionable talent. He maintains that this restaurant responds to the current need for culinary zapping. There's no real menu. You pick something from column A, something else from column B, and maybe another something from column C. He calls it 'modular mix and match.' If you want béarnaise on your salad along with sushi doused in pickle relish, why, just go right ahead! This is Fusion 2.0."

"Sounds like fun. If I ever get pregnant this is where we'll come. I still don't understand why you hate it so much."

"Let me put it this way. Jean-Louis once told me that he thought he was the only one of his three-star peers who really deserved to be called 'Chef,' and I think he's right. All the others have become mere businessmen. They want to open as many operations as they can, and so they opt for formula restaurants in far-flung corners of the world that are based on grossly overpriced fashion food and outlandish decors. Jean-Louis likes to say he would rather sell crepes from a street stand in front of a department store on the boulevard Haussmann than spend his time flying to Las Vegas in a private jet. That way he would at least have the feel of food in his hands and the smell of cooking in his nose."

"Poor Jean-Louis. A little giggle now and then wouldn't hurt him. Especially right now."

Despite Alexandre's muttered stream of invective, Capucine was delighted with her dinner. From the youmkoumg consommé brimming with squid and shellfish to Hand's version of a BLT—Batavia lettuce, watercress, heirloom tomatoes, and grilled pancetta on a brioche roll delicately anointed with balsamic mayonnaise—to her dessert of bubble-gum ice cream, she loved it all. Alexandre, even though he didn't admit it, also seemed to enjoy his squid with a sauce of chopped preserved lemon followed by a designer version of mac and cheese. As Capucine pecked at her ice cream Alexandre ordered shōchū, which the waiter assured him was the classic Japanese worker's liqueur. It arrived in a thick-bottomed shot glass that would have been at home on the set of a Western.

"This is a long, long way from Diapason but probably better than their staff meal, isn't it?" Alexandre asked.

"Actually, the food was not bad at all. The problem was that just as I was getting them to loosen up Perrault made them all go back to work. It was highly frustrating. I'd love to get my hooks back into that restaurant but Tallon's dead set against it."

Alexandre sipped his shōchū and made a face. "Bleech. This stuff tastes like watered-down vodka. What do you mean Tallon's against it?"

"His new thing is that he's got his heart set on tagging Martin Fleuret. He ordered me to stop everything else and has my three brigadiers, as well as six others he's assigned to the case, following Fleuret around the clock. He even got Madame d'Agremont to sign off on level-one wiretapping, which is a huge deal because it means that real people listen to his phones all day long instead of the usual computers. In the Police Judiciare world this is a full-court press."

"And has all this produced anything?"

"Of course not. What we did find out is that Fleuret's a workaholic. At his desk by eight, lunch in his office or something gobbled at a café counter, home by nine to eat a dinner prepared by his housekeeper. No social life. The phone taps yielded nothing more arousing than conversations with his clients and corn-fed good-night chats with Karine Bergeron. If you ask me, there's no way this Fleuret can have had anything to do with the murder. Tallon's wasting our time. The solution is bound to be somewhere in the restaurant. I told Tallon. Actually, we even had words about it."

"Your first tiff, how charming" Alexandre said sweetly.

"I know I'm a newbie at homicide and he's the grand old man with the brilliant reputation, but I still know I'm right. I trust my instin—" She was interrupted by the quiet buzzing of her cell phone.

"Lieutenant!" Isabelle said with suppressed urgency. "He just drove out of the underground parking lot in his car. We follow him, right?"

"Absolutely. Get going, but stay on the line."

Capucine heard the sound of running footsteps, a car door slamming, the distant voice of Isabelle talking to someone, no doubt Momo, who never relinquished the wheel.

"Okay," Isabelle said, "we're on him. That was totally weird! We could see the light of his TV and it sure looked like he was hunkered down for the evening, but all of a sudden he comes tearing up the ramp in his big fat-cat Mercedes 500. Now he's doing sixty down the avenue Henri Martin. We're a couple of hundred yards behind."

Capucine pressed the MUTE button on her phone and turned to Alexandre. "Maybe Tallon was right after all. This is my three musketeers. They're chasing Fleuret across Paris."

"This is going to be better than the movies. Do you want some popcorn or will a drink do?" Alexandre beckoned the waiter over, pushed the still-brimming shot glass over to him, and mouthed "Cognac" with two fingers raised.

For the next fifteen minutes Capucine listened to Isabelle's slightly breathless reports and commented them to Alexandre. The brigadiers followed Fleuret out of the Sixteenth and into the avenue de Neuilly, a broad avenue lined with small office buildings erected on tight plots that had formerly held stately townhouses.

"Okay," Isabelle said, "he's just turned down a ramp into the garage of one of these office buildings. All the window are dark. Looks kind of deserted. What do we do now?"

"You and David get out of the car and stake out the front. Have Momo drive around the block and see if there is a back entrance."

Three minutes later Isabelle was back on the line. "There's nothing in back. The only ways in and out are the front entrance and the garage door."

"Good. Tell David to use his post-office passkey and get into the lobby, but have him stay out of sight and be sure not to turn on any lights. Have him watch for any movement of the elevator. You and Momo stay outside in the car and watch the front of the building."

"What's this about a post-office passkey?" Alexandre asked.

"I thought everyone knew that. The postal service has a passkey that opens every apartment building in Paris so they can get in to deliver the mail. The post office was kind enough to give us a few copies."

"The things I learn, even at my age."

Capucine picked up her cell phone. "Oh, yes, and have David call me on 06 23 26 89 97 and leave the line open. I don't want to call him and have his phone ring while he's staking out the lobby."

"That's my number!" Alexandre said.

"The show's going to get better. From now on it's surround sound. I'm requisitioning your phone."

In less than five minutes Alexandre's phone buzzed like a bee trapped under a glass and scuttled sideways across the table as it vibrated.

"Hey, Lieutenant, it's David. I'm in the building lobby. Both the elevators are here on the ground level and they just wouldn't be programmed to return automatically. The building's way too small to have elevators that sophisticated. I have this feeling that our boy's still down in the garage. There's some weird shit going down here."

Capucine did not answer. She stared fixedly at Alexandre without seeing him. After five seconds David asked nervously, "Lieutenant, are you still there?"

"Sorry, I was just thinking. I can't imagine why a high-priced lawyer would be hanging around the garage of a empty office building, but, still, I think you might be right. Look, can you guys open the garage door?"

"Of course. The post-office key always works on those, God knows why."

"Okay. I'm going to have Momo drive the car down the ramp and see what's going on. You stay in the lobby. I'm coming down there. Call me if anything happens."

Capucine stood up and pecked Alexandre on the forehead. "You can grab a cab, right? And you don't need your phone, right? I'm off."

"You women are all just the same: any excuse to stick us with the check."

Capucine barely heard. She was striding urgently across the restaurant.

Capucine had parked the Clio with its front wheels on the sidewalk in front of the restaurant, a parking habit unchanged from her student days. Of course, she told herself, the beauty part was that she no longer had to worry about parking tickets. She put both phones on the passenger seat and bounced the car off the curb. There was nothing but silence during the ten-minute drive to Neuilly.

When she arrived at the address, the front was deserted. She picked up Alexandre's phone and asked, "David, are you still there?"

"Oui," came the whispered reply.

"What's happening?"

"I don't have a clue. I heard the garage door roll open and I guess Momo and Isabelle got down there. Me, I'm sitting here staring down the elevator display lights. And they're staring back at me. Two big zeros, like tiger's eyes. So far neither one of us has blinked."

"Don't get poetic on me, David. Hang on. I'm going to check out the garage door."

Capucine walked down the ramp and pressed her ear against the metal door. It was unexpectedly cold. Capucine had the fleeting sensation she was listening at the

door to a morgue cubicle. She could hear a man screaming, "*Salaud!* Traitor! Whore's son! You deserve to be killed.
You worm of no honor. You're like a mangy, maggot-
infested dog!" She hammered violently on the door. There
was no response. Exasperated, she walked to the front entrance and banged on the glass door. Again no response. In
a rage, she walked back to the Clio and picked up one of
the phones. "David, will you open the fucking door!" No
response. She realized she was yelling into her phone, not
Alexandre's, and tried again. "David. It's me at the door.
Will you hurry up and open it, for Christ's sake."

Once inside, she hit the light switch, found the stairwell,
and beckoned David to follow her. They inched down a
short flight of stairs and Capucine eased the door open
with her foot while she and David took cover at either
side, Sigs drawn and held rigidly in the air.

Momo and Isabelle were standing rooted, facing the
garage door, their guns anchored in both fists, aiming at a
dark car, packed with passengers, which sped up the ramp,
its tires squealing and smoking. Inexplicably, they did not
fire.

Martin Fleuret lay collapsed on the cement floor, his
limbs akimbo and his neck twisted so impossibly far back
it looked broken. Blood dripped from his slack mouth and
made a small puddle on the floor. The representation of
agony was so vivid it looked fake, like a death scene in a
particularly lurid B movie. Fleuret jerked in a convulsive
spasm. Capucine wondered if he hadn't just died for real.

Chapter 28

Momo's and Isabelle's story didn't even fill the wait for the ambulance. They had opened the garage door with the postal service key, driven down the ramp hoping to look like regular tenants arriving to park their car, and found a gang with Asian features vigorously kicking a supine Fleuret. Momo had been impressed with the professionalism of their endeavor. The two brigadiers had jumped out of their car, badges in one hand and guns in another, and approached the group, who had turned tail, run to their car, and driven off at speed. Unsure of who was whom, neither brigadier had fired at the car. It was at that point that Capucine and David had appeared.

When the ambulance arrived the paramedics had been utterly indifferent to Capucine's Police Judiciare card and even less moved by her insistence that the victim was key to an important murder case. They shouldered her aside roughly to examine Fleuret, and it had been all she could do to jump aboard the ambulance as it drove off with its earsplitting *pam-pom-PAM*. Capucine was relegated to a far corner while the paramedics, with the studied calm of great emergency, clapped an oxygen mask on Fleuret's face, inserted an IV drip in the back of his hand, and glued a seemingly infinite number of electrocardiogram sensors to his chest and legs. The ambulance lurched off, rolling from side to side sickeningly as the driver wove sharply through traffic. One of the paramedics held a running dialogue on the VHF radio, to all evidence with a doctor somewhere, and gave crisp directions to his partner, who injected a series of drugs into a rubber stopper connected to the IV, consulted the electrocardiograph with furrowed brow, consulted his colleague, and continued giving injections. Capucine's repeated questions as to how Fleuret was doing fell on disdainfully deaf ears, but it was clear things were touch and go. Eventually the ambulance backed into the loading bay of an emergency room. Capucine had no idea where.

Inside, Capucine continued to be ignored. Fleuret was placed on a gurney and, surrounded by a team in scrubs covered with transparent yellow plastic aprons, rolled at speed down a corridor. As he was pushed into an operating room the smallest of the group, a very short and very round woman, wheeled and peremptorily insisted Capucine go to the waiting room if she was family or leave the hospital if she was not. Intimidated in spite of herself, she dutifully went off to the waiting room wondering what Rivière would have done and, biting her lip, announced to the duty nurse that she was Fleuret's wife.

After an hour a very young doctor in blood-spotted green scrubs, a face mask pushed down around his neck, came up to her smiling in the carefully constructed grandfatherly way he had been erroneously taught is reassuring to patients' families.

"Madame Fleuret?"

"Not exactly," Capucine answered with a smile, brandishing her card. "Police Judiciare. Your patient is a suspect in a murder case and this attack may well have something to do with it. How is he?"

"He'll be fine. He probably owes his life to the ambulance crew. In addition to three fractured ribs, he has a ruptured spleen, a number of very nasty contusions, and a deep cut in the tongue. When they picked him up, his B.P. was seventy over ten and his heart was at one eighty and very thready."

Responding to Capucine's blank look, he explained. "A blood pressure reading that low with a very high and weak pulse rate meant he was very close to death. But his vitals are now back within normal range. There's no doubt he'll recover."

"Don't you have to operate for a ruptured spleen?"

"That was in the old days. Now we just keep the patient in the hospital and let the spleen heal itself. If all goes well he'll be on his feet and out of here in a week or ten days at the most."

That was the good news. The bad news was that he had been heavily sedated on top of a healthy dose of morphine. Fleuret wasn't going to say anything that made any sense until the next day at the earliest.

Purely out of a desire to take some kind of action, Capucine stationed a uniformed gendarme outside Fleuret's door and beat a retreat to the Quai.

At six the next morning Capucine arrived with Fleuret's breakfast tray. His eyes had sunk deeply into dark hollows in his paper-white face. He seemed to be in pain despite the drugs. He looked up and frowned at Capucine.

"What are you doing here?" he growled hoarsely.

"Maître, I think your guardian angel would like you to show a little appreciation that my people were following you and divined you were coming to no good in that garage. If they hadn't driven in you'd be in a whole lot worse shape right now, wouldn't you agree? From what I hear, your little playmates were just getting warmed up. So, what exactly was going on?"

"This doesn't concern you since I'm not going to press charges."

"Actually, it does concern me. You're a possible suspect in a murder case and everything unusual you engage in is very definitely the subject of police scrutiny."

Fleuret's lips puffed a protracted "Pfffff!" of derision and he twisted painfully, reaching for the nurse's call button.

"I wouldn't be too quick to do that if I were you. You can easily be transferred to a police hospital where I doubt you'd find conditions as comfortable." Capucine prayed Fleuret wouldn't know the most she could do was what she'd done already: post a gendarme at his door. "I'm going to insist you make a deposition."

"All right, all right, anything to get you out of here. That was a meeting with the client of a client of mine." Fleuret smiled ironically. "Or I should say ex-client of an ex-client of mine since when I declined to advise my client regarding the transaction in question I was fired and as a result he abandoned the transaction. I imparted that fact to the ex-client of the ex-client and, as you saw, he was somewhat less than pleased. Voilà. If you type that up I'll be happy to sign it."

"Maître, impressed as I am by your heroic sense of humor, I'm sure you can understand that the Police Judiciare does not appreciate levity. Let's hear your story." Capucine sat on the edge of the bed.

Fleuret poured himself a cup of coffee and dropped a paper packet of sugar into the cup as he tried to open it.

"Here. Let me do it. Do you want milk as well?" Capucine fished the packet out with the spoon, poured in the contents of a fresh one along with soy milk from a little plastic container.

The epidermis of Fleuret's antipathy softened slightly as Capucine stirred.

"You're right, I doubt I have any choice. It's all a matter of record anyway. As it happens, in addition to my high-net-worth clients I also represent a number of French manufacturers of tactical assets and handle the legal side of the commercialization of their products to foreign nations."

"By 'tactical assets' I'm guessing you mean 'arms,' right? Exactly what are we talking about? Airplanes, missiles, assault weapons?"

"Okay, 'arms,' if you prefer. France exports a full range of weaponry: sidearms, airplanes, and everything in between. The bigger the asset, the more complex the contractual agreement. My specialty is missiles, which usually involve elaborate maintenance service contracts, but I've done pretty much a full range of deals. The transaction in this case was a sale of missiles to an Asian nation. Upon reflection, I decided that this particular sale was unethical and informed my client that I would not be able to assist them. As a consequence they felt they had no choice but to abandon the transaction and asked me to inform the purchaser. That's really all there is to it. Obviously, the purchaser was less than thrilled with the news and chose to take it out on the messenger."

"I see. Now, who is the ex-client and who was the purchaser?"

"Lieutenant, that's irrelevant history. Just before the meeting I received a call from my client informing me that I was no longer on their roster of lawyers and that they had the intention of blackballing me with the other arms distributors. So that's all a closed chapter of my career."

"Maître, I wasn't asking you about your career, but I do need the names of the seller and the buyer, here."

"That, Lieutenant, is client confidential, very definitely so. A few of my transactions are a matter of record and I'm sure you could easily have divined the nature of that side of my practice, which is why I've given you the information you already have. But to think I'm going to violate client confidentiality is naive, to say the least. Now, I'm going to have to ask you to leave me to my breakfast or I really will call the nurse."

* * *

That afternoon she received a call from Fleuret. "I've just had your juge d'instruction on the phone, a very irate and unpleasant woman, but a very well-informed one nonetheless. She spent some time quoting to me from legal texts. She's very knowledgeable about the niceties of the attorney-client privilege, and she succeeded in convincing me that if I don't make a fully detailed deposition I face a risk of immediate incarceration. I know it's an imposition, but I wonder if I could ask you to come back to the hospital. I'm sorry, but I'm afraid it's impossible for me to get to you."

Madame d'Agremont's stock rose significantly in Capucine's books.

Fleuret's story was straightforward. Matra, the automobile, communication, and weapons conglomerate, had negotiated with the Taiwanese government for the sale of a large number of multihead missiles to be used with their 47 French Mirage 2000 fighter jets. Everything had been arranged, even the tricky negotiation of the extension of the existing missile maintenance agreement to the new weapons. All that had been left to resolve was the relatively simple agreement on the price of the missiles themselves. The meeting in the garage had been with the secretary to the Taiwanese minister of defense and, of course, the inevitable bodyguards. The secretary had not wanted to be seen in public, hence the underground venue. Fleuret knew the Taiwanese would be greatly disappointed at the loss of the deal—after all, a Mirage 2000 loaded with French-made multihead missiles would be a big step up from the Russian Su27, which was the top of the current Chinese fleet—but he had hardly expected the violence of their reaction.

"But why did you change your mind so close to the end of the transaction?"

"That's a bit complicated. I think, when all is said and

done, it was to honor the memory of Jean-Louis Delage. You see, it was my idea to have dinner that night, but generous soul that he was, he insisted on paying. I wanted Jean-Louis to approve my participating in the deal. Most of my weapons practice had come from his contacts and I wanted to make sure he would not object. It was a sort of moral obligation, if you can understand that."

"Why wouldn't he approve if he had encouraged you to do this sort of work in the first place?"

"Oh, you just don't understand Jean-Louis. He was first and foremost a statesman, not an industrialist. He saw the success of Renault, and France itself for that matter, as coming from skillfully concocted international alliances. As you probably know, Matra manufactures a good number of components for Renault and the links between the two companies are well known abroad. Over dinner he told me he was certain that this transaction would put Renault on the Chinese blacklist along with Matra. He thought it was a criminally stupid thing to do just as China's industrial star was rising. In fact, he was almost irrationally hostile to the whole thing. So hostile that I was sure he was thinking of negotiating some form of alliance with the Chinese the way he already had with the Japanese."

"So it was during dinner you agreed you'd drop the deal? I understand it ended quite amicably."

"This is the part where I blush. I'm afraid I did give Jean-Louis my word at the table. I really had no choice. You don't know how single-minded he was when he got going with his international agreements. Besides, he would have gone over my head and bullied the bigwigs at Matra if I didn't agree. But after the dinner was over, I changed my mind. My fees would have been enormous. I also doubt that the Chinese will be able to maintain their silly attitude toward Taiwan for very much longer. So in spite of my promise to Jean-Louis I kept on with the transaction. But after he was no longer with us, going against Jean-Louis's wishes seemed an insult to his memory. Something I just couldn't do. Does that make sense?"

Just as Capucine was launching into a second round of questions, ones she knew would just be gilding the lily, Karine Bergeron arrived, clucking like a chic mother hen, encumbered with bags and packages, all presumably intended to make Fleuret's stay in the hospital more bearable. Karine glared at Capucine, obviously unhappy that he was being disturbed in any way. A polite but painfully self-conscious conversation ensued. Capucine felt excluded, somehow at the mercy of her suspects, not the reverse. On her way down in the elevator she ground her teeth and wondered for the hundredth time what Rivière would have done.

Chapter 29

Early the next Saturday morning Capucine bundled a very testy Alexandre into the Clio for the forty-five-minute ride to the town of Versailles to attend the baptism of one of her cousins' first child.

"I don't understand why anyone would choose to live in Versailles," Alexandre whined, "and if they absolutely must, why do they find it necessary to baptize their scrofulous little urchins at the crack of dawn?"

"They live in Versailles because Marie-Chantal is a bit of a snob and Aurélien doesn't make very much money in his job selling insurance. It's less expensive than Paris and Marie-Chantal feels it's just as chic as the Sixteenth Arrondissement. And I hardly think eleven o'clock counts as the crack of dawn."

Capucine was enchanted with the church, a small but delightfully proportioned example of early French baroque architecture complete with an inverted-bowl cupola, delicately carved oak paneling, and a lavishly gilded baptismal font. To her utter amazement Cousin Jacques was standing by the basin, proprietarily resplendent in a Prince of Wales check suit, clearly unwilling to relinquish any of the godparental limelight as he unabashedly upstaged the horse-faced godmother. Dimly Capucine recalled that Jacques had been at boarding school with Aurélien but she had had no idea the unlikely friendship had survived into adulthood.

As tiny Marie-Aymone's head was dipped in the chilly holy water, she burst into muted wails that politely ceased the instant Jacques wrapped her in a white lace baptismal shawl that had been in the family for generations. Capucine's throat caught and her eyes misted as she realized that she had been baptized in the selfsame shawl. Biting her lip was no help at all, and she was forced to conjure up an image of Rivière smirking disdainfully at her before she could regain her tough-girl flic's demeanor.

After the ceremony, the forty or so guests were gently herded into the enclosed garden of Marie-Chantal and Loïc's small stone house. Over the phone Marie-Chantal had explained to Capucine with a titter that the house— which she insisted had been built by one of Louis the XIV's foremen during the construction of the château— was just too bijou for so many guests and so they were going to have a garden party even though the garden, so sadly, was hardly at its summer best. A small table placed in a corner held two crested silver dishes that offered a meager pile of finger sandwiches, and a rococo silver wine cooler abstemiously proffered four bottles of champagne.

Alexandre was aghast. "Here I am, hauled all the way out to the very marchland of French culture and when I arrive it turns out I'm to be denied even basic human sustenance." With alarm Capucine recognized this as the preamble to one of Alexandre's lectures and could easily imagine him searching out the priest to make wittily acerbic comments about Jesus' self-proliferating loaves and fishes for the multitude. Still, she fully shared his dismay. Two or three miniscule sandwiches and a few sips of champagne did seem well beyond parsimonious under the circumstances, particularly as her stomach was beginning to growl.

From behind Capucine heard a familiar mocking voice directed at Alexandre. "Fear not, dear cousin. I took the liberty of booking a table for the three of us at a lovely restaurant with a charming view of the chateau's famed royal vegetable gardens. Since this little hostelry sports a Michelin star, your day may yet be saved," Jacques said.

Capucine cringed again. Alexandre had always been—completely foolishly, of course—a little jealous of Jacques, but, to her surprise, Alexandre warmly grasped Jacques' hand and, without even a trace of irony, said, "Cousin, you are a ray of sunshine in my bleak day."

"Well, then," said Jacques, "let's not stand on the order of our going; let's just get rolling. If I hear one more iteration of 'Jaaaaaques' in that god-awful Neuilly-Auteuil-Passy lockjaw or have to kiss one more wrinkled, geriatric hand I may find myself teaching this branch of the family a few words they don't know," Jacques said, leaning back languidly against an ancient wooden door in the stone wall, which gave way under his weight with a loud cinematic creak. The three slipped out and made for the Clio.

The Relais du Potager du Roi's long suit was its panoramic view of the royal kitchen gardens, which had been painstakingly restored to the original ornate checkerboard and populated with fruits and vegetables guaranteed to be identical to those present in Louis XV's day. Happily, despite the restaurant's pronounced vegetarian bent, in deference to the French veneration of protein, game held pride of place on the menu. Capucine opted for partridge, Jacques for pheasant, and Alexandre for French grouse, which he delightedly explained was now almost impossible to find.

By the time the birds were nearly consumed—the shot delicately removed from mouths and placed on the sides of plates with a satisfying little ping—and a second bottle of

Nuits-Saint-Georges was uncorked, Capucine felt the day might turn out to be a success after all.

Jacques put his hand under the table and squeezed Capucine's leg just above the knee. Alexandre's face tightened.

"So, cousin," Jacques asked with a knowing smile, "how goes your famous case? I read your report on the Trag agent who was impersonating one of our people. What a jolly time you must have had catching him."

"All in a day's work," Capucine said, removing Jacques' hand. "Actually, we have a suspect, but I can't make myself believe he had anything to do with the murder. Other than that, I'm dry."

Jacques produced his little Cheshire grin and put his hand back on Capucine's leg. "I would have thought you'd be up to your eyeballs in international intrigue by now."

The bubble of Capucine's contentment burst. "Jacques, are you keeping something back from me? Tell me right now!"

Jacques giggled and pinched Capucine's kneecap, making her squirm and Alexandre frown. "Little cousin, you love to think I'm hiding secrets from you. I think it's because your id is begging you to offer me sexual favors for them." Capucine was obliged to calm Alexandre with one of her most severe looks.

"Actually," Jacques continued, "there are no secrets, just pure logic. Didn't you ever ask yourself how Trag just happened to know about Project Typhon?"

"Of course. It seems they just guessed Renault would be working on improving gas mileage and used Delage's death as an opportunity to plant a spy."

"That's exactly what they did. But you never stopped to think there might be other Trags at work, did you?"

"There can't possibly be other firms like Trag, can there?"

"Good Lord, there are any number of private firms, most much smaller, of course. And then there are all the national intelligence services who can be even better than Trag and twice as unscrupulous even though their employees earn far less. I'm willing to bet Renault is like a big steaming cow pie alive with industrious little beetles tunneling in and out."

"But Typhon is top secret. How could it attract that many people?"

"Project Typhon may be a secret but the fact that Renault is working on gas catalysis is an obvious truism. You see, technological leaps invariably turn out to be a race between a number of competitors and Renault is such a strong technical player it will obviously be in the race."

"I don't get it," Capucine said.

"I see his point," Alexandre said. "Let me try to explain. When most major scientific and technological discoveries are made it always seems that any number of different people in different places are working on exactly the same thing at the same time. For example, we like to think that only Santos Dumont and the Wright brothers had a monopoly on cooking up the airplane. But no one ever talks about Karl Jatho or Traian Vuia or Jacob Ellehammer, who all flew airplanes in different countries at about the same time. The point is that when technology is ready to pop, it pops all over the place like ripe pieces of fruit dropping off a tree."

"I still don't get it," Capucine said.

"Look, cousine, it's the same thing with this gasoline catalyst," Jacques said, "people are working on it all over the world. It's ready to drop off the tree, as dear cousin Alexandre says. Its time has come."

"And what does all this theorizing about the nature of technological discovery have to do with the case?" Capucine asked.

"Remember my cow-dung heap?"

"How could I forget? Such a charming metaphor to use at lunch."

"You see, it's not just the number of beetles crawling in and out, it's the fact that there are different kinds."

"I suspected the metaphor would get even more delightful. Let's hear it."

"Industrial spies come in two basic types: moles and hackers. Moles look like trusted employees and spirit information out. Hackers burrow in from the outside and bleed information out of your computer systems. You were confronted with such a rare type it's almost never seen: a scam artist. They're so unusual you should have pickled the one you caught in formaldehyde and put him on your desk."

"That's exactly what Commissaire Principal Tallon wanted to do."

Capucine removed Jacques' hand from her leg and placed it firmly on the table with a loud thunk. "It took a while, but the penny finally dropped."

Chapter 30

At ten the next morning—heeding her mother's dictum that it was not proper to make phone calls before ten in the morning or after nine in the evening—Capucine called Florian Guyon to announce she would be stopping by his apartment that evening to ask him some questions. Guyon sputtered, both at the early hour of the call and at the Sunday invasion of his home, but finally agreed to see her.

He received her with a coolness that verged on ill grace and led her almost reluctantly to the living room. Capucine suppressed a grimace. The entire space—walls, floor, and ceiling—had been painted in the same stark, relentlessly gleaming, high-gloss institutional white that looked like it had come from a hospital supply outlet. A monstrous kinetic sculpture dominated the room, looming from a towering white pedestal. It had countless shiny stainless-steel parts that plunged, rotated, swiveled back and forth, and spun hypnotically within other parts, clanking and clattering noisily as if the machine had been carelessly assembled and was about to come apart.

"I didn't think there were any Kanamgires outside of

museums," Capucine said over the din. "I understand he's very particular where his work goes."

"I wouldn't have thought a police officer would recognize his work," Guyon replied with obvious delight. "I knew him when we were students. I was very fortunate that he allowed me to purchase one of his earlier pieces. The motion is precisely ordered by a tiny computer hidden inside. It is both unstoppable and unfathomable. That is its message. It's an inspiration to me."

"You're lucky to have it, Monsieur Guyon. Sit down. We need to talk." Capucine noticed she had raised her voice in an unthinking shout the way she did when speaking into a cell phone with a bad connection.

"I trust the subject is important enough to merit the invasion of my home in this manner," Guyon said. The tone was such that he could just as easily have been attempting levity or showing bad temper.

"Monsieur Guyon," Capucine said loudly over the background noise of the sculpture, "when we last spoke you told me that you found it natural that the DGSE send an agent to interview you and inspect Project Typhon. I had the impression that you were almost expecting someone from the DGSE. Why was that? Had you asked for assistance?"

"Madame, as I recall telling you at the time, Project Typhon is of national interest. It was entirely natural that the DGSE would have sought to investigate that security was up to the required level."

Capucine smiled a complicit little smile at him. "So, I was mistaken. The visit just came out of the blue?"

"Where are you attempting to go with this line of questioning?" Guyon asked, even more loudly than the level of background noise required.

"Oh, it's nothing complicated. It just struck me that something out of the ordinary might have happened and I was trying to figure out if the DGSE had been alerted."

"In fact, it is true that there had been mild concern that some sort of leak might have occurred. Personally, I was quite sure there was no danger at all, but, of course, it never hurts to be too careful."

"So you did call the DGSE?"

"Of course not. It came up in a routine meeting with Président Delage. He became unreasonably alarmed. Later I assumed he had taken it upon himself to contact the authorities even though I told him it was entirely unnecessary."

"And what was it that aroused your suspicions of a leak?"

"It was nothing. I was at a conference in Seoul and a rumor was going around that could have led one to believe, if one were in the right frame of mind, that someone had some knowledge of the substance of Project Typhon. It was foolish, really."

"Have there been other indications of breaches of security?"

"Of course not, madame. Who do you think you're dealing with? Project Typhon has the most sophisticated security system of any industrial project in France. No one can enter any of the Project Typhon sites without an extremely high-tech security badge that is impossible to forge. On top of that employees are screened when they come to work and when they leave. They go through a metal detector and have their briefcases and handbags run through an X-ray machine to see if they have cameras or any other means of secreting data. Naturally, they are not allowed to take laptop computers in or out of the building. No, the system is completely foolproof. That's why I'm sure there were no leaks. Utterly impossible."

"That sounds impressive."

"It's as impressive as it is unnecessary. Don't forget that our staff are real engineers. Professionals. All handpicked by me. I would know instantly if there was a fake, a mole as they call it. He or she would be detected immediately."

"When you say everyone goes through the security check twice a day, do you really mean everyone?"

"Of course! No one at all is exempted."

"Absolutely no one?"

"Of course not. Obviously, the président didn't have to go through, nor do I. That would be unthinkable."

"And what about the président's and your staffs?"

"My secretary certainly doesn't go through security checks, nor does Président Delage's. They have our complete trust. But just to show you how strict we are, the acting president has to go through," Guyon said with a vindictive little smile.

"So in fact there are still at least three people who are completely free to take whatever data they want from the Typhon sites. It's a good thing that 'Etienne' turned out to be a fraud. A real DGSE agent would have given you a scathing report. There would have been hell to pay."

"What do you mean?" Guyon said angrily.

"It looks like there have been at least two breaches of security. Who or whatever it was that fed the rumor at Seoul and the Trag operative, who was not only given a grand tour of the installation but had a free lunch thrown in as well."

"How did you know about the lunch?" Guyon's gestures had become jerky and he was no longer able to look Capucine in the eye. "Oh, yes, it had to be that imbecile Vaillant. He's left the company, of course."

"Are you sure he didn't take a briefcase full of data when he went?"

Guyon glowered. "Madame, I find these insinuations insulting. My security measures—Renault's security measures—are none of your business. I admitted a DGSE agent to the company on the assumption that it was at my président's behest. No problem there that I can see. Also, there were rumors at an industry convention. I'm sure there are even rumors at police conventions if you have such things."

"Monsieur Guyon, I beg your pardon. I thought you said the président had merely expressed concern about Seoul. Now it seems he actually ordered you to contact the DGSE."

"Madam," Guyon said through clenched teeth, "I said nothing of the kind. These kangaroo court attempts to put words in my mouth are as laughable as they are offensive. I have no more patience for this interview. And you have no right to be here without my invitation. I must ask you to leave immediately."

Capucine basked in the feeling of peace when the door closed behind her. It was just as satisfying as the sudden quiet when she turned the vacuum cleaner off.

Chapter 31

Karine Bergeron sat demurely in the ground-floor interview room wearing a maroon cashmere twin set with a single strand of pearls as she stirred the inevitable flaccid plastic thimble of machine espresso that passed for hospitality at the Quai des Orfèvres. She was radiant.

"Lieutenant, it's very kind of you to receive me at such short notice. You were so nice the other day I feel I can treat you like a friend. I've made a few decisions and I wanted you to hear them from me directly."

"Good things, I hope."

"Oh, yes! I told you I had been thinking about accepting Martin's proposal, and I have. We're going to be married the week after next in the church of his village in Brittany. We decided while he was in the hospital. He seemed so weak and defenseless and he wanted me so much, I just couldn't say no."

"That seems quite sudden."

"Yes, it is. And there's even more! He's going to change his life for me. I was very moved."

"What do you mean?"

"Martin is an avid sailor. He keeps a big boat in Brittany and sails all the time in the summer. We've decided to take a year off and go around the world in it. That was one of the reasons he wanted to get married right away. The weather is still warm enough for us to leave France and the trade winds are perfect right now. We're going to go to Guadeloupe and then figure out the rest of our route when we're there."

"But what about his practice? He's going to walk away from that?"

"Well, you know about his specialty, this arms business. Almost all of his clients came to him because of Jean-Louis's position. His most important clients have already dropped him and he's convinced the others will as well."

"That's a shame. It must have been a lucrative practice for him."

"Oh, it was. But he was also traveling constantly and dealing with some absolutely horrible people. A lot were even worse than those you saw. He sold weapons of all types. Sometimes even small things like pistols and hand grenades and whatever. Often those were sold to the shadiest possible people. It was awful. Very unlike Martin. I'm so relieved that part of his life is over. Right now we're going to go around the world and just think about ourselves. And when we come back he can just build up a whole new practice, but a nice, normal one."

"I'm happy for you. I'll certainly authorize the trip to Brittany for the wedding but there's absolutely no question of Maître Fleuret leaving the French territory."

"Why ever not?"

"Maître Fleuret may well come to trial for the murder of Président Delage."

"Good God." There were tears in Karine's eyes. She took a paper tissue from her bag and patted her lower lids, careful not to smudge her makeup. "That would destroy Martin. How can you suspect him?"

"He had a motive. It could be argued that Président Delage was the main obstacle to his marriage to you. His desire to leave the country reinforces that logic."

Karine's tears cascaded. There was no saving her makeup now.

"B . . . but he left right after the dinner. He . . . he came to see me. I told you that."

"Yes, let's do talk about that particular visit."

Karine sobbed quietly, making gentle hiccoughing sounds. "He came to try to persuade me to marry him."

"After a long night out on the town? He has a curious sense of gallantry. What time did he arrive?"

"Oh, quite late. A few minutes after eleven. I was watching a film and it had just ended. It was a movie about a woman detective in the Police Judiciaire. She was completely unlike you. Very punk and tough. In love with a drug addict whom she had to arrest at the end." Karine laughed through her tears.

"I've seen it. My husband teases me about it all the time. But you're quite sure he was no later than eleven? He must have come straight from the restaurant. It would have taken a good twenty minutes to drive from there to your apartment."

"Absolutely sure. The eleven o'clock news was just starting and I asked him if he wanted to watch it. He didn't. He wanted me to take his ring, which I was too stupid to do right then. I had to wait until he was all broken to see how much he really loved me."

"Karine, I really am happy for you, but I must warn you to be careful. Make no attempt to leave the country. The consequences could be quite serious for you both. It's important you use your influence to prevent Maître Fleuret from doing anything foolish."

Later, Capucine gazed at Karine as she walked across the courtyard to the porte cochere and wondered about Fleuret. It would hardly be a dilemma, choosing between your livelihood and the love of your life. Not a difficult choice at all.

Chapter 32

Taken by surprise Capucine suddenly found herself hard in the grips of a deep depression. She tried telling herself that she had every reason to feel pleased with the way the case was going. The pot was boiling away cheerfully, brimming with enough ingredients to promise a rich and fulfilling denouement. She insisted to herself that La Crim was turning out to be exactly what she had hoped for: cases with countless convoluted threads intertwining through real people, requiring unraveling with infinite care and finesse. So very different from that pointless white-collar work where the suspect was identified from the onset and the challenge was simply to produce a file thick enough to send to court.

But the forced logic had no effect on either the stale brown taste in her mouth or the sinking certainty in her gut that none of the threads in hand would ever lead anywhere, much less to a solution. The whole thing seemed an exercise in futility. She was doomed. The case was unsolvable. She hated the whole business and rued her decision to try and make her way in the Brigade Criminelle. What a childish fool she had been. The more she thought about it the worse it got.

Of course, it was far from the first time she had felt this way about her life. Once, she remembered with painful clarity, at Sciences Po she had quit a class on literary theory in the middle of the semester while in exactly the same mood of despair. It was a decision she still bitterly regretted. At the time, once she had calmed down, she realized that it was nothing more than intellectual overload. It had been a demanding course and she had overinvested herself in it. The solution would have been simplicity itself: cut the class for a few days and wait for her enthusiasm to return, which would have happened quickly enough. Everyone burns out every now and then. It was perfectly normal. Wasn't it?

The more she tried to reason with herself the more her little homilies rang hollow. She knew she was on dangerous ground, an inch away from storming into Tallon's office and plunking her badge and gun down on his desk—or was it just in American movies that one did that?

She reached her three brigadiers on the phone—she was so close to tears she didn't have the courage to face them personally—and assigned them to a further round of computer background checks she knew perfectly well was useless. But at least they wouldn't pester her for a while. She then decided to devote the day to the most frivolous and futile pursuit she could come up with—keenly aware that the frivolity itself was the essential reagent—and wound up spending the day wandering through the fashionable boutiques of Saint-Germain fingering expensive clothes. She even went so far as to leave her Sig behind, something she had never done since the day she was inducted into the force. She felt even more denuded than if she had forgotten her wedding ring on the side of the bathroom sink.

The afternoon turned out to be a sweet and sour dish of pleasure and angst. The chic Latin Quarter boutiques, with their astronomic prices and rarefied ranges of clothes, turned out to be an effective opiate. She was far away from the police, embraced by a life that would have been hers by default if she had not made it a full-time job to resist it. Ironically her sense of relief brought home how easy it would be to quit. And that realization brought with it the shock of catastrophe and the terror of an empty life. By late afternoon she had only a pair of backless Italian mules to show for her efforts and was exhausted enough to call it quits. She squeezed into a seat on a café terrace facing the church of Saint-Sulpice. As the sun went down releasing the crisp odor of fall she nursed *kirs* and navigated the labyrinthine editorials of the final edition of the *Monde*.

By her third kir there was hardly enough daylight to even pretend to read and she was numb enough from the cold and the wine to feel that the whole world was safely at arm's length. No solutions had presented themselves, but she had the feeling that somehow she had tipped over to the other side of some sort of some unnamed watershed. It was time to go home and let Alexandre tease her about how useful her purchase would be on duty. The thought made her very happy.

Chapter 33

In the morning Capucine awoke to find her calm and sense of purpose intact. At the Quai, ever mindful of her mother's injunctions, she waited patiently until just after ten A.M. and dialed Grégoire Rolland's home number. He was clearly taken aback. In the high-pitched tone of a socialite she invited him to come down to the Quai, entirely at his convenience, to "brainstorm" with her. She complained she was making no headway in understanding the workings of the restaurant and he was the only member of the staff "really on her wavelength." The sense of Rolland preening himself oozed through the receiver. She reiterated that the visit must not inconvenience him in any way and that he must tell her with perfect honesty when he had free time. Together they decided that two days hence at three thirty, after the luncheon service was over, would be just perfect. As she hung up she imagined Rivière's mocking sneer if he had been privy to her approach and laughed, the first time in days.

Rolland arrived in an open shirt and decidedly un-French, close-fitting suit that, while expensive-looking, still smacked of the marked-down rack, perhaps an Armani on closeout sale from one of the *grands magasins*. He was more at ease than she had ever seen him, neither obsequious as during the staff meal nor inscrutable as during his restaurant service. Capucine wondered if this finally was his true persona. His attitude was of someone on a purely social visit. He could almost have come with a box of chocolates in hand.

Rolland spoke first. "So, Lieutenant, tell me how I can be of service to you."

"Oh," Capucine said, "it's really quite simple. It would be helpful to know more about the restaurant and I have no one else to turn to. As you can imagine, I can hardly speak freely to Chef Labrousse."

"Of course. But I'm afraid I don't know all that much about what happens outside of my own area."

"Well, why don't we start with that, then. Tell me, how does one become a sommelier?"

Rolland was delighted to talk about himself. He launched into the sort of rambling self-description that reminded Capucine of French talk shows: irrelevant, self-serving anecdotes stitched together with pointless digressions. He had grown up in Montargis, fathered by a postman, and had no fond memories of either. He had detested grade school, and had escaped to a vocational lycée in Paris to train for the restaurant and hotel industries. Even though the lycée had liberated him from the provinces, the victory proved Pyrrhic since the hot kitchen of the school turned out to be even more loathsome than grade school and he was allowed so little free time that Paris remained just as remote. It was only in his last year that his extraordinary nose was noticed. An instructor with the mission of teaching spontaneous recipe creation had presented a table full of raw produce—beef, artichoke, orange, asparagus, eggs, and chicken, each in a separate bowl—to the blindfolded class. As usually happened, none of the students could identify more than half of them. Except for Rolland, who sniffed them all out unerringly. It had been Rolland's big break. The instructor as-

signed him to the advanced wine class that same afternoon, a course he had been previously denied because of
his mediocre grades. He quickly became a school phenom-
enon and secured a spot as apprentice sommelier at the
Troisgros restaurant in Roanne that summer.

He explained happily that the rest was history. He
began to collect awards. Best Young Sommelier in France
three years out of the lycée, then Best Sommelier in France,
and finally, the crowning honor, Best Sommelier in the
World before he was thirty. But he insisted these awards
were meaningless. What mattered most was his reputation
within the community of sommeliers and there it was
known he had no equal.

He had no desire for a family. In his view women and
children were incompatible with the hours of the restaurant
business. He was really only interested in associating with
initiates of the world of enology. The bit between his teeth,
Rolland had become transfixed. He had the distant look of
a visionary or a dinner-party bore. Capucine felt that if a
video were being made it could easily be dubbed over with
the voice of a man describing his life's work of constructing
a ten-foot-high model of the Tour Eiffel with matches.

In an attempt to drive the conversation back to Diapason, Capucine feinted with, "Isn't there an element of
pride in being on the team of one of the most illustrious
restaurants in the world?"

"I hardly think of myself on anyone's team. Labrousse
does his job and I do mine. I don't doubt that he's an admirable cook. It's just that . . . how can I explain it to you?
. . . the food is merely a support for the wine." He paused
with wrinkled brow. "It's a poor comparison but think of it
this way. It's like the cheese on the bread. The bread must
be good, of course, but the important thing is the Reblo-
chon. When I serve, say, an Haut-Brion '78 I am happy to
have one of Labrousse's little dishes as a backdrop, but of
course it's the wine that triumphs. It's obvious, no?"

"And do you think Chef Labrousse sees it that way?" Rolland laughed raucously. "Who knows what these cooks think? Personally, I think their brains must be addled by all that heat and sweat."

Like a drover coaxing a recalcitrant cow back into the herd Capucine tried repeatedly to prod Rolland into talking about life at Diapason, but he was not to be moved. Only "his" wine mattered. The sole merit of the restaurant was its ability to attract a worthy clientele. The less he knew about the steamy mechanics of food preparation, the happier he was.

After another half an hour of monologue about himself, largely focused on the theme of his current desire to spend six months in Australia to develop a "visceral understanding" of a *vignoble* that was increasingly becoming worthy of his attention, he suddenly jerked a look at his watch. "Good Lord! Look what time it is. I have to rush back to the restaurant. I'm going to be late. I hope this has been of some use to you. It's certainly been extremely enjoyable for me." Rolland, ever the well-mannered guest, beamed and stood up, offering his hand.

Capucine pushed a button under her desk and the door opened quietly as Momo entered wordlessly. "I'm sorry, Monsieur Rolland, but you're going to be spending the night with us. I'm placing you on *garde à vue*. You'll be here at least until tomorrow, possibly longer. Momo, take Monsieur Rolland down to the detention cells."

"You can't do this! I have to get dressed for the dinner service. How will the restaurant funct . . ."

Capucine jutted her chin sharply and Momo placed a meaty hand under his armpit and squeezed just hard enough to shut him up and start him toward the door.

"Don't worry, I'll give Chef Labrousse a call and let him make arrangements for the dinner service. Good night, Monsieur Rolland."

Chapter 34

This time imagining herself into Rivière's persona was no help at all. Capucine had already felt highly guilty about assigning her brigadiers to pointless make-work duty just so she could have a day off to go shopping and now she was going to put them on something even more crushingly boring.

Once they had shuffled in and coiled into the Police Judiciare's ubiquitous bent metal chairs, she announced with the forced cheerfulness of a Club Med host, "It's time we changed tactics. We're going to do a round-the-clock tail of Guyon's and Delage's secretaries. We'll have some backup but we're going to have to do most of the tailing ourselves. I know it's a huge pain in the ass, but I think it's going to give us our first really solid lead."

Capucine cringed internally, bracing for the outburst. Astonishingly, all three brigadiers erupted into joyous smiles and high-fived each other with raucous, "*Eh bien,* voilàs," and "*Enfins!*" How unlike the fiscal brigade this all was. It was really true, in La Crim they were only happy if they were out on the street.

When the buzz died down she assigned David and Isabelle to Thérèse Garnier, Guyon's secretary. "You'll have backup from the pool but I want you to stay on the subject when she goes to work in the morning, when she goes home, and for at least two hours after her normal bedtime. That's going to be a long day but we can't afford to delegate the important hours. Momo and I are going to tail Clotilde Lancrey-Javal. I want to review the setup with you back here tomorrow night at midnight when you hand over to the pool guys but after tomorrow you can go straight home and report in by phone."

At the meeting the next day David and Isabelle were like bouncy puppies. Unbelievably, the day's tedium had actually invigorated them. It turned out that Thérèse Garnier lived in Fontenay-sous-Bois, a low-income suburb to the east of Paris, with her husband and two small children. She had risen at six, fed her family, taken the RER rapid transit train to the Châtelet station, had been herded for fifteen minutes through a tightly packed tunnel to another RER train, and had been spewed out at Issy-les-Moulineaux, where she had caught a Renault shuttle bus. The trip took an hour and a half and she entered the building at eight forty-five, fifteen minutes before her boss. In the evening she had left at six thirty, reversed the process, reached home a little after eight, fed her family, watched an hour of TV, and had been in bed by ten.

"I tell you, Lieutenant, every time I want to bitch about the job, all I have to do is think about the way women like that live. I'd rather be a nun," Isabelle said.

"But just think about all the great sex you'd be missing out on," David said. Seemingly playfully, Isabelle punched him in the arm, but he recoiled sharply and pursed his lips, obviously in pain.

Thérèse's routine was repeated every day that week. When Saturday arrived Isabelle was proved wrong. The outing, which did in fact include the entire family, was only to the Monoprix at the end of the street. The Garniers didn't own a car. The level-three wiretap that Madame

d'Agremont had authorized revealed nothing more interesting than a Friday-night call from Guyon ordering his
secretary to be at work at seven thirty Monday morning to
type up a presentation he was going to write over the
weekend. Thérèse's comments to her husband had not
been recorded but Capucine had no trouble imagining
them.

Capucine had not tailed anyone since the police academy, and even then it had been far from her favorite subject. Becoming invisible just went too much against her
grain. Fortunately, Momo revealed a talent for gently
prodding her into the thick of the crowd or behind a corner just in the nick of time and the shadowing of Clotilde
Lancrey-Javal passed without mishap.

With her increased workload as administrator of the
bureaucracy of the office of the president, Clotilde didn't
leave the office until seven thirty at the earliest. In compensation, her transit time was considerably less than her
colleague's. She took the same RER train but changed to
the metro at the Odéon in the Latin Quarter for a short
ride virtually to her door. The trip rarely took more than
half an hour. Of course, the last fifteen minutes on the
metro could occasionally be tense. She lived on a small,
twisted street that snaked down the side of Montmartre
toward the boulevard de Rochechouart, in the heart of
Paris's notorious North African quarter, an area where
even the police in uniform were often uneasy.

On the second day of the surveillance, once Clotilde
was safely ensconced in her office, Capucine went back to
Clotilde's neighborhood to get a feel for the environment.

"Lieutenant," Momo had said. "Let's be careful here.
This ain't one of your vacations in Marrakech."

Capucine bit off her acid retort and strode purposefully
at Momo's elbow. The streets were jammed with North

THE GRAVE GOURMET 179

African men, bored, loitering, strolling, lolling, smoking, jeering at passersby, the detritus of a neighborhood where unemployment for those with papers topped thirty percent and the majority of inhabitants were unemployable illegals. What little French was spoken on the street was drowned in the macaronic singsong of Arab argot. As a couple Momo and Capucine sparked a good deal of interest. Momo was bombarded with comments. The few words that Capucine could understand seemed to indicate a consensus that his choice of a woman not from the bled must result in a very tame time in bed and even worse food. Most of the time Momo just laughed. Once or twice he turned in anger, causing his mocker to vanish in deference to Momo's bulk.

Clotilde's building was a nondescript dark, narrow four-story structure built in the late nineteenth century on a plot undoubtedly previously occupied by a small town house. Surprisingly for the neighborhood, a concierge was on her knees scrubbing the tiny tiled foyer with a stiff brush and a green plastic bucket of bleach water. She wore a shapeless housedress, a well-worn lemon-and-white striped apron and ancient carpet slippers. Her face was decorated with faded harquus tattoos on her chin and under her eyes.

Momo whispered in Capucine's ear. "Boss, let me deal with this woman. She'll give us a look at the apartment. No problem. Just step away a little and let me handle it."

He walked over to the kneeling concierge and bent over her threateningly. "Woman, you've been bad," he said in a strong Maghrebian accent. "I'm going to take you in and put you in GAV and keep you under arrest until you talk. You be there long time. Do you understand?!"

The woman was terrified. "No, no. I no do anything. Why you say that? Don't take me down. I have to feed my little ones."

"You have bad person living here. You bad, too. A *blanc* called Lancrey-Javal. You tell me about her."

"*L'Ancre Naval!* She lives under the roof. Go see if you want. I have keys. She not from the bled."

Momo turned to Capucine. "We're in. She calls her the Naval Anchor because the name is too complicated for her. Just don't smile at the woman. She'll only cooperate if she's terrified and thinks we're going to let her rot in GAV for weeks on end, which happens often enough to these people." Capucine was surprised to see that he hadn't bothered to show his police ID.

They followed the woman as she shuffled up three flights of shabby but spotless stairs and stopped at a final set so steep it was almost a ladder. Normally this would have led to the dormers, the floor that had been built to contain tiny cubicles for servants, devoid of plumbing except for a single cold-water tap and a hole-in-the-floor "Turkish" toilet in a closet at the end of the hall. But the top of the stairs was blocked by a wooden door painted in brilliant lilac.

"It's here that she lives, the Ancre Naval." The concierge extracted a trousseau of keys from her apron, singled one out, and handed the bunch to Momo. "You go look. I stay here. Say nothing."

The apartment could well have been featured in *Madame Figaro*. The partitions of the cubicles had been knocked down and the area transformed into a single long loft brightly lit by six windows. The ceiling had been knocked out and the roof beams exposed, stained, and waxed, creating a pleasing feeling of an antique barn. A large double bed covered in pillows was at the far end. The middle consisted of a living room of beige leather furniture clustered around an onyx fireplace. Several large portraits trimmed in ornate gilt frames stretched from floor to ceiling. The area closest to the door was occupied by a brushed stainless steel kitchen area equipped with the latest in German appliances.

"Wow!" Momo said.

"I told you she wasn't from the bled," the concierge shouted happily from the bottom of the stairs.

Later that night Capucine and Momo returned to the Quai des Orfèvres after examining the contents of the apartment. Other than the neighborhood, they found nothing that was not consistent with the dwelling of a relatively well-to-do single woman. Capucine, interest piqued, went straight to her office and turned on her computer. In less than an hour she strode into the bridadiers' office, her eyes alight with the joy of discovery.

"That Naval Anchor apartment gets stranger and stranger."

"She won it in a lottery?"

"Not even close. There are four separate apartments listed on that floor of that building. One of them is in her name and three others in the names of Jean, Bertrand, and Lisette Moreau. All four have post office mortgages. The values listed are ridiculously low, even for Barbès. What do you make of that?"

"Beats me, Lieutenant. I'm just here for the heavy lifting."

"Lieutenant, I may have fucked up. Badly," Momo said, his voice clear enough on the cell phone to be audible to the others in the room. By mid-week the surveillance of Clotilde had revealed nothing of interest. Impatient, Tallon had convoked Capucine to review the case at the end of the day. Capucine had followed Clotilde home on the metro, handed her over to Momo when she went upstairs, and had then come back to the Quai des Orfèvres for the meeting. Half an hour into the session Capucine's cell phone had vibrated in its irritating way.

"What happened?"

"Well, about an hour after you left the subject comes down with a newspaper under her arm. You know, the *Monde*, the small one, folded in half, like."

"Momo, I know the *Monde*. Go on."

"So she hangs around, like she doesn't know where to go. That looked odd. Then she walks down the street and starts poking around the stuff this store has out on the sidewalk. You know, pots and pans, suitcases, djellabas hanging on the wall, all that stuff."

"I remember the store."

"Anyway, this Asian guy comes up. Suit. With a *Monde* under his arm. He starts looking at this junk, too. At one point he brushes up against the subject and apologizes. They don't talk after that and he just walks off. Looked odd to me. Who in hell reads the *Monde* in Barbès? I think they switched papers. After the fact it struck me that the *Mondes* were fatter than they shoulda been."

"Then what happened?"

"The subject just goes back upstairs. I know I fucked up. I should have tailed the Asian guy, but I didn't want to leave the subject without orders."

"You did the right thing, Momo. I should have been with you. It sounds like a drop, all right. Stay with the subject. I'll be back there in half an hour."

Capucine looked at Tallon pointedly. "Seems like Clotilde Lancrey-Javal just passed something to someone on the street. Momo couldn't follow him because I wasn't there to back him up."

Tallon beamed. "Don't worry about that. Put more people on her surveillance. Upgrade the priority level on her wiretaps. Get going. Things are looking up."

Chapter 35

Capucine let Rolland sulk in his cell until late in the afternoon of the next day before bringing him up to her office. Despite his wrinkled suit in which he had obviously slept for two nights, it was the same affable Rolland who still gave every indication of being on a social call.

"Monsieur Rolland, pleasant as our conversation was the other day, we really didn't spend as much time talking about the restaurant as I would have liked. I gather that there's no love lost between you and the kitchen staff but, nevertheless, Diapason is your place of business. A man has been found dead, people come and go in the middle of the night dragging heavy bags: obviously there must be a good deal of discussion about these things."

"If there is, it isn't with me. I've already told you, Président Delage was not a devotee of wine. He possessed the rudiments, of course, but preferred ordering safe, solid, costly but dull wines of no particular interest. There was no pleasure in conferring with him. I'm sure his death was a tragedy, but not for me."

"And the mysterious visit in the middle of the night?"

"I know even less about that. Who can say? Some sort

of produce delivery, no doubt. As I'm sure you've been told, Jean-Basile Labrousse is famous, or shall I say infamous, for ordering his produce in minute quantities from small farms all over France. There are deliveries all the time. Obviously, avoiding the wholesale distributors is a good thing. I myself mistrust the large *marchands de vin* and buy a good deal of my wine locally direct from the châteaux. But there are limits. Apparently the kitchen is continually in fear of having to withdraw a dish from the menu in the middle of the service, which would just not do in a three-star restaurant, particularly if the wine I had chosen for that dish had already been uncorked."

"But there is the question of the key. Would a farmer, if that's who it was, be given a key?"

Rolland laughed. "Madame, I couldn't care less who has keys or who makes deliveries. My wine cellar has a steel door as solid as a safe's. It has to meet the insurance company specifications. As long as they can't get into it— and they certainly can't—I don't give a damn who traipses around the restaurant, day or night."

Capucine looked at him sharply. "Who has keys to the cellar?"

"Just Labrousse and myself." Rolland paused and stared at the floor. "But I don't allow anyone in there without my being present." He raised his head and his eyes traversed the room slowly like the twin barrels of a shotgun until they stared hard into Capucine's. "You can't imagine how painful it is for me to think of my *aide sommelier* pawing my bottles without my supervision."

"Oh, I'm quite sure he's been perfectly trained by you and is a credit to the restaurant."

"Lieutenant, how long is this going to go on for? Are you going to allow me to work tonight?"

"Not tonight, no. Let's hope we can make more progress tomorrow." Capucine stood up as Momo arrived and turned her back on Rolland. Without a word Momo escorted him from the room.

The next day Capucine again waited until after lunch to send for him. Even though Rolland was now haggard and his suit frankly scruffy, smelling faintly of urine and industrial disinfectant, he still hung on valiantly to the shreds of his affable tone. Capucine continued their discussion, hardly an interrogation, into the late afternoon. Rolland reiterated his utter lack of interest in pastimes that didn't involve enology and his disdain for the pedestrian domain of food preparation. At precisely four o'clock Capucine stopped the conversation short and conspicuously pushed the button that summoned Momo.

"Your forty-eight hours of garde à vue are up. I'm going to have you driven home. You're in no condition to be on the streets."

When Momo arrived she beckoned him to the window and whispered almost inaudibly in his ear. "Use my car. Drive him home. Take him up to his apartment. Make sure he steps over the threshold. Then arrest him immediately and bring him back. I'm not through with him."

Momo did a double take but walked Rolland out the door without comment.

Within an hour Rolland was back in his old cell, untouched since his departure. Capucine had no difficulty imagining his dismay at the evening meal, which would probably consist of a glutinous heap of tasteless, unsalted white beans with a few unidentifiable shreds of meat serving as a backdrop for a glass of tap water drawn from the cold-water sink in his cell.

Capucine again left him to his own devices until the next afternoon, when she had him brought, not to her office, but an interrogation room on the second floor of the Quai. In a Chanel suit and the extravagant mules she had acquired during her antidepression spree Capucine looked jarringly out of place in the depressingly drab room with its cheap felt carpeting, sound-deadening foam wall tiles, and gray Formica table with four—inevitably—bent metal chairs. Even more out of place was the bottle of wine on a small table next to the door.

When Capucine had asked Alexandre to name the wine that would be most likely to attract the attention of a sommelier he had hiked his eyebrows and intoned a bored litany as if it were a Gregorian chant, "lafitelatourmoutonhaut-brionmargauxyquempétrus-romanéeeeeaycontiiiieeiieeii."

"No, no silly, not the obvious ones. I know all of those. I want something outstanding but relatively unknown. And if it works, I might even give you the bottle."

"Ah. That changes everything." He thought for a moment. "How about a bottle of La Mouline? It's a Côte Rôtie. Superb, little known, and almost impossible to get. They only make three hundred cases a year. I saw a bottle of the 1991 the other day for a little under a thousand euros."

"Perfect. That exactly the sort of thing I'm looking for."

"What sort of up-market mouse do you expect to catch with such a luxurious cheese?"

"It's not going to be used as cheese. It's what they called a 'stressor' at the academy interrogation classes. If it works I'll tell you all about it tomorrow while we're drinking the damn thing."

As a uniformed policeman led Rolland into the interrogation room he held back for an instant to stare at the bottle lying in an open wooden box like a dead body at a viewing. Capucine placed him at the table half-facing the bottle, at which he darted frequent nervous glances.

This time around Rolland seemed unable to muster his cocktail-party persona. He breathed audibly through his mouth. The ammoniac jail-cell acridness was more pronounced and was now enhanced by a musky smell of body odor. He was as gray and gaunt as if he had moldered in the depths of a dungeon for decades. Sitting on the corner of his chair he shifted nervously, mute while Capucine drummed her fingers inaudibly on the table. The eternity of a minute passed as Capucine's little smile ebbed like a parting tide. "Well?" she asked finally.

Rolland paused, twisted on the corner of his chair, gulped, stared at her, then at the bottle, then back at her, and finally, in a small voice that needed to be primed by a cough, said, "Okay, okay, it was me. I confess."

"Of course you do. Everyone loves catharsis. But to what exactly do you confess? Be specific."

"It was me bringing the bag into the kitchen. The other man was a, well, an associate."

"Grégoire," Capucine said, falling into the first-name and familiar "*tu*" the police invariably use with the criminal classes. "Why don't you just get on with it and tell the story instead of being coy. We'll both get where we're going much faster that way."

"Lieutenant, believe me, it's nothing. It was foolish of me not to tell you from the beginning. But once I had fibbed I had to stick to it. You'll laugh when I tell you."

"Out with it, Grégoire."

"See, I actually do have a little pastime. I like to gamble. It gives me a big thrill that relieves the tension. You wouldn't think there's a lot of tension in my job. But there is. Anyway, you know how it is with gambling. Sometimes you win, sometimes you lose." He stopped, uncertain how to continue.

"When you say you gamble, what do you mean? You buy lottery tickets at the café?"

Rolland sneered. A bit of his bravado had returned. "Hardly. Sometimes I go to casinos for the weekend, sometimes I gamble in Paris. I'm sure the police know that there are a number of private clubs that cater to gambling even if it stretches the law a little. For the gambling to be a thrill the sums have to be important and the atmosphere has to be correct."

"And what does your innocent little pastime have to do with carting bags around in the middle of the night?"

"I see that, like most women, you disapprove of gambling. But over the years I've won more than I've lost. How many people have a pastime that costs nothing and actually brings money in? Of course, every now and then your short-term losses are more than you expect. It's the way it works. But I always get it back. Always. Well, anyway, a while ago it happened that I owed a certain man— I most definitely won't tell you his name—a bit over fifty thousand euros. Unfortunately, I didn't have the money in the bank, so I did the honorable thing. I sold some of my wine to a marchand to pay him. Not much at all. Just two cases, actually."

He paused and looked at Capucine, as if for approval. She stared back, expressionless.

"A week later I won big, as of course I knew I would. So I went to an auction at Drouot and bought two cases of the same wines I had sold. In fact, I got lucky and bought them for quite a bit less than I had received from the marchand. Since I certainly wasn't about to make a profit out of the transaction I also bought a case of a Forts de Latour that we were nearly out of at the restaurant. I gave the wine delivery man from Drouot a huge tip to make a delivery in the middle of the night. Those guys will do anything for a few euros. Voilà! Everyone was a winner. Even my cellar, which got an extra case of a wine for free. Wasn't it foolish of me not to tell you from the beginning?" Rolland seemed relieved and confident he was restored to Capucine's good graces.

"Simply put, you're telling me that in order to finance your gambling losses you steal wine from the cellar at Diapason? Is that it?"

"Hardly stealing!" Rolland looked shocked. "Yes, I sent some of my wine to a dealer but I knew I would replace it in a matter of days. I was careful to select the standard classics that are always on the market. There was no risk. I always recoup my losses quickly. I would never take any chances with my wine." He gave a comfortable little chuckle of complicity.

"Do you realize, Grégoire, that a theft of this value is considered grand larceny? You could go to prison for over fifteen years. Worse, you've betrayed Chef Labrousse's trust. Hell, you've betrayed your profession. You're a discredit to the restaurant industry. It makes me happy to think of the years you'll have in jail to think it all over."

"Lieutenant, now it's you being childish. I stole nothing. The wine is happily back in my cellar sleeping soundly. If anything has changed it's that I added a case. That's hardly a crime."

For a second it was as if Capucine was back in the financial brigade. Rolland had the same self-satisfied, supercilious smirk plastered on his face that had never failed to enrage Capucine in her former role. It was clear Rolland felt he was fully entitled to his actions. For him it was Capucine, with her Little-Goodie-Two-Shoes morality, who was at fault and had to be handled carefully.

"Lieutenant, seriously, what sort of case do you have? There's no evidence. The Drouot commis will say he was home in bed. There's nothing missing from the cellar. There's just an extra case that I carelessly failed to note down when I bought it. Big deal." He persisted with his maddening smirk.

Capucine clenched her teeth, her lips compressed into the beginning of a pucker for a long moment as she contemplated letting him rot in the cells downstairs for the rest of the month. She could probably get away with it, too. It was just the sort of thing Tallon liked to do. Finally, she sighed and shook her head in disgust.

"All right. You were lucky this time. But it's not going to be that easy for you. I'm going to give you a choice: either you quit Diapason and leave Paris or I'll have a chat with Chef Labrousse and make damn sure that he drums you out of the business and destroys your reputation. If you're a good boy and leave Paris by the end of the week I won't say a word to Chef Labrousse. He's suffered enough as it is. But God help you if I ever see you in this town again."

"Lieutenant, you're the most charming policeman I've ever met, but I really do think you've seen too many Westerns." Rolland walked out of the room as jauntily as when he had first come in four days before. Capucine had a hard time restraining herself from throwing one of the bent chairs at him.

Chapter 36

"Fucking tie! What's the point of being plain clothes if you have to dress like a goddamn clown? Might as well be directing traffic."

"Momo, calm down," Capucine said.

"Lieutenant, he nearly killed the whole operation," Isabelle said. "He went into this burlesque Arab routine that he thinks is funny. If that poor woman hadn't been stressed out of her gourd she would have smelled a rat."

"All right, all right, start from the beginning," Capucine said, acutely conscious that setting up a conference call to listen to the two brigadiers report at the same time on their cell phones had been a big mistake.

"There we were dressed up like the Gestapo . . ."

"Momo," Isabelle interrupted, "that's the Renault security uniform. There's nothing we could have done about it." She added for Capucine's edification, "Monsieur Momo took offense at the Sam Browne belt."

"All right, guys, enough of this. There you are manning the security checkpoint at the Renault headquarters in Renault security staff uniforms and what exactly happened?"

Isabelle picked up the thread of the narrative. "Okay, Lieutenant, around seven thirty along comes Miss Princess, the Naval Anchor. She tries to walk around the metal detector and Momo starts doing his thing, you know, the sycophantic illiterate North African. 'So sorry, Madame, you must go through the detector or de boss man, he fire me.' It almost didn't work."

"But it did, didn't it, dipshit?" Momo pointed out.

"Yes, it did asshole. Lieutenant, she tried to pull rank. She tried to say she was exempted from the security check. She tried to turn around and go back. But in the end we made her open her briefcase."

"And what was in it?" Capucine asked.

"A folded copy of the *Monde*, a Fred Vargas paperback thriller, a pack of Marlboro Lights, and a sealed manila envelope about an inch thick." Isabelle answered self-righteously. "We pretended it was nothing. That we were just looking for stolen laptops. But we hit pay dirt. That's why we're calling you."

As Clotilde walked up the steps of the Marcadet-Poissonniers metro stop into the cool evening Capucine was a few steps behind her. Two brigadiers waited at the top of the stairs while David and two other brigadiers were placed at strategic locations on the path to her door. In her desire to take no chances at all Capucine had planned her surveillance with such textbook precision that the exercise could have been videotaped for training sessions.

One brigadier remained on post at the metro. Capucine followed Clotilde for two short blocks and was smoothly replaced by two other members of the team. Another brigadier was loitering across the street from Clotilde's door. Anticlimactically she went straight into her building; the lights in her apartment were seen to go on, and after a short pause the blue glow of her television appeared. To all indications she intended to spend a quiet evening in.

Capucine admired the forbearance of her team as they

settled into what was likely to be an all-night vigil the way a ship's crew anesthetizes itself as it sinks into a night watch. They paced quietly, smoking, lost in reverie but still keenly observant, becoming almost invisible in the shadows. Capucine walked to the corner susurrating into her radio, raising the team one by one and positioning them in a broad arc spanning the three blocks in front of the building door.

For Capucine the time passed with agonizing slowness. She stared at the faint blue flicker in the center window and calculated her next moves. She would wait a full two hours after all the lights had gone out before sending the team home and would leave a brigadier in front of the door all night long just in case.

Without warning the front door opened and Clotilde stepped out briskly, still in her work clothes, a copy of the *Monde* folded under her arm.

Capucine pressed a button on the radio. "Subject moving."

Clotilde turned left, walking up the steep hill in the direction of the Sacré-Coeur, purposefully, rapidly, as if she were late for an appointment. Capucine followed, fifty feet behind. It was the least expected route. The point officer, lounging a hundred feet up the hill, was Momo. He and Isabelle, who would be easily recognized, had been assigned the positions farthest away from her front door to allow them plenty of time to get out of sight. Capucine pressed the button on her radio again.

"Momo, she's coming your way."

Momo stepped through a rickety glass door into a minuscule café. The façade was of dirty glass down to the shin level allowing a full view of the room inside, no bigger than ten feet by fifteen, packed with men, many in flowing djellabas with kufis perched on the backs of their heads, sitting on benches drinking mint tea in ornate gilt glasses or espressos from thimble-sized cups. The crowded

room was completely free of the odor of bodies or cigarette smoke. Momo positioned himself at the end of the
bar farthest from the door and asked for a mint tea. He
could still see the narrow street from his vantage point but
was confident he would be imperceptible among the other
North Africans. Without thinking he had almost asked for
a beer, which he would have relished, but realized in the
nick of time that he was in a deeply religious part of the
quartier and a request for alcohol would have earned him
a stern reprimand from the barman and probably cries of
"shame" from some of the patrons. There was even a
chance of an uproar and his being thrown out of the café.

Directly opposite, Clotilde walked up to a short Asian
man in a suit and accosted him angrily. The man seemed
evasive and attempted to walk by her, making a pantomime show of embarrassment. As if in exasperation she
thrust her *Monde* at him, turned on her heel, and stalked
irately back down the hill. The man wheeled and walked
in the opposite direction slowly, as if he were continuing a
leisurely stroll. A few seconds later Capucine arrived,
walking up the sidewalk following the Asian while whispering animatedly into her radio. Momo threw some coins
on the bar and walked out after her. In his rush he took no
notice of the number of men who shuffled out after him.
At the corner the Asian man paused as if uncertain which
way to go.

In the next street a loudspeaker suddenly blared out a
wailing melismatic chant, the recorded voice of the
muezzin rising hauntingly. *"Allahu ākbar, allahu ākbar,
ash'hadu ān lā ilaha illā-allah,"* it began and continued on.

The street filled with men. All silent. Most carrying
rolled-up rugs. The urgency in the air was palpable.

The Asian man turned to the left and walked into a narrow street, a tight fit for even one car, now as thronged as
the metro at rush hour. The loudspeaker, which was in the
middle of the block, blared again, much more loudly. *"Al-*

lahu ākbar, allahu ākbar, ash'hadu ān lā ilaha illā-allah,"
with the muezzin sounding more stern and commanding.
Quickly the men slipped off their shoes and pointed
babouches, jockeyed them with their toes into neat rows
against the building walls, formed into a tight phalanx,
shoulder pressed against shoulder, began the prayer, and
then dropped as a single man to their knees on rugs that
had been spread out on the cobblestones. The Asian was
halfway down the block on the sidewalk, inching down
the street crabwise, back to the wall, squeezing past the
kneeling men, clearly unnerved by the spectacle. At the
next chant from the loudspeaker the men in the street
pitched forward, foreheads hard down on the rugs, poste-
riors high in the air, palms flat on the ground beside their
faces. The distances between the rows had been so well
learned by endless repetition that heads were less than an
inch away from feet in the row in front. The street was a
tightly woven carpet of humanity. The recorded muezzin
chanted on through his hidden loudspeaker. The prostrate
men in the street chanted in response.

Capucine started forward in pursuit. Momo arrived
breathlessly and seized her upper arm.

"Lieutenant, it's the *Salat-ul-Isha*, the night prayer. We
cannot intrude."

Capucine tried to pull her arm away. "What we can't do
is let him get away." Momo tightened his grip.

"No. Blancs are not welcome at the prayer. And if they
discover we are flics, there will be an incident."

The Asian man reached the bottom of the street, turned
the corner, and vanished.

Chapter 37

"All right, where's the subject?" Capucine barked. "She just walked back into her building." David's voice crackled over the radio.

"David, stay put. I'll be right there. The rest of you can go back to the Quai."

In a few minutes Capucine arrived a little breathlessly at David's side. "We lost the pickup. We're going up and see what we can worm out of the subject. We walk in, show our cards, you say nothing. Got it?"

"Lieutenant, don't we need a warrant? It's after nine o'clock."

"What we need is not to dither around here. What you guys need is to stop telling me what to do. Let's get up there."

Clotilde came to the door in her stockinged feet but still in her street clothes, a half-empty glass of wine in her hand. She had been crying hard. The mascara had run down her cheeks in two straight lines, giving her a pathetic Marcel Marceau look.

Capucine and David stood at the door holding their ID wallets menacingly at face height. "Madame Lancrey-Javal? Police Judiciaire," Capucine said.

"I knew it would come to this! Am I under arrest?"

"Not quite," said Capucine. "But I do need to talk to you."

Clotilde turned and walked back into the apartment. Capucine followed her in. David hung back, a languid sentry at the door.

"Sit down," Capucine said. "Tell me what happened."

"How much do you know?" Clotilde asked, her voice choked from the crying.

"Why don't you just assume I don't know anything. Start at the beginning."

"I have no idea how he found me. I was shopping at the Printemps one morning. In the housewares section. I needed a new set of pans. He was there next to me. He asked my advice on a skillet for omelets. We talked. He was very attractive. Such deep eyes. Very polite. He said his name was Dac Kim Chu. He was Vietnamese. We talked for a while in the store. He asked me to a snack in the department store coffee shop. Then we had dinner two days later. A few days later he offered me a lot of money to do some very little things. It was the solution to all my problems. Money has been so very, very difficult for me. I don't know how he knew. That's all there is to it. Really."

Once it was obvious the story would be forthcoming Capucine relaxed. "Let's start at the beginning. Why is money such a problem?"

"Three years ago my husband ran out on me. I had no warning at all. One day he just left for the United States with his secretary. He took all our money, everything in the banks, sold our stocks, everything. The worst part was that he owed an enormous sum to the tax people. It seems that I am responsible even though I knew nothing about how he handled his financial affairs. So even though he deserted me I still have to pay all the taxes he owes. The tax people are terribly aggressive. I was lucky to get a reasonably paid job. I hadn't worked for twelve years. But I have to pay nearly two-thirds of my salary to the *fisc*. I have barely enough for necessities with what's left. You have no idea how awful it was. I spent every hour of every day thinking about making silly little economies, thinking about how I could scrimp to pay for things that three years before I would have thought nothing about. Money worries rule my life." She paused. "Do you know what it feels like to borrow money from your children so you can eat? Can you imagine the look in their eyes?"

"But you have this wonderful apartment. How did you manage that?"

"That was one of my husband's sharp tricks. He opened up a postal savings account for each of the children when they were born. The interest you get is almost nothing but the accounts give you a subsidized mortgage at a very low rate after fifteen years and you can use the principal of the savings account to make the purchase. He used the accounts to buy four maids' rooms, which he rented out. When he ran off we let the tenants' leases expire, and then the children and I knocked down the walls and turned the four rooms into a single apartment. The kids all took out mortgages to decorate it. The tax people can't seize it because it's in the children's names except for my little part. That's not illegal, is it?"

"Well, I don't think that was what was intended when the postal act was written, but I don't see what anyone can do about it. It's a clever enough trick. It's been done before. So this charming man that you met at the Printemps offered you money. For what, exactly?"

"That's just it. For doing virtually nothing. All I had to do was go into the ladies' room at work and pick up an envelope that would be inside the paper towel dispenser, on top of the towels. Then I would put that envelope inside a copy of the *Monde,* go outside an hour after I got home, and walk around my neighborhood. The man would come up and exchange newspapers with me."

"And how would you know when to do this?"

"I would find a flower on my desk. A white hibiscus in a little plastic water glass from the water dispenser. That meant I had to pick up something in the ladies' room. If Dac Kim wanted to deliver something to whoever in Renault these things came from, I would place a pink hibiscus on my desk and then put whatever it was in the paper towel rack. Everyone thought I had a secret admirer in the office."

"Were there many deliveries?"

"Oh, no. Once or twice a month most of the time. But sometimes there would be a flurry back and forth. A delivery a day."

"And how much did you get for this?"

"Every time I gave him something there would be an envelope with money in the newspaper he exchanged with me. At the end of the month it was as much as my salary. It was a godsend—with no taxes, of course. It changed my life. It was like being free again."

"Very neat. But I don't quite see how you fell into such an elaborate plan on the strength of one quick lunch and one dinner."

Clotilde stared at the floor for a moment reddening slightly. "I'm afraid there was more to it than that. We had several dinners. We became . . . well . . . intimate. He even spent a few weekends here. Actually, I never went to his apartment. He always came here. He was the first man I slept with after my husband. I had come to feel no one wanted me. The money only came later. One day I told him how desperate I was about money. He offered to help me. At the time I really thought he was doing me a favor because of what he felt for me. I didn't know what I was doing. I still don't." She drained her glass of wine. "I'm going to have some more wine. Can I get you some?"

"Thanks. I will take some. I'll pretend I'm not on duty."

"What about him?" Clotilde asked, indicating David.

"He's not allowed to pretend."

When Clotilde returned with two glasses Capucine asked her, "And what would you guess all this is about?"

"I have no idea. Really no idea. It has to be some sort of industrial espionage thing. That much is obvious. But I can't imagine what it might be. I mean, what else could it be? I'd guess it was the new model designs or something like that. Or colors, maybe. They're enormously secretive about those things."

"And you never asked him?"

"Well, after I started giving him envelopes, our 'relationship' died down," Clotilde said, making quotation marks in the air with the first two fingers of each hand. "He told me he didn't want to mix business with pleasure. His personality changed. He became tough, almost brutal. I became afraid of him. Like tonight, when I told him I wanted to quit he told me I had no choice. If I tried to quit he would come around with some friends to make sure I would continue. He is a tremendously powerful man. I'd never been with a man as strong as he is. Very frightening. He made love very roughly. Very roughly. He always hurt me. I think that was the part he enjoyed."

"What happened tonight? Why did you tell him you wanted to quit?"

"Renault has toughened its security measures. I'm not sure, but I think it might even have something to do with all the papers I am giving him. There are new security staff and everything. Tonight I nearly got caught. The security guards wanted to go through my briefcase. If I hadn't complained they would have opened the envelope I was taking Dac Kim, but I got strict with them and they let me go. I don't think they noticed anything but I panicked completely anyway. I told Dac Kim that I wanted no part of it anymore. I gave him his envelope but refused to take his money. That was when he told me I had no choice." She drained her wine.

"I know I made a huge mistake. But it was so nice to be with someone after those years of loneliness. And then it was even nicer not to have to worry about money all the time. I knew it was very wrong, but I pushed it to the back of my mind. Are you going to arrest me?"

"No. Nothing you've done is criminal. I'm sure it violates Renault's employment regulations and could possibly expose you to a civil suit, but that's hardly a police matter. We're interested only because it relates to a case we're working on. Tell me, how do you contact this man?"

"I have a cell phone number for him. I call it when I get an envelope. He doesn't answer. I just call and hang up. Obviously, his phone records my number. And he meets me that evening. Or he will call my cell from a pay phone and tell me he wants to see me in such and such a place."

"Give me the number. I'm sure it's a prepaid phone that was bought anonymously, but it still needs to be checked out. With a little luck you'll get out of this mess," Capucine said. "But be very careful. You're dealing with a highly dangerous man. Go on doing what you were doing. You'll hear from me in the next day or two. If anything happens call me at this number," she said, giving Clotilde her card. Capucine smiled at her gently and patted the back of her hand. "Don't despair. With a little luck things will work out, you'll see."

Capucine swept into the restaurant and pulled up short at the end of the bar. Alexandre wasn't hard to spot. He was at his usual corner. Tables had been pushed together and a crowd of ten or twelve were well into dinner, rowdy enough to verge on the obnoxious. She walked across the room grinding her teeth. It was Alexandre's coterie of journalist cronies. None of them were devotees of the police and she suspected some would be delighted to craft an editorial pearl around any grain of gossip she might drop.

As she approached the table the portly waiter came up

and handed her a tall glass with two ice cubes and four fingers of amber liquid. "Scotch, Lieutenant. You look like you've had a hell of day."

She was greeted boisterously. People moved around to vacate the chair next to Alexandre for her. A very pink and very corpulent man exclaimed in stentorian measured tones, as if he were proclaiming Racine, "Ah! The advent of our gorgeous and intrepid detective. Just in time to cast the pall from our gloomy gathering. My dear, have your efforts in repressing the forces of evil been crowned with success?"

"On the contrary, Robert, I've left my evil hare free to make another lap around his field and am concentrating on oppressing his victims instead. Just to keep my hand in, of course."

"Alexandre, do you ever know what she's talking about?"

"Never. It's the secret to a perfect marriage. All one says is 'Yes, dear' over and over again with suitably adoring looks and then one reaps the rewards. A technique you really should try on your next wife."

Halfway through her titanic Scotch Capucine sank into the general hilarity, losing herself in the sexual peccadilloes of the candidates of the upcoming senatorial elections.

Much, much later she and Alexandre found themselves at the virtually deserted Deux Magots, sitting at the celebrated corner table in the window made famous as the second home of Sartre and Simone de Beauvoir. They drank coffee and bad cognac in miniscule snifters, made even worse by being several drinks too many.

"Doesn't sound like it's going all that well," Alexandre said.

"It's going and that's what counts. The problem is that the guilty consistently turn out to be innocent. They are even victims." She told him about her evening and the Asian agent who had vanished.

Alexandre was silent for a moment and then motioned to the waiter for two more cognacs. "If this is really the work of spies, it'll get wrenched out of your hands. Marie-Hélène will have no choice but to call in the DGSE, even if it does drive her up the wall."

Capucine laughed. "No, my love. For once you're wrong. It's going to stay a police case and the police will get the murderer. I think I can promise you that."

Chapter 38

"Sometimes it takes forever to get here. Monsieur Guyon was very annoyed this morning. But what can I do?" Capucine had arrived at Guyon's office at nine thirty. It was obvious that Thérèse Garnier had just arrived herself. She informed Capucine that Guyon would be with her shortly and began setting up for the day. She hobbled rapidly and erratically around the office, the staccato of her heels broadcasting her verve. Eventually, she perched behind her desk, applying makeup carefully, looking intently into the mirror of her powder compact, peering over the top as she recited her morning epic. "The flat escalators at Le Châtelet were broken and the tunnel was completely jammed." She brushed her hair back vigorously. "Then the train never came." Her eyes seemed to widen with the effort. "And when it finally came we were packed in like sardines." She shook her head. Her lips turned up in the beginning of a smile. She still wasn't attractive, but the abject look was almost gone and her eyes hinted at the mischievous. She reached into her bag and produced a tiny bottle of perfume, held it between thumb and middle finger, inverted it, and delicately touched the recesses under the lobe of each ear. She smiled. "I guess it's not all that bad. I'm going to run down the hall and get some coffee. Want some? I'm sure Monsieur Guyon won't keep you waiting long." As she stood up her square frame looked almost elegant in the inexpensive tan suit. The transformation was complete. It was impossible to imagine her existing outside the luxury of leather and chrome and soft, indirect lighting.

Half an hour later Guyon opened his door and beckoned Capucine in brusquely. "Voilà, mademoiselle, let's get going. I have a very busy morning."

Once inside the office, he waved her to a chair with an authoritative gesture. "You're making progress, mademoiselle. I see you have capitulated to the elementary rules of politeness and deigned to have these sessions in my office," Guyon said, delighted he had kept her waiting so long. "What is it today?"

"Monsieur Guyon, it appears that your department has been infiltrated by some sort of espionage activity. Normally, that wouldn't concern me, but there's a chance it's connected with the murder of the président."

"My good woman, we went through all that the last time. You claim that this fake DGSE agent worked for some American company. So be it. But he didn't steal anything except a free lunch, so I don't see what the problem is."

"This is something altogether different. We intercepted one of Renault's employees handing an envelope to a man on the street. Even though we weren't able to obtain the contents, it very much looks like the envelope contained confidential data coming from your department."

Guyon sneered. "I don't understand. You saw one of our people on the street handing someone something. But you seem to have bungled again and never saw the contents of the envelope. Why ever would you conclude that it was theft of secrets? Sometimes I wonder about your mental processes. The less efficient you are, the more you see crime on every street corner. It's an obsession."

"For some time our officers have been assisting the Renault security guards at the building security checkpoints. They intercepted an employee who was taking materials out of the building. That employee was followed and was seen to hand those materials over to someone on the street. Our guess is that this is an entirely different operation from Trag's."

"This is an outrage! You've planted flics on the Renault staff? You're following our employees around? On whose authority? And who is this person you're accusing?"

"Monsieur Guyon, these issues are irrelevant. For what it's worth, the human resources department cooperated fully with us in integrating police officers into the security team. But, since it's part of a murder investigation, the identity of the person in question will remain confidential for the time being. The reason I'm here is that you clearly have a serious leak in your department. I should say 'another serious leak.' Obviously, you are going to want to take steps, but I want those steps to be coordinated with our investigation. Do you understand?"

"And what do you expect me to do? You're the police officer. Not me."

"Industrial espionage is rarely a police matter, as I'm sure you know."

"So you come in here and tell me these things, but you don't have any suggestion as to what I should do."

"Monsieur Guyon, you have two possible routes. You can go to the DGSE or you can hire a private company. I do think you need to do something, but it's important you keep us informed. In fact, it's even a legal requirement."

Guyon paced in front of his desk. "Well, Lieutenant, what do you think I should do?"

"At one point you seemed to think the involvement of

DGSE was logical. Given Typhon's importance to the nation that makes a certain amount of sense. I can give you a contact there if you want. He's a man who is very easy to get along with. He will tell you if they can be of value or, if not, recommend a private firm."

"Lieutenant, you apparently don't have the slightest notion of how corporations work. Do you really think I have the authority to go whining to the DGSE? What would the board think? How would our acting president react? You're out of your mind."

"If you feel it would require the involvement of the acting président, then why don't you see him?"

"How little you understand. He's the chief financial officer. He's been placed in a temporary position until the board chooses to name a new président. He's not there to make decisions. He doesn't even sit in the président's office. The président's former secretary remains at her desk. She handles everything that goes into the office of the président. Do you think I should ask her to handle it? Wouldn't that be clever?"

"That's an idea with more merit than you suspect, Monsieur Guyon. But, you must take steps. You can't just ignore this. At the very least you have to alert the acting président. This could possibly be very serious for Renault."

"Very well, I'll go see him. But I can tell you right now what he'll say."

"You do that. And if you two decide to go to the Ministry of the Exterior I'll be happy to give you a contact." Capucine got up. "Call me and let me know what your decision is. You have my number."

On her way down in the elevator Capucine regretted her cockiness with Guyon. It was true she felt the case was heading to fruition almost of its own accord, like a pimple that invites being popped. But that didn't mean she had the slightest idea what to do next.

Chapter 39

Jacques met Capucine at the elevator bank on his floor of the Pool in what she assumed was carefully calculated to be his hard-at-work outfit: no jacket, a brilliantly striped Turnbull and Asser shirt that fit his torso so perfectly it could only have been made to measure, gold cuff links in the shape of decorative nautical knots, and a solid navy blue tie of rough silk transfixed by a gold hunting pin. He held an uncapped clunky gold pen as if he had torn himself away from composing a note so confidential it could not be entrusted to a computer.

"Cousin, thanks for seeing me at such short notice," Capucine said.

"Who can resist the irresistible," Jacques said, wrapping his free hand around her waist and tickling her rib cage. Capucine giggled and struggled to get away while Jacques pulled her closer. "Jacques, if you get a drop of ink on me I'll never forgive you."

"Petite cousine, I never would have dreamt you were such a slave to fashion. Why don't you be like me and put material things behind you. You'll see it's the only path to happiness."

"Jacques, be serious for once. I need your help."

"If we're going to be serious, we'll have to go into the little cupboard I've been given for an office. We can lock the door," he said with a leer. "Follow me."

Jacques' office really was little bigger than a cupboard, barely large enough for the magnificent eighteenth-century mahogany rolltop desk that filled most of the room. Capucine vaguely recalled having seen it in Jacques' family château. The top of the desk was shut tight. Maybe Jacques really had been working on something highly confidential. Jacques installed Capucine in a wooden armchair with delicately curving mahogany armrests and pulled up its twin so close that his knees touched hers.

"Chère cousine, do you really need help, or is this just an excuse to spend the afternoon ensconced in my little lair?" Jacques burlesqued a dirty-old-man's laugh.

"Jacques, just stop it. This is serious. Just as you predicted, we found another cow-dung beetle rooting around in our cow pie."

"How wonderful. I want to hear all about it."

"We caught Président Delage's secretary sneaking an envelope out of the building and handing it over to an Asian man, who we lost in the evening prayer in Barbès."

"Prayer does have a way of putting a damper on things. That's why I avoid it at all costs," Jacques said. "Your chase sounds as much fun as hare coursing. Tell me everything."

Capucine gave him a succinct résumé of the incident and the subsequent interview with Clotilde.

"Actually, your little drama does smack a good deal of a foreign espionage agency," Jacques said, "even though it's a bit amateurish. Sticking envelopes in the towel dispenser in the ladies' room is what they call a 'dead-letter drop' in trade school. Your secretary doesn't have a clue what lies beyond that dispenser. The sloppy part is that the people on the other hand know who she is because they have to put the flower on her desk. That's very unprofessional.

And the Asian contact is even more sloppy. Of course, the only hard link with him is his cell phone, which is easy enough to drop off a bridge into the Seine if the need arises. But still, sleeping with an agent is unforgivable. That sort of stuff went out with Mata Hari." Jacques made an exaggerated frown of revulsion as if he had poked his head into a restaurant kitchen and discovered a chef committing some major culinary solecism such as opening a package of instant béarnaise.

"So you want us to root around in Renault and figure out who these people are, is that it?"

"That's the last thing I want. I'm not here about the secretary. I've already got her well in my net. It's all the other little dung beetles that might be in there that worry me. I need to know how much other espionage activity is going on. Searching for them is beyond the competence of the Police Judiciaire."

"That's for sure. Counterespionage is a bit more complicated than rounding up the usual suspects." Jacques giggled his childish shriek.

"Do you think the DGSE could look into this for us?"

"It all depends on if my masters can be persuaded that your Project Typhon is a national security issue. One never knows what they'll do next. But I'll tell you what. We have an operations committee meeting this afternoon. I'll bring it up and see if it makes the operations executive a little stiff. I'll call you as soon as I know something."

"Jacques, I can't thank you enough."

"Well," Jacques said, standing up and giving her a vaudeville wink. "I'm sure I could think of a way or two."

As she rode down in the elevator, Capucine had a déjà vu sensation that Jacques had known everything she was going to say before she said it and was far—very far—from telling her all he knew about her case.

Chapter 40

"Sweets! Two!" A piercing shout, strident over the din in the kitchen. "Sweets! Two!" Achille shouted back. Sweetbreads, chestnuts, and black truffles. His dish. With his hands he scooped three pale fat white globules out of the turgid brown liquid in a metal bowl, pinched it between his thumb and first two fingers, and began slicing thin slivers. He hunched over the table and squinted in concentration. A bead of sweat fell on the first perfectly formed disk, an eye with a jet black iris of truffle surrounded by a sclera of pale lamb thalamus. *Don't sweat the sweat, that's what makes restaurant food taste so good.* The corners of his lips turned up. *Okay, okay, it's a little more than that. But this dish isn't all that hard to make. Really. Of course, here it's different. Chef gets all this stuff from weird places. Or at least he says he does. These lamb sweetbreads come from lambs bred on a farm he owns somewhere or other. He probably personally sodomizes each one before it comes here, to make sure it's extra tasty.* He carefully placed the second sliver, precisely the same thickness as the first, on the cutting board. *Naturally, we can't use the whole damn sweetbread, only the big fat nut at the end.* Another sliver. *What time do the*

prep guys start this thing? Eleven? Another sliver. *Soak for
two hours in an ice bath. Change the water and the ice
every half hour. Parboil in Chef's secret stock three times
with an ice bath between each time.* Another sliver. *De-
membrane the fucker. Then simmer an hour in another of
Chef's secret stocks. Chef certainly isn't going to let us see
what he puts in those stocks.* Another sliver. *Then stick
your finger through the thing and shove in the truffle seg-
ment.* Another sliver. *And pray the damn thing doesn't
break apart like it always did when I used to prep the little
fuckers. Hey, the slices are all done. Good.*

He pulled a much-dented steel skillet, burnished to pure
chrome on the inside and left flame ebonized on the outside, from the hottest part of the *piano* where it had been
heating up and dropped in a large nugget of butter. The
butter hissed and tore around the skillet as if in agony.
With his fingers he placed the medallions in the skillet and
shook it back and forth vigorously so they wouldn't stick.
*So far so good. It sure is funny how you can tell things are
going just by the smell. Done!* He picked each one up between finger and thumb and flipped them over. The last
one stuck a little and he swiveled on planted feet to grab a
spatula from the counter behind. No spatula. He stepped
over to the counter, rooted around, found it. *Way too
long. Fuck! If you move your feet at this station you're
fucked!* He teased the spatula under the recalcitrant disk
and flipped it over. *Uh oh . . . not a beauty that one. A bit
darker than it should be.* It wasn't burned, or even really
overcooked. It was just a hair past the precise golden hue
required by Chef. He looked around furtively to see if the
eagle eye of his *chef de partie* was on him. *That poor
fucker is so tense with his lobster aiguillette, I could be
reaming a waitress in here and he wouldn't notice. Not
that we have waitresses. That'd be the day.* He lined up the
last medallion with the others.

No American tourist is going to have a clue. Chef's not

going to notice either, the way things are going around here. He glanced at Labrousse earnestly cooking at a range on the opposite side of the kitchen. *What's that fucker doing? Oh, I know. I've seen that. It's his famous fluffed omelet. He beats the shit out of it with a whisk for twenty minutes and then loads it with powdered sugar and crumbled bits of chocolate. Some fucking tripper must have brought his brats. To a three-star! Instead of throwing the fuckers out, Chef's making kiddie desserts. Man, this place sure is going downhill fast.*

He placed the empty skillet back on the hot center of the piano, grabbed a small, squat *clavelin* labeled *"Salins les Bains—Vin Jaune,"* and splashed a liberal quantity of the wine into the smoking hot skillet. It boiled instantly, spitting lustily. In a few seconds the urine-dark yellow of the wine had become clouded with the deposit of the sweetbreads. He scooped in some crème fraîche with the tip of his tongs, a pinch of salt, four twists of pepper, a double pinch of a mix of herbs from a round bowl, a triple pinch of finely chopped truffles from another round bowl, moved the skillet to a less hot part of the stove, and contemplated the bubbling mixture intently, swirling it occasionally. Like a Method actor, he identified so strongly with the sauce it was as if he had oozed into it, becoming a part of it, his consciousness gently swaying as the sauce rocked back and forth in its skillet, as tranquilly satisfying as a dinghy undulating on a mooring.

Funny how the police still can't crack the case. That flic *who seems to be in charge is a real hottie, though. When she interviewed me I spent the whole time checking out her boobs. She definitely wasn't wearing a bra, that's for sure. I'd really like to get my hands on those. I thought her guy must have been some super-stud cop type with three-day stubble like in the movies. Man, was I floored when it turned out it was that pudgy food critic that's here all the time. That's the thing. You have to be rich or famous, or both, to get the girl. Looks don't count for dick. That's why I'm going to be a celebrity chef. I'm going to get all the girls. And everything else.*

When you think about it, the story going around the kitchen that it was Chef who smoked that guy might actually pan out. Chef is one intense fucker. The way they tell it, that automobile big shot snaked Chef's girl away from him way back when, when he was interning at Bocuse's. Couldn't have been all that hard to do. When you work from seven thirty in the morning to midnight you certainly aren't going to get it up for any girl. They say he's had it in for the guy ever since. Wouldn't surprise me. He's one mean fucker when he gets pissed off.

The sauce was reduced by half. He put the sweetbreads back in, let them simmer for a moment, removed the skillet from the fire. *Let's plate these little fuckers.* Without moving his feet this time, he swiveled and pulled two highly polished individual-sized steel-and-brass chafing dishes from a rack behind him, held the sweetbreads down with his spatula, coated the bottom of the chafing dishes with the sauce, and then meticulously placed the medallions on the dish, interspacing them with slices of extra-large chestnuts that had been simmering all afternoon in a truffle stock until they were precisely the same texture as the sweetbreads. He was careful that the offending slice was good-side up in the center of the militarily arrayed alignment. He picked up two small sheaves of julienned Jerusalem artichokes that had been deep fried in walnut oil and tied them into small bundles with strips of dried green onion. He carefully set up the sheaves so they leaned back at fifteen degrees from the vertical. *Gotta have verticality or you're not in a restaurant.* He cleaned up the rim of the dishes with his sweaty side towel and yelled, "Ready! Sweets! Two!"

A kitchen runner rushed up and placed the dishes on the service table next to the door. Labrousse ambled over to the service table apparently without purpose. Almost as an afterthought he picked up the dish with the overdone sweetbread, stared at it for a moment and unerringly turned over the offending medallion with his index finger, revealing the darker side. Without any expression at all he opened his hand and let the dish fall to the floor. It clanged. The contents splattered. "Achille! Replate! I smelled it was burned to a crisp the same moment you saw it was. Where the fuck do you think you are? McDonald's? Get it right this time."

The waiter, followed by two commis bearing silver trays, advanced with almost comic solemnity like acolytes participating in a ritual in a vampire movie. He reverently removed a small metal platter of sweetbreads from the tray and placed it piously before Karine Bergeron. The first commis retreated three steps and was replaced by the second. The waiter turned and repeated the process for Martin Fleuret. *"Ris de veau poêlé et châtaignes médaillonées à l'effilade de truffes noires des coteaux du Saumurois,"* he intoned as if in incantation.

Both Karine and Martin were silent for a moment as the humus aroma of the truffles blended with the tartness of the sweetbreads and nudged the boundary of corruption and decay.

Martin looked deeply into Karine's eyes with the liquid tenderness of a puppy. "We won't be eating like this tomorrow night." He gave her hand on the table a squeeze.

"I'm nervous about leaving like this," Karine said. "You're more or less a suspect. I really don't think we can go without the permission of the authorities."

"That's just why we're going. We've been over it a hundred times. Soon the weather will turn. The sea will start to chill and the trade winds will lose their strength. If we ask permission to go, we'll be stuck here for months. We won't be able to leave until the spring. That's an awful time to go. The sea will be cold and the weather fluky. Even dangerous. We have to go right now."

"But what about the murder investigation?"

"What about it? They'll find the culprit soon enough. There's nothing we can do to help. It has nothing to do with us."

"I don't know. Isn't it illegal? You and I were both warned not to leave France."

"Who's going to know? The boat is provisioned and ready to go. We just hop in the car around two in the morning and we'll be floating out on the tide at dawn. There'll be no one to stop us. Once we're at sea we'll be invisible. When we get to the other side we'll log on to some newspaper's archive and read all about how they caught the killer in some old news story. They'll have forgotten all about us."

"But if we do something illegal can't they impound your bank accounts or something?"

"Legally they might be able to, but I took the precaution of moving most of my money to offshore accounts. I have enough so we can live abroad on a boat almost forever if we want to."

"You make it sound so final. As if we won't be able to come back."

"Dear, you're overreacting. Don't you want to make this trip? Think of us in three weeks in the Caribbean sun, without a care in the world. Just you and me and nothing else."

"Of course I want to go. It's just that I'm nervous about sneaking out like this. I'm sorry. It's just me. I'm sorry." She reached out for his hand. "These sweetbreads are astonishing. I never thought anything could taste as wonderful as this."

Rivière examined the little harbor with wide, disarmingly childlike eyes. Capucine looked at her watch and suppressed a yawn. The basin was fully encompassed by a stone wall save for a single thirty-foot break cut into its top. The water level inside was exactly at the level of the bottom of the cut. Beyond the wall the sea was a good twenty feet below the level in the harbor. Inside, boats docked to jutting piers were as static as if on a gaudily colored postcard.

"How does this work? Is it done with pumps?" Rivière asked.

"Jeanloup, you're such a city kid." Capucine laughed. "The tide here goes up and down over thirty feet every day. Sometimes almost sixty feet in the spring neaps. Most of the harbors around here are dry half the day. The boats are held up by crutches. In Granville they built a retaining wall. At high tide that cut is ten feet below the water level. When the tide goes out the water stays in and the boats in the harbor remain afloat."

"But then you can't get in or out. I get it. So where are our little chickens?"

"Right there." Capucine pointed. A stubby, powerful-looking motorboat lettered POLICE on the side of its hull became visible through the cut a short distance from the wall, inching from stage left, making a deep sensual throbbing noise, to disappear stage right. After it passed a towline appeared and, attached to the line, eventually a large elegant sloop, its mainsail down and sheathed in a blue cover, the boat's name, EUNOMIE, lettered in white. Ten minutes later the procession would return from stage right proceeding to stage left.

Capucine looked at her watch again. "A good four hours before they can get in."

"Four hours! Great. I know something we could do that would take about four hours if we got going right away. What do you say?"

"Why don't we have lunch instead? That little café over there," she said, pointing at a tiny *café-tabac* a short way from the docks, "actually has a pretty decent *moules mari-nières*. The mussels aren't from around here, but don't tell anybody."

Halfway through the luncheon bottle of ubiquitous Sancerre, Rivière's lascivious banter mellowed and he looked at Capucine with something that came close to sadness and affection. "You probably already know, little sister, that you're losing the best mentor you ever had. You're on your own now. I'm being transferred. I got promoted. I made *capitaine*. I guess because of my brilliant work catching that metro hacker in record time. But the fuckers are sending me to Bordeaux. Pisses me off big-time! Will you miss me?"

"Jeanloup, who wouldn't?" Capucine laughed. "Anyway, I'm sure you'll figure out a way to get transferred back to Paris in no time."

"I'm not sure why Tallon ordered me here with you. I guess he wanted two officers present at the arrest of the murderer of a bigwig or maybe I'm supposed to give you some last pearls of wisdom before I exit your life forever." Rivière perked up. "Or maybe he was just giving me a reward for my brilliant work. What's that old movie where the guy chats up the hottie in some seaside restaurant like this and at the end of dinner calls the waiter over and asks him if they have rooms?"

Capucine erupted in laughter. Rivière looked hurt. "I'm sorry. But the thought of you cast as a Jean-Louis Trintignant was just too much. Anyway, you're out of luck. They don't have rooms here." Rivière looked even more hurt.

"You know, Capucine, when I first met you, I thought you were super hot but you also looked like the world's biggest asshole. A useless, stuck-up society girl with attitude. But it turns out you've got street sense. I don't know where the hell you got it, but you definitely do. I like working with you. And it's not just because of your boobs.

If you give me another glass of that wine I might even be tempted to say you're not half bad."

"But still a society girl?"

"Obviously. Who else would know about the tides in a Normandy yacht basin? Not a poor kid from the projects like me. Seriously, though, I'd like to work with you again someday. You taught me a bunch of stuff I'd never have come across otherwise. Or maybe we could just have a drink sometime if you ever make it down to Bordeaux. We could even have dinner or go away for the weekend."

"The feeling is mutual. Absolutely. About the work part. Even the drink."

As the shadows began to lengthen the police cutter tugged the sloop over the cut with only inches to spare under its keel. The boat made a slow but tight turn and released the towline as the sloop was halfway through its wider turn behind. The yacht was gently catapulted sideways toward the pier. It slowed to a stop only inches away from the dock. Two waiting black-clad policemen with large embroidered red CRS badges on their shirt fronts expertly made the sloop fast to cleats on the dock. Not one word had been exchanged during the entire exercise. Not one gesture had been anything but relaxed and casual.

"I don't know dick about boats, but that was pretty impressive," Rivière said.

Next the police boat came up to the pier and was held alongside by two crew with boathooks. A black-clad CRS adjudant stepped off and saluted Capucine and Rivière smartly.

"I have your detainees, if you'll sign for them. We're going to impound the boat. No need to sign for that."

"Did they give you any trouble?" Capucine asked.

"None. They hove-to when we came up, no problem. They seemed a little surprised, that's all. They didn't say anything while on board with us."

Karine and Martin were led up by a stony-faced CRS, their arms handcuffed in front.

The four-hour drive back was peaceful, at least for Capucine and Rivière. They chatted contentedly about office gossip, recent promotions, who had good appraisal reviews, who had bad ones. Apparently, Rivière felt flirtation was inappropriate in front of detainees. Given the police argot and endless acronyms, the conversation was incomprehensible to Karine and Martin, silent in the backseat. After a while Karine slept fitfully and Martin gnawed his lip and stared out the window.

At the Quai des Orfèvres Martin was taken to an interview room and Karine was told she would be released. "But what about Martin?" she asked Capucine. "I can't just leave him here."

"My dear, he's a suspect in a murder case who just got a whole lot more suspicious. You have no choice."

"But why aren't you holding me? I violated the instructions, too."

"You're not a suspect."

In the elevator up to their offices Rivière asked Capucine, "Do you think they'll be able to tag him?"

"I don't think he'll even be charged. I doubt he has anything to do with the murder. Of course, he had access to the poison through his clients, but neither the timing nor the scenario work. I think Karine would have lied for him, but I don't think she'd have been solid under questioning and stuck to the precise times unless it had been true. And, most important, I think I have an idea who did do it."

"Could've fooled me. He looks like just the kind of guy who should go down for something."

The genial policeman and the venomous one alternated hammering at Martin all night long. But to no avail. So when Capucine arrived at six in the morning to take over the interrogation she spent no more than half an hour before releasing him and then going to the *boulangerie* for a croissant for her breakfast. Martin left for home in a taxi, still a suspect, but at least able to sleep in his own bed, or the bed of the person he chose. On the way back from the boulangerie Capucine let herself be invaded by the yeasty, doughy aroma of the croissant and the feeling of peaceful solitude as she walked the empty streets in the snappy morning air. She was beginning to feel happy about the case.

Chapter 41

In a cashmere- and lamb's-wool-blend suit from Lanvin and bespoke John Lobb shoes from an Hermès atelier, Jacques had reached a sartorial apex. He contrasted dramatically with the two other men at the table. One, in a short-sleeved polyester shirt and drooping knit tie, looked every bit like a *Doonesbury* character. The other's hair was greasy enough to stick together in clumps. His front teeth were mottled with gray stains. His fingers were so grimy Capucine had been reluctant to shake his hand. Now they both stared bleakly at her across the table.

"Capucine, as I told you over the phone," Jacques said crisply, "the director has asked me to act as the liaison officer with the Police Judiciaire to make sure we do not interfere with your murder investigation, which, he has made quite clear, is of the 'utmost importance.' This meeting will bring you up to speed as to where we are with Renault."

Capucine nodded. So this was Jacques on the job. Astonishingly, he really was efficient and authoritative.

"Hyppolyte and Armand here are our best cybertechnologists." He looked at the two men with fondness and a certain amount of tender revulsion, as if they were aged family dogs that had sadly begun to smell a bit and let themselves go on the carpet. "They have just spent three nights at Renault's R & D department and have found some extraordinary things. Hyppolyte, can you explain this to the lieutenant?"

Hyppolyte spoke to her as if she were a slightly retarded, but nonetheless charming, ten-year-old. "Lieutenant, we spent two nights in the department checking their computers. Looking for things like worms and viruses and things like that. Viruses are—"

Jacques interrupted him gently. "I'm sure the lieutenant knows what a virus is. Why don't you just tell her about what you found?"

Hyppolyte looked hurt. "We found a very complex worm had been introduced into the system. Actually, it was beautifully written. It worked on the KaZaA application on the LAN's P2P file-sharing feature."

"Sorry, Hyppolyte, you may have to dumb that down a bit after all," Jacques said.

"It's simple. A virus needs a file to live in. A worm lives happily on its own. That makes it much, much harder to detect. This worm simply went into all the files on the network, chose the ones it wanted, sent them out to an e-mail address, and then laid low. It was taught about three or four hundred key words and sent out anything that contained those words."

"Did it send out a lot of data?" Capucine asked Hyppolyte.

"Hang on a minute," Jacques said, cutting off Hyppolyte. "It seems the focus of the worm's little vocabulary was something the Typhon team calls the 'nozzle.' Do you know anything about that?"

"That doesn't surprise me," Capucine said. "The disgruntled employee who tipped me off to Project Typhon said it was the bottleneck. 'No nozzle, no Typhon,' was the way he put it. And he said they were stuck."

"We looked into it ourselves," Jacques said, "and they still don't seem to have made much progress with their little nozzle."

Hyppolyte pouted like an adolescent, his chin tucked into his throat.

"I'm sorry, Hyppolyte," Jacques said, "you were about to explain why almost no data got out."

Hyppolyte beamed. "That's right. You see, all of Project Typhon is on a single LAN except for the nozzle team. They have their own LAN that is not hooked up to anything else. Since the worm wasn't in the nozzle department LAN, all that got sent out was administrative stuff on the nozzle department—you know, salaries and things like that—but nothing technical about the nozzle itself." Hyppolyte brought himself up short. "Oops, I'm sorry, Lieutenant, do you know what a LAN is?"

"Yes, a local area network, a group of computers that are networked into each other."

"Good for you! Case closed, except for one thing."

"What was that?"

"At first we couldn't figure out how the worm was introduced. See, they have firewalls up. Quite good firewalls, actually." Hyppolyte paused politely. "Know what a firewall is?"

Capucine nodded.

"OK, then. Their firewalls are excellent, certainly good enough to prevent the introduction of this worm through the Internet. It contained a tremendous amount of code, you know. We were stumped. Then Jacques here told us that they had had an unauthorized visitor. So that was it. You know what he must have done?"

"What?" Capucine asked.

"He must have had the worm on a USB flashdrive. These things are fabulous." Hyppolyte produced a small metal lozenge shorter than his thumb. "This little gizmo slips into the computer's USB port and it can upload or download anything up to a couple of gigs faster than you can sing the first stanza of the "Marseillaise." They're all over the place now. You can even get them on Swiss Army knives. I'll bet he just asked to go to the john, walked by a computer at an empty desk, and did the deed."

"But do you know who planted the worm?"

Jacques raised his eyebrows in mock astonishment. "You persist in thinking you're dealing with the DST. Actually, it wasn't all that difficult. I figured that part out myself. After all, we had the e-mail address the data was sent to. I had an excellent idea of who it might be, of course. So I called one of my American spook chums. Our little community is very palsy, you know, especially when our bosses aren't looking. They had to do a bit of research, which took them all of several minutes. It was a private e-mail address registered to the child of a Trag employee. Yes, that's right: Trag."

"That bastard," Capucine said, slapping the table in anger. "That two-faced bastard!"

"Well, it's been put paid to. The worm is gone and I believe the director himself will be speaking to the CIA tomorrow so that someone there will have a word with these Trag people. I really think we've seen the last of them," Jacques said.

"And what about the envelopes in the ladies' room?" Capucine asked.

"That's a whole other kettle of worms," Jacques said. "These two gentlemen's time is precious. We'll let them go, and then I can take you out to lunch and fill you in on that part of it."

The restaurant turned out to be an authentic example of a Paris institution that had only recently been wrested back from the path toward extinction: the traditional bistro. Just when it had looked like those tobacco-darkened rooms ringing with boisterous chatter would be replaced by more sophisticated, "modern" formats it suddenly had become chic for vanguard chefs—with restaurant critics like Alexandre riding point on the movement—to open one or even two. Capucine had no illusions; they were doing it to flaunt their virtuosity, or to underscore their deep ties to authenticity, or more likely just to make a few more euros. But still, bistros were definitely back, even if they were copies. This one, however, was the real thing, staffed for the last hundred and fifty years by broad-beamed men in broad, starched aprons for whom lunch was clearly a three-hour affair, preferably topped off with one or more glasses of Calvados.

"This is your hangout?" Capucine asked her cousin.

"Not every day, but often enough. Ever been before?"

"No. But it's one of Alexandre's favorite places. I doubt they'll be happy to see me have my usual salad and half bottle of Badoit."

"Cousine, you haven't changed a scintilla since we were kids. Do I look like I'm troubled by cellulite?" He opened his double-breasted jacket to show off his ballet dancer's torso.

"And I thought I only had to put up with force feeding from Alexandre. Fair enough. You order and I won't comment. Just tell me about what else you found at Renault."

But it wasn't to be that quick. There was the sacrosanct litany of menu and wine list to be dealt with first. The meal of wild boar fillets preceded by a blood sausage terrine left Capucine with little hope of afternoon productivity. As the sommelier retreated to his lair with his order Capucine turned to her cousin. "All right, out with it. I need compensation for the three thousand calories you're shoveling down my gullet."

"Ah, gratitude! Where is thy radiant face? All right, the director asked two or three of our best operatives to review the situation. They concluded this secretary you picked up is the conduit for at least one, and maybe more, 'hidden assets,' to use the phrase."

"Do they think it's also Trag?"

"Almost certainly not. Their guess is that this is someone else entirely. They also feel that given the potential importance of this Typhon it's also possible that there are even more espionage activities going on that haven't been detected yet."

"And is there any chance of finding these other moles?"

"Very doubtful; nothing is harder to find than a mole. They are only vulnerable when they try to pass information. If threatened, they just disappear."

"So Typhon's a lost cause?"

"My dear sweet cousine, don't be such a fatalist. Relax. Have some more of this Minervois. It becomes a different wine when it's allowed to breathe. Is the boar hearty enough for you? It's beginning to get chilly out there." Jacques thumped his nonexistent belly.

"Oh, Jacques, do shut up. You know how worried I am about this case."

"Sorry. The director is going to take action. Actually, he was pretty forceful about it. He wants the whole project handed over to the government and moved to a military installation as soon as possible. That would mean that the security level would increase enormously and that all the personnel would have to go through the most rigorous military security clearance procedures. It would be like flushing a toilet to clear everything out. Not only would anything that even looked like a mole be found but if they were working on something that belonged to the military they'd get a serious jail sentence instead of just a scolding, which is all they face now."

"So Renault will have to give up the project?"

"They wouldn't give up anything. They would merely subcontract to their largest shareholder, the government. Honor would be saved. And once the thing was ready to go into production it might even be handed back to them. Anyway, they don't really have any choice. To all intents and purposes they are still a government company. So it definitely is going to happen, but there's a big but. And I don't mean yours." Jacques shrieked in childish laughter.

"Jacques, please. You're not ten anymore."

"That's why I get to put this yummy lunch on my expense account and don't have to ask Daddy to pay. You're not finishing your boar? The director has asked me to tell you that nothing will happen until the murderer is found. Let me put it this way. I don't want this to go back to your people, but it has been impressed upon the director that finding the murderer is actually more important in the upper echelons of government than bringing off Typhon. Can you believe that? It may be that they don't really believe that cheap gas is feasible, but I personally suspect that a senior official getting murdered in Diapason is just too close to home for comfort. It's the sort of thing that just can't be permitted." He allowed himself a purely cynical and definitely adult laugh.

"You're becoming a true politician."

"So I'm told. Anyhow, here's my official message. The DGSE is not going to appear to intervene until you—by which I mean the PJ, of course—come home with the croissants, as it were, as long as that happens in a reasonable time frame."

"And how long is that?"

"More a question of days than weeks, little cousin. Personally I think it's absolutely shocking that under the circumstances you elect to spend the afternoon flirting with golden youths while overeating and overdrinking at the poor downtrodden taxpayer's expense. Shouldn't you be out there herding up suspects with a cattle prod or whatever it is you people do?"

"Jacques, I absolutely loathe you," Capucine said as she walked out of the restaurant. Very stealthily Jacques slid her order of boar, almost untouched, onto his plate.

Chapter 42

A week later Capucine received a call. "Petite cousine, I'm standing at attention itching and horribly uncomfortable in full dress uniform wearing all my medals because this is an official communiqué from on high. There is a troop of buglers behind me at the ready to sound a clarion. Attention! Are you prepared?"

"Jacques, dear, I don't have time to be teased by you. I'm in the middle of a case, as you fully well know."

"Actually, cousine, I *am* calling about your case. There have been developments."

"I'm all ears, then."

"You remember last week I told you the director was keen on having that project taken away from Renault and handed over to the military, who could keep a proper lid on it? But he had had instructions that your investigation was the top priority?"

"Of course I remember."

"Well, it seems that we may have misread the atmosphere of the upper echelons. You see, prior to Delage's death my masters' masters really didn't know much about the Renault project. Actually, no one had heard about it at all. But it's big news now. Typhon's potential has suddenly dawned on them. And there was less than unmitigated pleasure at what was viewed as free access readily granted to any and all foreign spies. Am I being comprehensible?"

"Entirely."

"So the topic made several laps around the corridors of power and a consensus has been achieved. The matter has been taken out of the director's hands, but the powers that be reached the same conclusion he had. The upshot is that Typhon will be moved to an armored cavalry garrison at Rambouillet that has been vacant for some time. It's more than big enough for all the equipment and test tracks and all that. It's going to be placed under the authority of the CNRS, which was the obvious choice since it's the largest research agency in the country and a tightly controlled government department. The project will be completely detached from Renault. Once the work is completed the government may, or may not, give it back to Renault for implementation."

"What happens to the staff?"

"As many as possible will be retained, but they will all have to go through full government security clearance procedures. A new project head is in the process of being appointed. We are to act as advisers on the security side of things, but the CNRS will be in charge. The general idea is to shut the thing down by the end of this week at the latest. Then everyone gets run through the security mill and the survivors start up at the other end in a few weeks. They'll lose a month at worst. The general feeling is that it's the only possible solution because the whole thing is out of control right now."

"That really was fast."

"But wait! Here's the fun part. You just have to love our masters. Apparently, it is also not wished that your investigation be hindered. You have carte blanche. But only until the end of the week. The fact that after that you might have some difficulties in investigating a unit that has been largely disbanded is apparently irrelevant. The intent is positive and that's all that counts."

"That sentiment will be enormously helpful. My boss is going to be delighted."

"Be sure you make him fully aware of the fact that the rapid success of your investigation is now even more anxiously awaited in high places. Of course, that, no doubt, has already been communicated to him directly." Jacques paused. His voice lowered a register. "Capucine, I am sorry, but there was nothing to be done. Between you and me, the director's nose is a little out of joint because he thought he was running things. I think it just dawned on people that this Typhon really could be hot stuff. They didn't have a clue before. I hope this doesn't make your job impossible. If there's the slightest thing I can do just give me a bell and I'll come running. In fact, even if there isn't anything I'll still come running."

"Jacques, you're a dear. I have to get off the phone. I need to go drop this bombshell upstairs."

Just as she reached the door her phone rang. "Lieutenant!" Guyon shrieked. "I have just had some very displeasing news and I suspect you've had a hand in it. I need to discuss it with you and not over the telephone."

"Monsieur Guyon, why don't you come to the Quai des Orfèvres this afternoon and we can chat."

"Come to the prefecture? Me?" Guyon paused. "Very well, I doubt I have any choice, but I want you to know how displeased I am by your conduct. I may be forced to make a complaint."

Capucine's tightly closeted meeting with Tallon lasted far longer than she expected, stretching into the early afternoon. Not only had her lexicon of invective been substantially enriched but she had been awakened to a new and distressingly dire vision of the shortcomings of the government. Still, the upshot of the meeting left her elated.

Either she was learning or Tallon was coming around to her way of thinking. But either way they were definitely beginning to sing from the same hymnbook.

Guyon had been left sitting in one of the ground floor glass-paneled interview rooms for over an hour.

"This is an outrage! And this coffee is filth! How dare the government inflict it on taxpayers."

"Monsieur Guyon, you're being ridiculous. Think for a minute what the majority of our reception facilities are like. Would you have preferred the sight of bars? You'll have to be brief. I'm going to have a busy afternoon. What's happening?"

"I was convoked by the acting president this morning and told that Project Typhon was to be relocated to a government facility and removed from my tutelage. Is this your doing? Do you have any idea what's going on?"

"It certainly was not a recommendation of the Police Judiciaire. The ministry must have reached its own conclusions. The results of the DGSE investiga—"

"What? The DGSE has been rooting around in Renault?"

"Monsieur, sit down and calm yourself. Yes, following that incident I reported to you, they were asked in."

"But you had no authority—"

"Actually, I do. Do you want me to go on or not?"

"I'm sorry, madame."

"The DGSE's investigation revealed a serious leak."

Guyon went pale. "What do you mean? They found out who was stealing information? Did they?"

"Monsieur Guyon, I'm not talking about the person we apprehended passing materials on the street. The DGSE experts undertook an examination of your group's computer system and found that it had been invaded by a worm and was transmitting information."

Guyon seemed to relax. "Oh," he said almost indifferently. "I see."

"They rectified the situation so there is no more problem on that account. But my guess—and this is only my guess—is that since this was the third instance of spying in your group it was decided to move the activity to a more secure venue."

"The acting president said nothing about any of this. That fool probably doesn't know anything anyway. He just told me the development work had been reorganized and the CNRS was going to assume responsibility for Typhon. I had hoped I would be going with it. After all, it's my creation. My brainchild. This is a catastrophe for me. Can't you do something?"

"Monsieur Guyon, don't forget I'm just a vulgar flic. Surely you don't think I can have the slightest influence on your career."

"Madame, I thought I could turn to you if I needed. I thought we had reached an understanding. I seem to have been mistaken. But I'll tell you one thing. This whole business is entirely unacceptable. I'm not going to take it lying down. You will see what you will see! My reach is long, very long." He stalked out, slamming the door hard enough to make the glass rattle.

Chapter 43

Capucine, flanked by Momo and David, took the steep flight of stairs two by two and banged loudly on the lilac door with the heel of her fist. The sound resonated like pistol shots in the narrow stairwell. "Police Judiciaire," Momo said in a deep, menacing voice. In a few seconds the door opened a crack and Clotilde peered out timidly. When she recognized Capucine she opened the door wide and retreated into the apartment.

"This time you're here to arrest me, aren't you?"

"Not necessarily," Capucine said. "It depends on how well you cooperate with us. Have you heard from your Asian contact since we spoke?"

"No. Thank God. I'm so happy that's over. But I am missing his money."

"The last time we met you told us that you reached your Asian friend on his cell phone. You said you called him, but he never answered and only called you back later. Is that right?"

"That's it. I'd call. He wouldn't pick up. When his voice mail message came on I'd hang up without saying anything. He would see my number on his caller ID and call me back. But I never knew when he would call. Sometimes it would be right away, sometimes the next day."

"Well, I need you to call him now."

"But the last time I told him I never wanted to see him again and refused to take his money. What could I say now?"

"Leave a message that Project Typhon is being transferred out of Renault and you have an extra-thick envelope for him. Spice it up and say you want double pay because it's an extra-special envelope."

"Are you behind that? The move of Project Typhon? There's a lot of gossip in the office about that." She paused. "Is that what this is about? I never made the connection."

"Don't worry about who's behind what. Clotilde, let me caution you. This is a very serious matter. I'd very much like to keep you out of trouble, but that's going to depend on your working very closely with us for a few days. Do you understand?"

The next day Capucine received a call from a very excited Clotilde. "He called me back this morning. Right here at work," she whispered into the telephone. "I told him that Typhon was going to be shut down and moved and that I had a big bulky envelope for him. I did just what you said and told him I wanted double my usual money and also the money I didn't take the last time."

"Good. When are you supposed to pass the envelope?"

"At eight tonight. He said he wanted to talk to me. We're supposed to meet at a café at the end of my street."

Capucine smiled up at Momo, who was hovering by her desk. "He bit."

I may have overdone it this time. If he gets away I won't dare show my face at the Quai, Capucine thought. *But so what? It can't be helped. This is our one shot.* She had been over the plan twenty times in the afternoon. Twelve brigadiers and adjudants were posted. Two in each of the three closest metro stops and six around the perimeter of the café. The evening prayers were already over, so there would be no repetition of that debacle. As instructed, Clotilde was sitting in the window of the glassed-in café terrace quietly reading *Le Monde* and sipping a kir. The stark blue-white of the neon light and the thick cigarette fog made her look tired and old. Behind her, three youths, who showed every sign of becoming future clients of the *Police Judiciaire*, were violently playing a pinball machine, thunking the buttons loudly with open hands and slamming the machine brutally against the wall with pelvic thrusts to make the steel balls rebound more vigorously. The café was on a broad avenue, making surveillance easier. There were more than enough passersby on the avenue to provide cover for the officers but not so many as to hinder pursuit. So far so good.

At exactly ten after eight the Asian suddenly materialized on the seat opposite Clotilde. Capucine was stunned. She had not seen him walk into the café. It was as if he had appeared as part of a magic trick. He must have been sitting at a table inside for hours before she came. *Thank God we took position with no commotion. Luck must be on our side today.* Clotilde and the Asian spoke for a moment. He appeared agitated. He asked questions with aggressive gestures, pounding on the table frequently. Finally, disgusted, he thrust his copy of the *Monde* at Clotilde. Capucine had procured several dated automobile engine design files from the CNRS and sealed these into a tear-proof mailing envelope in the hopes that the Asian would not be inclined to struggle with it in public, or if he did, would be lulled by a quick glance at the contents. It was an unnecessary precaution. He grabbed rudely at the

Monde shrouding the envelope, tucked it under his arm, and stormed out.

"Subject leaving the café." Even over the radio she could feel the entire team become tense. The Asian turned left and walked up the avenue toward the Barbès metro station. Capucine alerted the team in that direction and followed three hundred feet behind. At the steps of the metro he stopped without warning, wheeled, and came back the way he had come. Capucine melted into a doorway, pretending to light a cigarette, muttering into her radio. As the man approached, he fixed her with a frank, appraising look and quickened his pace. He turned right abruptly into a narrow street, no wider than a passageway.

Capucine and one of the brigadiers reached the street at the same moment, just in time to see the Asian rounding the corner ahead at a dead run. Before she had the chance to alert her crew her radio cheeped and someone spoke. "Okay. I see him. He's sprinting. He's just ducked into the rue Pilon moving fast. Adjudant Chauvau, he'll be at your end in a few seconds."

Capucine pushed her transmit button. "Adjudant, don't try to stop him. Let him go by but keep after him."

"Très bien, mon Lieutenant," came the reply. The Asian sprinted toward the boulevard Clichy, running as fast as he could down the steep slope. The sidewalk was packed with a mulling, sullen North African throng, mostly too poor to have even a few euros to spend in a café, passing the time on the street before going to bed, taking advantage of the last few days before it would become too cold to saunter.

The momentum of his run down the steep hill projected the Asian into the boulevard at speed, the two police officers well behind but still obvious to all on the street that they were flics in pursuit. The crowd came alive, muttering, gesturing, indignant. The short half block of chase had fanned their hatred of the police to the flash point. As they ran down the boulevard, the two officers were continually shoved and bumped. One nearly fell. Losing his temper, he drew his gun and waved it in the air, warning the crowd back. A cry went up and grew into a wailing ululation. In a second they would attack the two officers, guns or no guns.

Capucine and Momo emerged into the avenue fifty feet ahead of the Asian. If he had had the wit to turn and run back into the crowd he could have escaped easily. But he kept on. Capucine drew her Sig, cupped both hands around the grip, dropped to one knee, and shouted, "Stop or I shoot!" The crowd scattered noisily like a flock of clucking farm chickens.

The Asian produced a pistol and fired a shot that went wild. Capucine forced herself into the discipline of the firing range, took a deep breath, let out half, locked her lungs, and gently tightened on the butt of her Sig. *Don't pull the trigger. Squeeze the whole butt as if you were squeezing the juice out of an orange,* she consciously reminded herself. The sound made the night white. The Asian spun almost a full circle on one foot, the other leg outstretched, like a toddler imitating a ballet dancer. For a split second a rosy nimbus of blood mist framed him in the harsh light of a street lamp. His gun flew into the air and bounced off a wall with an innocent tinny sound, unnaturally clear in the silence following the deafening report. He fell and stayed on the ground. Capucine and Momo advanced toward him, crouched, separated, guns held out stiffly in front on straight arms, as cautiously as if he were a growling, fire-breathing demon waiting to pounce.

Momo glanced over at Capucine as they inched forward and said out of the corner of his mouth, "Lieutenant, were you really aiming for his leg?"

"Actually, I was trying to hit the other one."

Chapter 44

"Hey, Lieutenant, ever seen one of these?" Momo asked, brandishing a short-barreled automatic pistol. "It's a Daewoo DP-51. I just looked it up. It's what the South Korean Army gets. Nine millimeter Parabellum. It's got a weird feature. You push the hammer back down once it's cocked. See." He demonstrated. The gun gave a little tick. "And then when you pull the trigger the hammer pops back up and fires. Like this." The empty gun clicked sharply. "That's what must have saved our butts. He must have shot involuntarily. Dumbass Daewoo shoulda stuck to stereos."

Capucine, sitting at her desk signing forms, did not react. "So what are we going to do with the guy?" Momo pouted, not altogether unlike an insistent toddler.

"He's carrying a South Korean diplomatic passport. We're supposed to check him out and if he's a bona fide diplomat drop him off politely at his embassy. But the juge d'instruction's signed off his garde à vue. She's even classified him as a potential terrorist so we can keep him for the full seventy-two hours. Apparently, she doesn't think diplomats should be able to shoot at flics on the street with impunity."

"How bad's he hit? He was bleeding like a stuck pig in the van."

"Just a flesh wound. In one side, out the other. Missed the femur and the femoral artery. Nothing to worry about. I've got to get back to the clinic. He should be ready to tell his little story. Here." She handed a thin sheaf of papers to Momo. "Can you walk these around to Records? It's the paperwork for the GAV."

Capucine had a *crise de conscience* over the Clinique Bayol, the existence of which was unknown in the fiscal brigade. It embodied the sleazy elasticity of French law. Even its charade as a prissy overdecorated private surgery emporium was offensive, probably because it was so well done. Still, she had to admit to herself that the damn place was essential. Under the circumstances her South Korean could hardly have been put in a public hospital where the press would have nosed him out in no time at all.

When Capucine arrived at her detainee's room, an over-fit officer clad in a black field dress and hobnailed combat boots sprang to attention and buzzed the clear Plexiglas door open for her. Inside, the Korean lay naked on a hospital bed, his arms handcuffed to the bed frame, a twisted bedsheet covering only one leg and his genitals, his tormented body as ingenuously exposed as a rococo sculpture. The visible leg was swathed in a thick bandage through which blood had seeped and was just beginning to turn brown. He was as thickly muscled as an Olympic weight lifter, his trapezius so well developed that his head seemed to fuse directly into his shoulders. Beside him a tall metal stand held a large, flaccid bag of clear plasma that trickled down a cannula, through a boxy, beeping, blinking flow-control device, and finally into a hole jabbed into the crook of his elbow. A smaller bag, containing morphine in a dextrose solution, dangled next to the bigger bag like an impish tag-along little sister ready to caper and make silly jokes. But the little sister's cannula had been choked off with a blue plastic crimp.

Two detectives sat side by side on chairs facing the bed, smoking, tipping the ashes into an empty glass, chatting in a whisper. One was the affable detective with a limp, the other Capucine had never seen.

Both stood up when she walked in. The amiable one smiled at her with his warm, confidence-inspiring smile, looking for all the world as if he was selling life insurance on TV. "He hasn't said a word. He's conscious all right, but I'm beginning to wonder if he speaks French."

"I'm sure we'll find out soon enough. Why don't you two go grab lunch. Let me see what I can do with him."

The two men shrugged with Gallic indifference, dropped their cigarettes in the glass, and waited at the door until the policeman at the desk buzzed it open. After they left the door closed on a hydraulic mechanism with a rich, oily click that somehow conveyed a note of utter finality.

The Korean continued to lie glassy-eyed, staring at the ceiling sightlessly like a fish on a slab. Capucine stood in front of him motionless, mesmerized by the gleaming drops of solution falling into the drip chamber one by one with the inexorable monotony of a metronome. His breaths rasped in the dyspnea of deep pain.

Capucine shook herself out of her reverie. "Remember me? I'm the flic you were shooting at."

No reply. He continued to stare emptily at the ceiling. Gradually consciousness seeped into his eyes. Then, suddenly, his pupils contracted and his irises darkened in anger. Still, no words. Then, with the anger intact, his lips twisted into the ghost of an imperious sneer.

"You do not know who I am," he said finally, in heavily accented French. "I am accredited diplomat. You are acting illegally."

"Actually, I fully well know who you are, and I'm afraid you're in a bit of a tight spot," Capucine said airily.

"You're not going to leave this room until we hear your story. No matter how long that takes."

No reply.

"Suit yourself. I'm sure you know your wound will get quite painful. Painful enough to make you think what you're feeling now is no more than an itch. I'm going to give orders that you are to talk to no one but me. Then I'm going home. My shift is over and tomorrow is my day off. Enjoy." She turned to leave.

"Wait," the man said. "I am truly a diplomat. A member of the consular service of the Republic of South Korea. When I not return to my embassy they register a formal complaint. You detain me illegally. This is serious international crime. I demand release."

Capucine snorted a disgusted laugh. "If you really believe that, you're an incurable innocent. And you also know nothing about French law. You are being held in garde à vue, under the terms of Articles 63 and 77, which allow me to keep you for three days, during which time you do not exist. You will have just disappeared. No embassy, no lawyer, no nothing; just here, you, me, and the pain."

The Asian looked stonily at Capucine and swallowed.

"In fact, I can keep you as long as I want. You were apprehended in *flagrant délit.*"

The Korean had raised a questioning eyebrow.

"That means you were caught red-handed committing a crime. Under French law that puts everything in a whole different context. Normally, I'd have you taken straight to a court that would certainly convict you on the spot for the most serious of crimes, the attempted homicide of a police officer. You'd go directly from the court to Fresnes Prison to start serving your sentence. However, since you're wounded, I can legally hold off sending you to court until you're healed and I'm the one who decides if you're healed or not."

The Korean stared at her, visibly concentrating on keeping his face expressionless.

"It is true that your embassy would eventually seek to obtain your release, but you have no idea how slowly we can make our bureaucracy move. Do you have any idea of how cop shooters are treated in prison? Think about these things. I'm going off duty. Do you want the lights left on or off?"

"Wait, wait, madame. Don't go. Please. I remember these abusive French laws from school. I will talk to you. But send me the doctor. I will talk more if he makes pain better."

"We'll see about the doctor. Let's see what you have to say for yourself first." Capucine went to the door, waited for it to be buzzed open, and spoke quietly to the guard. In a few minutes a uniformed officer arrived with a stenotype machine on a small stand, which he set up in a corner opposite the bed.

"The officer will note everything you say. The machine will then be plugged into a computer and the text will be printed out. I will ask you to sign each page. Is that clear?"

The man nodded.

"All right, let's get going. Name, date and place of birth, current address, profession?"

"Kim Park; July 15, 1974; Seoul, Republic of South Korea; Korean Embassy, 125 rue de Grenelle; I am a third secretary in the commercial section." In the corner the officer silently typed at his tiny keyboard, pressing multiple keys at the same time in the unfathomable way of stenotypists.

Capucine waved the envelope that Clotilde had passed him inside the *Monde*. "Tell me about this."

"I did not open it. I think it contains technical informations about Renault cars." He fell silent.

"Kim, let's not play games, here. I want to hear what this is about, and quickly."

"Yes. Yes. One of my assignments is to obtain technical informations on certain Renault manufacturing processes."

"How do you do that?"

"I have an assistant. Inside Renault. In the research and development department. He obtains the informations and gives to a woman, a secretary, who gives to me. She was the woman who passed me the envelope."

"What is the name of your plant, your assistant, in Renault?"

"Nguyen Chapellier."

Capucine went to the door, walked out when it was opened, and returned in less than a minute.

"All right. Back to you. How did you manage to place Nguyen Chapellier in Renault?"

"Very easy. I found engineers who would do such work. I have studied as engineer and I went to many trade conferences. I met many people who would be happy to take the money I offered. I chose the three best and told them to make application to Renault. Two were chosen. One was put in a division that was not serviceable. Nguyen was put in the correct research group. If he had not been chosen for right place I would have begun again.

"That is easy part. Placing assistant. It always is. Much harder to get informations. Renault e-mail is checked so it cannot be used. The informations must go out on paper. Renault checks all documents that leave building. But my assistant Nguyen told me that the top boss-mans' secretaries not checked and that the president's secretary is juicy girl. So I meet her and take her to dinner and she happy to bring me informations from Nguyen. Very efficient."

The door opened with its loud buzz and a uniformed policeman entered and spoke softly in Capucine's ear. "They've found him. They're on the way to pick him up and bring him to the Quai."

"Good," Capucine replied. "Could you ask the doctor to come in and start the morphine drip in his IV. Oh, and give him some ice chips. That'll give him something to chew on while I'm gone."

She looked at Park. "Enjoy your lunch. I'll be back in a little while."

Chapter 45

Nguyen Chapellier stood rigidly in front of Capucine in abject terror, his eyes round with fear.

"So," said Isabelle, "we pick this asshole up in his cubicle at Renault and make as little fuss as possible, just like you told us, Lieutenant. Hell, we didn't even cuff him. And so what does the little jerk do? He comes on to me in the elevator. Can you believe it? What a fucking sicko."

"Still, Isabelle, you went overboard," David chimed in. "Lieutenant, Isabelle decides to cuff him but instead of normal steel cuffs, she gets him in those nylon jobs and pulls them tight so they really hurt. And while she's doing it she clips him a few times in the kidneys pretty hard just so he doesn't miss the message."

"Well, asshole, it wasn't me that punched him out, was it? Lieutenant, when we dump him in the backseat of the car, he starts screaming; I guess because his poor sweet little wrists hurt. Anyway, in the middle of all this he wets himself, and pretty-boy David here goes bananas because he's peed on the car seat and hauls off and whacks him a good one in the mouth. When the little asshole comes around David starts yelling at him and keeps it up all the way down here. All in all, it was a totally fun ride," Isabelle said with heavy sarcasm.

Capucine held her hand up for silence and addressed Nguyen. "We're holding your little friend, Kim Park. He's already told us his story. Let's hear your side of it."

"I don't know anyone called Kim Park," Nguyen muttered sullenly, exploring the inside of his mouth with his tongue while darting terrified glances at David.

Capucine looked at David with eyebrows raised in exasperation and jerked her head at the door. He eased out of the room with his ballet dancer's fluidity. Capucine turned to Isabelle. "Brigadier," she said formally, "do you think you could get us some coffee?"

With the two brigadiers out of the room, Nguyen relaxed visibly and his shoulders dropped a good two inches. Capucine smiled her protective big-sister smile. "You probably don't know him by that name. Beefy Asian guy. No neck. Pays you to stuff things into paper towel dispensers. Ring any bells?"

His eyes morphed from saucers of fear to saucers of astonishment. Capucine was amazed the difference was so obvious.

"Oh, gosh. *That's* what you arrested me for. Dac Kim— that's what he told me his name was—told me it wasn't criminal. The worst that could happen would be a civil suit and even then they would settle out of court."

"Look around and tell me how civil you find it here." Capucine looked at him stonily. "Let's hear it."

"Gee, there's not all that much to tell. Renault has this project that will make internal combustion engines totally more fuel efficient. Dac Kim—I guess he's some sort of secret agent or spy or something like that—hired me to apply for a job at Renault to get as much data on the project as I could. I got lucky and they put me in the right department. So I'd Xerox stuff and get it out through the president's secretary. She was never checked by the security people. It wasn't any more than that. Really. Just Xeroxing some stuff every now and then."

"How much did you get paid?"

"Twice as much as my salary. It was great. I was making more than three times as much as my last job and all I had to do was make a few copies every now and then. Took me no more than a couple of hours a month and I'd get a big fat envelope stuffed with five hundred euro notes hidden in the paper towel rack in the ladies' room of the executive floor. How smart was that?"

"Selling corporate secrets worth multimillions and risking a long jail sentence for a few thousand a month is smart?"

Nguyen looked crestfallen. "Actually," he said like a scolded schoolboy, "I had it all set up so I was going to get the big bucks."

"What do you mean?"

"After a couple of months of rooting around the department, it became obvious that the key part was this thing they called the 'nozzle.' It's supposed to inject the catalyst into the engine. The invention was going to be a complete dud without it. So anyway, the problem was that the nozzle group had its own security system that I had no access to. But I solved it, let me tell you. I was good to go. And I convinced Dac Kim that I was going to need a big lump-sum payment if I produced the goods on the nozzle. A whole year's pay, that's what I was going to get!"

"And how were you going to get the info on the nozzle?"

"What do you think?" Nguyen said, raking Capucine with frankly lascivious eyes. "I hooked up with this girl in the nozzle team. She was really ditzy and geeky but totally hot once you got her clothes off. Anyway, she was spending her weekends at my place. The plan was to 'borrow' her badge." Nguyen crooked the first two fingers of each hand to signify quotation marks and smiled a sly smile. "See, I was going to sneak it out of her handbag and use it to get into her work area on a Saturday. I figured she'd never notice. Worst case, she'd think she left it somewhere, she was that ditzy."

Isabelle walked in with three flaccid plastic thimbles of espresso. Nguyen met her gaze confidently. His self-esteem seemed fully restored.

"So you got the plans?" Capucine asked.

"No way. I had really bad luck. At first it went off like a charm. I wormed the password out of Marie, that's the girl's name. I got her to play a guessing game. You know, 'I bet I can guess this or that.' So I bet her I could guess her computer password. I got it the third time around. The name of her cat, 'Rutabaga.' But she goes, 'Oh, wait, you lose. I stuck a 7 right in the middle, right after the first 'A,' to make it more secure.' She's that ditzy. She told me right off."

"Then what?"

"Marie comes over on Friday night for the weekend and I cook up this seafood lasagna. It's my specialty. I use scallops, mussels, and a lot of clams. It's a lot of work but it's worth it. The seafood all has to be cooked separately first. You have to steam the clams over chopped onions, and—"

"We'll do the *Bon Appétit* TV show later. Stick to the story."

"Okay. But trust me, if this gig doesn't pan out I could become a chef, I'm that good. So Dac Kim gave me some white powder and said to put just a pinch in Marie's food. Man, I really felt bad about crapping up my lasagna, but work is work, right? Anyway, she was sick as a dog the next day. I tucked her up in bed and she must have slept twenty hours. She only got up to barf. I spent all of Saturday going through her area at work but I couldn't get into her files. I had the code to Marie's terminal, all right, but I didn't have the goddamn codes for the files, so no cigar."

"So you gave up?"

"For those kind of bucks, are you kidding? I kept going back on Saturdays to see if I could crack those files. I didn't even have to dope up Marie. She just sat around reading or whatever while I was gone and never noticed a thing. But nothing doing. And obviously I wasn't going to get the code out of Marie. I mean, what was I going to say? 'Hey, sweetie, I just happened to notice that you have separate passwords on all your nozzle files. Can we play a guessing game about those?' " Nguyen laughed happily. He could have been at a bar chatting the two women up.

"So then what happened?" Capucine asked.

"Everything got crazy. First off, in the middle of the week it must have been, I'm talking to my boss, Lionel, and he tells me that Monsieur Guyon, he's the head of R & D, is in a state about some security leak and the président himself was going to go to the government to get the spooks or whatever to plug up the leak. You can imagine how that made me feel."

"I'm amazed you didn't give it up right then and there," Capucine said encouragingly.

"Hey, I'm a pro, remember. No way I was going to forgo all that cash. So, I did my super-sleuth routine. I wrote Dac Kim a little note. Stuck it inside the paper towel holder in the ladies' room. How Dac Kim dreams this crap up is beyond me. Like it's not risky to be going in and out of the ladies' crapper all the time. So he gets my note, but instead of sending me a note back like he usually does, I get a call that very night from the big man himself. 'Meet me at thus and such café on the boulevard Saint-Michel at nine o'clock.' A first.

"So anyway, Dac Kim has a big plan. I'm supposed to e-mail the files out and not even try to open them. He says once he has them he can figure out a way to have someone crack the code. So, I'm supposed to go to Marie's area on the next Saturday and do my stuff like there was no problem. Sure, there was no problem. For him. He wasn't going to be there."

"Did you have any luck with the file?"

"Not the slightest. Those files were wrapped up in the tightest security I've ever seen. I thought the game was over and that security would get super tight. Then on Monday they found Président Delage dead. Remember that? I always wondered if there was a connection. I guess not. I was sure that they would really clamp down on security then, but nothing changed. So I was able to go back the next two weekends. I never could do anything with those files, though.

"Then one day, out of the blue, they tell us they're moving the whole project to a military base and that everyone has to get a government security clearance. Hey. Fuck that. I quit as of next week. I'm history on that project. A buck is a buck, but I have no intention of winding up in a maximum-security prison. Renault is one thing, but a government installation is a whole other kettle of fish."

Nguyen gave Isabelle a sly look out of the corner of his eye. Capucine guessed he was hoping she would be impressed with his story. Left to his own devices she wouldn't have put it past him to try to hit on her again.

Chapter 46

Some of the color had returned to Kim Park's face. A drop of morphine often goes a long way. "I've just come from being entertained by your colleague Nguyen Chapellier," Capucine said to Park.

"Yes," he said serenely.

Capucine walked over to the IV stand and clipped the morphine drip shut. Enough was enough.

"Let's talk about the weekend of October twenty-sixth. Were you in Paris?"

"Yes."

"October the twenty-sixth was the day the president of Renault was killed. Do you know anything about that?"

"I read about in newspaper. Soft-bellied bureaucrat. No connection to my duties." His voice was barely audible.

"Monsieur Chapellier tells me you had received news that security measures at Renault were about to be increased and that weekend was his last chance to obtain critical data."

"Nguyen is French. He like tell story. Say they would tighten security. Not important. Nguyen try to use story to get more money from me."

"Did you think Président Delage had anything to do with security controls?"

"No. Président no do real work." Park paused for several beats. "Not care. I here only to collect informations. Not to get involve in French stories. Président of Renault not stop my collection of informations. If president of company die from bad oysters, no worry for me. No business of mine. No business of mine. No business . . ." Park's voice trailed off, his eyes shut, and a small stream of drool trickled out of the corner of his mouth.

The submarine hatch slammed shut. Careful! The enemy ships on the surface might hear. The sound rolled out into the sea disastrously like a sonar pinging and pinging until it faded far away.

Shit. What was that? Must have been the door. The policewoman left. My leg's still throbbing. That bitch must have cut the morphine off. Good for her. She's not some dumb juicy girl. She has the soul of a man. The pain will clear my head. Make me think sharp. Get me out of this filthy stinking French pigsty even faster.

Getting shot is always the same. When it hits you feel nothing and then slowly it gets worse and worse. But it's good. You melt into the pain. It makes you one with your being.

I'll go home to Korea now. The assignment is blown. For damn sure. Very soon the embassy will send an ambulance. They must be worried I'll talk. Probably put me straight on a plane. Just like the last time. I woke up in first class with curtain around my gurney. That time I was a hero. Not now. They'll put me in economy. Ha ha. But I'll be on another assignment in a month or two at most. Maybe they'll find me one at home. It's terrible being abroad. There's nothing to do. The hwa-byung *just gets worse and worse. You drown in a sea of foreignness.*

France is the worst place I've ever been. It's supposed to have the best juicy girls and the best food in the world. That's a load of crap. When I arrived I went to a bunch of expensive restaurants. Big fucking joke. All of them were disgusting. Not at all like Korean bab. Lumps of half-cooked meat floating in syrup that looked like snot. It wasn't even prepared right. Just thrown on a plate. You had to cut it yourself and then spear it with that funny spiked tool thing they give you. Savages.

I asked the receptionist at the embassy which was the best restaurant in town. She said it was a place called Dia-pason. But it was even worse than others. It didn't have any taste. It was like someone had already sucked on the food and spat it out. One dish was rotten. It had little black bits in it that smelled like a dirty foot. I asked for chopsticks. The Best Restaurant should have hand-carved ivory chopsticks. The waiter looked at me and said nothing, but I could hear him laughing inside. The stupid man came very close to dying. The hwa *boiled up inside me. The blow was ready in my arm. He would just have fallen down dead. No one would have seen what happened. It would have felt very good. It was hard to keep my arm down. Very hard.*

Shit, all there is to do in Paris is eat in Korean restaurants. Of course, that's not all you can do, but the other is as bad as the food. And smells just as bad. Except for the juicy girl from Best Restaurant. I saw her when I was trying to swallow that rotten garbage. She had those bug eyes like all the long-noses, but she was still something. That's for sure. She was maybe even better than a Korean woman. Ha ha. I saw that all the way across the room.

Here Park fell asleep and dreamed he was back in Seoul. At a dinner he had been to just before he had come to Paris. It had been his send-off and he had been invited by his best *chingu.* A group of ten men went in a rented white stretch limousine to what they liked to call a *kisaeng* palace, but which was really just an expensive room salon. The girls pretended to be geishas but were just prostitutes. But it was still very nice. They would come into the room with elaborate hairdos and lovely billowy chiffon dresses like in an old Elvis Presley movie. They kneeled next to you and fed you with chopsticks. Performers came and played stringed instruments and sang. It was very refined and elegant. Every man had a whole bottle of whiskey in front of him and his girl would mix the drinks. Every once in a while you let her have a drink and she was very, very grateful and whispered her thanks in your ear. Of course, the girl didn't eat. She would feed you with chopsticks and murmur in your ear. But never when you were telling a story. Her leg touched yours and, as the meal went on, with the men joking and sparring, she got closer and you felt the warmth of her body. When the dinner was over she disappeared and came back dressed in jeans and something modern and sexy. Then it was time to go. There was a car outside. The girl went back with you and did whatever you asked, without speaking, without complaining. Sometimes there was blood. Sometimes someone had to come to take the girl away. That was the way it was meant to be. When he floated back into consciousness he wasn't sure if he had been dreaming or remembering.

No, the last part had to be a dream. There was too much blood for it to be real. That Best Restaurant longnose girl liked to do all the things he had done in the dream. She wasn't as pretty as a Korean girl, of course. But she had been as obedient. Appreciative. A real juicy girl. Just like home. And useful, of course, very useful. Stop, it's very important not to think about that now.

Then there was the other one, the président's secretary. She was huge. And smelled like an old hag. Not a juicy girl at all. It was like fucking a fat monk. Of course I've been trained to fuck anything, so it didn't make any difference, but even a boy would have been better. The worst part was

*how she moaned and clung to me like a sick, stinking oc-
topus. I hate these foreign assignments. I hate these foul-
smelling French.*

*But the Best Restaurant girl was good. She liked going
to the Korean restaurant to sit quietly and look at the peo-
ple at the table even though she didn't understand a word.
She learned to feed me with chopsticks. Just like a kisaeng.
She liked that. Of course, it was a game for her, but inside
I know she liked it.*

*I always wondered if she really believed my story. I
needed a reason for being in Paris. Telling her I was opening a restaurant was a good idea. Except that it made her
talk about the Best Restaurant too much. If she wasn't
talking about that, she was talking about clothes. But the
stupid girl made the hwa-byung go away, even if she wasn't
Korean.*

*It's important not to have hwa-byung. It makes you
make mistakes. Like that waiter in the Best Restaurant.
That could have been bad but I was lucky. Like that policewoman I shot at. I wasn't so lucky there.* He barked a
laugh, but the flash of pain cut it short. *That was a very
bad mistake. But the gun had just appeared in my hand
and went off by itself. No wonder I didn't hit her. At home
they will get very mad about that. Good, so don't send me
out of Korea next time. Plenty of work to do at home. But
all the more reason the embassy will have to get me out
quick. I won't be a hero, that's for sure, but they'll get me
home quick. What's that? The door? Maybe I'm going to
go now. It's about time. I'm tired of this shit.*

Chapter 47

"Those two really are pieces of work, Lieutenant," Momo said.

"Who? What? What are you talking about?"

"David and Isabelle. The way they made the arrest. I'm surprised they don't get hauled in front of the review board more often. Someday they're going to get fired."

"The girl's downstairs, right?"

"Of course she is. It's just that when they went up to her place she opened the door stark naked. David thought that was great. So he handcuffs her before she can get dressed and he's holding onto her arm while she's yelling and throwing a fit. Then it turns out there's this naked guy in the bed."

"That's the way it's usually done," Capucine said. "Both people get naked."

"Right, but I guess the guy got all excited at seeing his girlfriend in handcuffs and he gets this pretty serviceable woody, if you understand me. That seriously pisses Isabelle off. You know how she gets. So she handcuffs the guy while he's still naked and tells him to stop doing it. Which he didn't. She went ballistic. Apparently it was Adam and Eve meet the Untouchables."

"I'm sorry I missed that. Is the girl wearing clothes now?"

"Unfortunately she is. She's really pretty hot."

Drama and no makeup suited Giselle. Her tousled hair looked as if the turbulence had been artfully created by a stylist. Her translucent skin was as luminous as porcelain. Her eyes were even deeper, more brooding, more movingly hunted. *Too bad Alexandre had to miss this. It would have made his day,* thought Capucine.

Giselle looked up sullenly at Capucine like a waif who expects to be slapped. The unsaid questions—"Why am I here? What have I done to you?"—were as articulate as if they had been spoken.

"Mademoiselle Dupaillard, you are under arrest as an accessory in the murder of Président Delage."

"B . . . but that's insane. I never knew the poor man. He just smiled at me that evening when he came for dinner. How could you think I had anything to do with it?"

"Mademoiselle, do you know a man call Kim Park who often goes by the name of Dac Kim Chu?"

"Of course I do. Dac Kim is my boyfriend. But I don't know anyone called Kim Park."

"But I understand that when my officers arrested you, you were in bed with a different gentleman."

"Oh, I don't even know that guy's name. Dac Kim is out of town, I guess. Anyway he hasn't called in a couple of days, so I went out and came home with that guy."

"If it's any help, I have his name and phone number right here."

"Oh, no thanks. After what that policewoman said to him I guess I won't be seeing him again. He really was cute, though."

"And how do you happen to know this Dac Kim?"

"I met him at Diapason. He came in for dinner. All by

himself. So lost and lonely. When he left he told me to meet him at a bar when I got off work. He was so forceful. He didn't ask. He just told me. Can you believe that? So of course I went."

"And he became your boyfriend?"

"Yes, it was very intense. He's fabulously physical. Sometimes he's so violent I'm afraid. Other times he becomes like a rock: silent, completely solid, very deep. I guess that's why I love him so much. He doesn't talk. He doesn't make any demands. Well, except in bed. And then I just love obeying him."

"And what does Monsieur Kim do for a living?"

"He's Vietnamese, of course. And he is working with some other people to open a very up-market Vietnamese restaurant. They're aiming for three stars in the Michelin. It's going to be the first Asian restaurant with three Michelin stars. Isn't that exciting? And I'm going to work there."

"Is that so?"

"Oh, yes. I'm already helping him."

"How?"

"Well, I have to tell him about everyone important who goes to Diapason. Particularly automobile executives. Dac Kim really likes cars. And he's very interested in knowing how Diapason works technically. So sometimes I give him my key and he goes in over the weekend and draws plans. There's nothing wrong with that, is there? It's closed then, so he doesn't disturb anyone. And he likes to know everything that's on the menu, so I tell him all about that. But I don't give him any recipes. I don't know any and, anyway, he's opening a Vietnamese restaurant, and that's completely different."

"Did you see him the night of October twenty-sixth? You know, the Friday before Delage's body was discovered."

"Who could forget that weekend? Dac Kim had a meeting with his restaurant partners. He came to my apartment very late. It must have been around three in the morning. He was especially passionate. It was really fabulous. I had bruises all over. On Monday I had to wear a long-sleeved top to work, I still had so many marks on my arms."

Chapter 48

"Monsieur Park, you're moving up in the world," Capucine said.

"Good. I go now? Embassy send ambulance?" Without the morphine Park again looked exhausted and drained. Even more yellow and brown spittle had caked on the sides of his mouth.

"No. You misunderstand. You are now also accused of the murder of Président Delage."

Park's head sagged. "That stupid. Why I kill anyone? Just here to get informations," he muttered.

Chapellier, his hands cuffed behind his back, appeared at the door held by two uniformed gendarmes. As he was led in Chapellier recoiled at the sight of Kim. "My God, what happened to him? What's going on here? I thought I was just going to answer questions. You're going to let me go, right?"

Chapellier was placed in the chair next to Capucine at the side of Kim's bed.

"Nguyen, I need you to corroborate some parts of your testimony with Monsieur Kim present," Capucine said. In his corner the stenographer typed silently.

"Of course. Anything. Will you let me go after?"

"Let's worry about that later. You stated earlier that you told Monsieur Kim that you had learned that Président Delage was going to go to the authorities to stop the security leak in Project Typhon. Is that correct?"

"Totally and absolutely correct. Kim, if that's his name, got really steamed up about the thing. I told him that that clown Lionel—my boss, remember—was just puffing himself up and the président wasn't going to see anybody, but Kim wanted to know everything. 'What exactly did Lionel say?' 'Are you sure he didn't say anything else?' Yadda yadda."

"And Park said he could fix it?"

"Absolutely. He said I was to go into the office with Marie's badge that Saturday because he would have taken care of everything."

Capucine made a gesture with her head. The two policemen removed Chapellier.

Kim lifted his head, which had fallen over on his chest. "This stupid. Will become an act of aggression against the Republic of South Korea. Nguyen's accusation ridiculous. He trying to drown own crimes by accusing me. He knows I cannot be arrested but that something very, very bad will happen to him. So he make up story to look like little fish. Little fish who escape when big fish caught. I insist you call embassy and tell them what happening. You must." For the first time there was a hint of entreaty.

The door buzzed opened again and two other gendarmes entered escorting Giselle, handcuffed, who was placed in the chair Chapellier had just vacated. Her hair had become even more tousled, her eyes even darker and more deeply set, her skin even more translucent and pure. She exuded the appeal of an injured gazelle. Capucine felt an inexplicable rush of desire to take her in her arms and shook her head in irritation.

At her first glimpse of Park Giselle registered shock, but it was quickly replaced by an expression of repugnance, as if she had caught him committing some disgusting act in the bathroom. She pushed back in the chair as if to get as far away from him as she could.

"Mademoiselle Dupaillard, is this your boyfriend? The man you know as Dac Kim Chu?" Capucine asked.

"Yes. It's Dac Kim. What happened to him? Was he in an accident?"

"He's under arrest for murder. We're trying to determine if you're his accomplice in the crime. The stenographer will take down everything you say and then you will sign it. You should know that it is highly likely that your deposition will be used in court."

"Oh my God!" Tears of genuine panic ran down her face.

"You told me before that Park asked you about the famous people who booked reservations at Diapason. Who did you tell him about for the week that preceded Friday, October eleventh?"

"Well, we had Georges Leprieur that week—you know, the big fat movie star. He took a table for eight. He always makes a lot of noise but Chef loves him and takes him into the kitchen to show him around. And, let's see, we also had Grazella Camões, that Brazilian supermodel who is about a hundred feet tall. She always talks to me. She's so beautiful. That was it. Oh, wait, I'm so dumb. We also had Président Delage, of course. That's what all the fuss was about. I'm so stupid."

"And you told Dac Kim all this?"

"Yes. He was only interested in Delage. I don't think he even knew who Leprieur was. I would have thought he'd be interested in Grazella because he likes girls a lot and likes us to watch a ton of porn; but, no, he got all excited when I told him about Delage, no one else."

"How do you mean, excited?"

"You know, 'What time is he coming?' 'How many are going to be at the table?' Stuff like that. He just asked me a lot of questions. He couldn't stop asking questions. Well . . . he got excited the other way too and told me I was the best girl ever and had made his life a lot easier. It was funny how Delage got him all excited. And then he asked me to . . . well, I'd better not go into that."

"Did he ask you about the week's menu?"

"Of course. He always did that. Sometimes I even snuck a menu out for him, but don't tell anyone. And I also told him about the *amuse bouches* that weren't on the menu. That week it was an oyster sorbet with a lemon sauce. Isn't that crazy? They let me taste it the first time they made it. It was really, really good."

"I'm sure it was. Did Dac Kim comment on that?"

"Yes, he did. It was later in the evening, you know, so he was pretty knocked out, but when I told him about the sorbet he said something like, 'This just keeps getting better and better.' At the time I thought he was talking about me. That was because he wanted me again right after he said it."

Kim, who had been staring straight ahead at the wall, roused himself. "You stupid hag, that all lies. You invent whole story. Why I be interested in corrupt bureaucrat? Your only brains are in ass. You only think with that!" Park spat on the floor. Capucine was amazed that he was able to produce the requisite fluid.

"How can you say that? I'd never seen you so happy. That was the day you asked me for my key to the restaurant so you could draw the layout. Don't you remember?"

"Ancient hag with claws! Wait until they set me free. I show you your place." Kim's color had partially returned and he strained at his handcuffs, growling deep in his throat, striving to rise, his neck corded with the effort.

"Mademoiselle Dupaillard, that's going to be all for now," Capucine said.

"Does that mean I can go home?"

"Not quite yet."

When Giselle had been taken away Capucine turned her chair around and sat down, splaying her legs and crossing her arms over the chair back. In her close-fitting pants and baggy-sleeved white silk blouse she looked like a Napoleonic light cavalry officer anxiously waiting for a cockfight to begin.

"Park, those two witnesses will be all we need to get you sentenced for premeditated murder. You had motive, you had means, you had opportunity, you'll get convicted. It's a tight case. Under the circumstances it will take more than your ambassador to get you out. It would have to be an agreement between the heads of our two nations. It will come out that you are an intelligence agent, that's obvious, and I doubt very much the government of South Korea will want to argue to the French government that the murder of the head of one of our largest industries was an act of state. Think of where that will leave you. They're going to need a fall guy and it's going to be you."

"You talk lot about international relations for cop."

"I hold a degree in political science."

"Diplomatic immunity sacred. Have been told by my superiors. You must let me go."

"Don't be silly. You're reasoning like a child. A few years back a deputy ambassador from the Republic of Georgia got drunk and killed a teenager in a car accident in Washington. Not some sleazebag spy like you with a trumped-up diplomatic job but the actual deputy ambassador. The Americans asked the Georgians to waive his immunity and the guy is now serving a twenty-one-year sentence."

"South Korea not former Communist country. Different."

"Right. Remember a few years ago when there was a demonstration in front of the Libyan embassy in London and some nut inside strafed the crowd with a submachine gun and killed a young policewoman? A cop shooter—just like you. The mild-mannered British bobbies laid siege to the embassy for nine days hoping to starve the man out. In the end he escaped and went home. So the British broke off relations with Libya. Know what happened?"

"No."

"The Libyans admitted responsibility, tortured their fake diplomat, and then made a big production of hanging him."

Park began to look worried.

"And if I talk to you, what I get?"

"It's more what you don't get. If you cooperate it will be taken into account. Your government will be consulted. There will unquestionably be a negotiation. Your sentence may be reduced. There is even some possibility that part of your time will be spent in a Korean prison. I don't know how much slack your government will cut you but it's bound to be a better deal than if you go to prison kicking and screaming."

"Still not like going home now on plane."

"Park, there's not a chance in hell of that happening. You're in a lot of trouble. Talking is the best thing you can do now. The worst thing for you is to get thrown into the bin as a cop shooter. Which is exactly what's going to happen this afternoon if you do nothing."

Kim paused for nearly a full minute. His head sunk progressively lower on his chest until Capucine began to wonder if he was losing consciousness again. Finally he looked up and said in a barely audible whisper, "I remember other cases of diplomats arrested. But get sent home after negotiations."

"Yes, deals can be made. But unless you cooperate, we're not going to be making any."

"Okay. I like make deal, then."

"The only way that could work is for you to tell your story in full. Then we'll take it to the French government and see what happens. In fact, you have no choice. If you get sent to court on a flagrante delicto charge it will be impossible to cut any deals."

Kim shook his head as if angry flies were buzzing around. "Yes, yes, yes. Okay, okay, okay. Why shouldn't I tell story. Just get me home faster. Back to duty quicker. Give me painkillers. Make talk easier."

An hour passed. The doctor had come, tut-tutted cynically, changed the dressings, and added four new drip bags alongside the big plasma sack on the IV. "He'll be a new man with that stuff," he said, "for a while, at least. You might even have to hold him down," the doctor had laughed.

The small clinic room filled with people. The last to arrive was Tallon, producing the usual tension among the officers present. Kim had responded well to the stimulants and looked at each new arrival with interest.

"All right, let's hear it," Capucine said. The stenographer straightened up and lifted his hands ready to type.

"I am a major in the NIS, the South Korean intelligence service. National Intelligence Service is like French DGSE and French DST combined. NIS work in Korea and abroad. I am specialist in industrial espionage. I joined long ago when service called Agency for National Security Planning and objective to keep out agents from North Korea who want steal our industrial informations. We best service in world in industrial espionage. Best. When attend five-year training course at the ANSP I also go to Yeungnam University and get master's degree in engineering.

"Korea does not need foreign technology. It is the reverse. But sometimes foreigners get good idea and we don't want good idea to be wasted in the hands of lazy incompetents. The NIS often act in those cases."

He paused. "Can have water? Throat is dry."

Capucine held a plastic cup with less than an inch of pale liquid to his lips.

"It's tea. The doctor says if you have too much liquid you'll throw up. Go on."

"As said before, assignment to obtain gasoline catalyst from Renault. For me is only one way to do this properly. With assistants on inside. Espionage services in West no longer like to use assistants. That is very wrong. In old days of ideological conflict it easy to obtain loyal and faithful assistants happy to die for cause. More difficult now. So CIA and everyone else now like only computers. Easy, safe, go home at five o'clock. But never get everything. And not fully understand what get.

"No. Must be assistant. But that now hard. Have to be bought. Have to know how to recruit. Have to know when they about to desert."

For the first time Tallon intervened. "Look, buddy, we're not here for a tutorial on espionage while you're sucking up free drugs. Tell your story and be quick about it." Capucine shot him an irritated look.

"Well, I tell policewoman," Park said, nodding at Capucine. "Arrive in France, recruit three possible assistants, and put one in right department Renault. For a while the informations come satisfactory. Then assistant get greedy. They always do. Important informations all in one department. Assistant not have access. Find girlfriend in section who let him in to get final informations. He want large bonus for this. Then he invent other story, claim management of the company find leak, so we need to get final informations immediately before everything shut down. In end, we never get informations.

"Police follow secretary who deliver informations and try to arrest me. Case a failure. Important I not get arrested. Fired shot over head of policewoman to scare away. Big, big mistake." Progressively Park's head had been sagging on his chest. Finally his chin rested on his sternum and spittle dripped from his slack mouth.

"The fucker's faking," Tallon said. "But get the doctor

just in case. Lieutenant, what the hell happened here? You said he was all set to spill the beans and you wanted to make him more comfortable. So he's had a happy little trip and all we get is laughed at. Get this guy back on the rails and call me when he's really ready. I don't want to hear Chapter One of the NIS espionage primer again. Got that?" Tallon strode to the door and made an irritated gesture with the tips of his fingers for the guard to open it. He stalked out, swearing under his breath. Gradually all the other occupants followed, leaving only Capucine and the stenographer, and of course, Park.

Chapter 49

"Pretty policewoman get scolded." Park laughed drunkenly. "Punishment for shooting me. But you good. Not weak like rest of French."

"Keep this up and I'm going to shoot you again. What the hell was that all about? Bullshit to get more drugs?"

"Yes. Pain very great. Did not like man who look like bull. I know I have to talk. But not to him. Talk now. Don't shut painkillers off. Please."

"Let's hear it, then. Did you kill Président Delage?"

"Of course. Only solution. Should have been easy for Nguyen to get informations over weekend if he not have interference. Killing président easy way to get needed time. No risk. No problem. Proper solution."

"Let's go through the events of the week. The first thing was that Giselle told you the président had a reservation that Friday."

"No, no. First, Nguyen tell me his boss tell him about coming crackdown. Very clear that Président Delage in charge. No doubts. Project very important to career of président, that why he take charge himself. Important man. Go to big boss in government. Things then happen fast. Just like Korea. Need immediate action. Had to do something before weekend."

"And you had no doubts that Delage was really on the verge of asking for the assistance of the DGSE?"

"I quite sure. Project of highest importance. I have many plans to keep Delage from meeting with government man. Hit with car or just kill on street. Not hard to do, to kill someone. But I find something much better." He paused for breath. "Giselle, juicy girl from Best Restaurant, tell me Delage come for dinner on Friday. Perfect. Easy to do then."

"How did you do it?"

"Easy. Very easy. We have excellent poison called TZ, made by CIA, we have plenty from days when CIA help create ANSP. Comes from algae saxitoxin like in shellfish. Excellent poison. Victim immediately passive and then die quietly. No noise. I also give same poison to Nguyen to give to girlfriend, but only very, very little, so she sick and quiet all day and he free to go to her office. So, I wait for Delage to leave restaurant, inject him under ear into carotid. Use small hypodermic that easy to fit in pocket. Delage get quiet right away. I walk him to my car and make him sit. Drive him around until he pass out. Ha ha, go to Bois de Boulogne to look at juicy girls in trees. I want his last hours to be happy hours."

"How considerate of you. Then what?"

"Drive back to the restaurant, put Delage arm around my neck like drunk, carry through door. Giselle give me key. Many police in area, guarding important buildings, but if anyone see, we just drunk workers of restaurant who forget something. Then put sleeping président in big refrigerator and all is finished. Giselle tell me restaurant always closed over the weekend so I know no one disturb until Monday.

"Then go back to the Bois de Boulogne. One of the girls

we see is real juicy and wanted her. But she gone, so I go to Giselle's apartment instead."

"Lucky her."

"Yes, she happy. Things work out good after removing président. Very successful plan. We not bothered for two weeks. But Nguyen not able to get into computers. Not have codes. Incompetent assistant. Then project shut down and about to be moved to military. My replacement not going to have easy time. No." Park laughed dryly.

Chapter 50

Capucine rushed through the plain aluminum-framed glass doorway. *Late again. I hope he isn't fuming.* She pulled up short in a small unassuming anteroom. A self-effacing man in a dark business suit left a lectern in a corner of the room and came up to her with the hint of a knowing smile, as if they shared a secret. At the mention of her name he nodded and led her down a hallway into a large, bland dining room. Not for the first time Capucine told herself that Tirel's eminently forgettable decor was hardly what you would expect at the best known of the three-star restaurants.

Nonetheless, the room was full of memories for Capucine. Tirel had been her family's venue of choice for celebrations. All the milestones of her youth had been feted here: birthdays, passing her *bac*, graduation from Sciences Po; it was even here that Alexandre had invited her parents for that memorable dinner to ask for her hand. In flowery hyperbole that made her mother giggle and her father frown Alexandre had explained that the paragon of restaurants was the only possible venue to ask for the hand of the paragon of women. The dinner had been successful enough to allay—but not permanently extinguish—

her parents' resentment that she was not making a more suitable marriage.

With its nondescript carpet and tan walls, the room exuded a sense of cozy opulence as comfortable as an old cashmere sweater. Capucine bubbled with a happy-little-girl-on-her-way-to-her-birthday-fete feeling as she walked toward Alexandre and Jacques in the far corner. Still, something nagged, scratching angrily across the surface of her contentment. Would she never free herself of that eternal fear of being sucked down into that hateful life of affluent insouciance so vital to her parents . . . and, for that matter, beneath all his bluster, Alexandre as well? By the time she reached the table most of the bubbles of her mood had gone flat and she hadn't had time to really understand why.

Jacques and Alexandre percolated at the edge of hilarity, obviously fueled by a bottle of Dom Perignon that, given its drunken list in the cooler, was already well over three-quarters depleted. They both half rose from their chairs and saluted with their flutes in a toast.

"Here's to your triumphal coup," Alexandre said.

"Oh, so this is a celebration, is it?" Capucine said, with barely masked irritation. "I had hoped it was just Jacques dipping into the bottomless well of his expense account so he could show off his new tie. I'm not really sure there's anything to celebrate." She gave Alexandre a withering look that would have been rude had he not been her husband.

With more verve than the situation really required Jacques asked brightly, "Oh, do you like it? How nice." He energetically flapped an Hermès tie dotted with blue and yellow butterflies cavorting on a salmon background, his pick of their fall crop.

"Cousin, it's precious. I just hope it's not something you intend to wear when you're stealing around incognito."

Jacques compressed his lips in a dramatic pout. "Cou-

sine, you delude yourself if you think that these august sur-
roundings will prevent me from pelting you in the kisser
with the bread roll you so richly deserve." He picked up a
roll and brandished it menacingly. Capucine wondered if
there was any champagne left in the bottle at all. "Also,"
he added in a hurt tone, "it just so happens that I can be
utterly invisible when I so choose."

"Now, now, children, behave. This is a serious occasion.
We are here to commemorate a truly Homeric achieve-
ment," Alexandre interjected.

Capucine shot Alexandre a look that was frankly rude
even if he was her husband.

"The paragon of restaurants for the paragon of detectives," Alexandre said dramatically. "No other place
would be suitable for such an occasion."

"I seem to have heard that line before," Capucine said.

Jacques clenched his teeth with a grimace of courageous
despair that made Capucine think of a Foreign Legion-
naire at Tuyen Quang trying to forget that he and his six
hundred colleagues were surrounded by twenty thousand
Chinese. "But, chère cousine, it's not going on my expense
account at all. Anyway, the director would never spring
for Tirel. This is Alexandre's treat. I understand he's even
going to pay out of his own pocket. I'm sure he asked me
along merely for comic relief."

Capucine ignored him and crackled in irritation with
Alexandre. "Good Lord, you sound as fatuous as an Arsène Lupin character. Only the top hat and waxed moustache are missing," Capucine said.

"My dear. I was being perfectly sincere. You really have
succeeded a major triumph and I honestly think this is the
only place that does it justice."

In spite of herself Capucine softened and her irritation
evaporated. Alexandre always had that effect on her. In a
mini-epiphany she understood that her annoyance didn't
have anything to do with her parents' lifestyle. The prob-

lem was that in her heart she didn't see the case as a success. The whole thing was so obvious it had just resolved itself.

"It's ridiculous to think of putting me in the same league as a Tirel, but I have to admit even that grouchy bear Tallon seemed pleased with the way the case worked out."

"Pleased? He must have been impressed as hell. You're a veritable Commissaire Maigret," Jacques said.

Feeling that their dinner had returned to an even keel Jacques waved a remonstrative finger at Alexandre and poured the last of the champagne, sparking the sommelier to rush up, distraught at not having been left to pour the wine himself. "*Mon vieux,* you're becoming a cartoon-strip husband. You project yourself into your wife. Who could be farther removed from that Belgian beer swiller with his huge appetite, vast belly, and pipe glued to his mouth than Capucine?" Jacques asked.

Alexandre laughed happily. "That's hardly it. I merely blush with pride when I recognize in her the virtues Georges Simenon bestowed on his character: the ability to plumb the unfathomable depths of people while having the courage to rely on his instincts."

"How noble of you. But wasn't the corpulent commissaire's motto, 'I don't know anything'? Our dear Capucine has been dropping hints that she knew who the killer was almost from the very beginning. It was a bit like the dance of the seven veils except less titillating," Jacques said.

"Well, I did have some ideas," Capucine said, beginning to enjoy herself.

"Do you mean you really suspected it was the Koreans even before you arrested that awful man?" Alexandre asked.

"Not from the beginning, obviously, but the picture became clear the minute we discovered the involvement of Clotilde Lancrey-Javal, Delage's secretary." The sommelier returned and released the cork of another bottle of champagne, producing a sigh even more discreet than Alexandre could manage.

"Once the Trag saga was put to rest it was obvious that there had to be another spy network in place. During his interview that Trag operative made it quite clear that he was convinced there were no other Americans involved. And it couldn't have been the Japanese, given Renault's involvement with Nissan; you know how disciplined they are. And it also seemed unlikely that it was the Germans or the Italians. I don't know why, but it just wasn't their style somehow. So who was left? The Koreans, voilà!

"Now, if I really were Maigret, I'd tell you that what tipped me off was that the hibiscus, the flower the insufferable Chapellier would leave on Clotilde's desk, is the national flower of Korea. But actually, I only looked that up this morning. Also, Maigret would have told you that Dac Kim, Park's nom de guerre, means 'acquired knowledge' in Vietnamese, but that's just Korean pedantry.

"Of course, now that I think about it, those are exactly the sorts of conceits that go along with an ego psychotically overinflated like Kim's." She paused in thought. "That ego is his stock in trade, essential to create deeply bonding codependences he thrives on."

"Jacques, does this sort of Saint-Germain cocktail party psychology go down at the DGSE as well?" Alexandre asked.

"Oh, yes, definitely. Intelligence work is all about exploiting psychological weakness. I'm told that in the bad old days people would be delighted to have their toes put to the coals just to validate their political beliefs. But now that ideology is a thing of the past you have to look for true neurosis if you're going to turn anyone. And you have to be neurotic yourself to be able to exploit it." Jacques cackled loudly.

"Just look at Park's victims," Capucine continued. "And that's just what they were, victims. Clotilde Lancrey-

Javal wasn't really attracted by the money. She fell for a personality type that was the same as her husband's: profoundly egocentric and brutally demanding. Park just filled the void of codependency left by her husband. The money was important for her self-justification. It wasn't a motivation in itself."

"Absolutely archetypal," Jacques said. "You have the insights of a true intelligence operative."

"And Giselle Dupaillard, with her compulsive sexual behavior, suffers from a classic narcissistic personality disorder. She is unable to feel empathy or to form mature bonds with people. Underneath a superficial glow of entitlement she feels continually empty and threatened. That's why she seeks to be dominated by a ruthless force who takes no heed of her personality. Park filled the bill perfectly."

"Yes, another classic stereotype," Jacques said.

"What a waste. She really is delectable," Alexandre said. "But you're not going to argue that Nguyen Chapellier was also a narcissist, are you?"

"No, he's a personality type the police are far more familiar with. A deeply flawed personality that seems to have no cause to be flawed. Like most of that type he also has a strong sense of entitlement. So he jumped at a chance to get the income he felt he deserved and also lash out at the establishment in the process. It's the psychological makeup typical of most professional thieves."

"Enough psychiatry. You're way ahead of your story. How did you know Park had killed Delage?" Alexandre asked.

"Oh, that was easy. He gave himself away. He had told a believable story about being on a plain-vanilla industrial spying mission. But at one point in the interview he let slip that the poisoning was related to oysters. That certainly wasn't anything we had released. Also, it was clear that the murder involved some sort of insider component.

Giselle's personality type was sufficiently obvious to make her easy prey for Park. Once we understood his motive, she was by far the best choice as his entrée into the restaurant."

"So if it wasn't for bad luck Delage would have survived?" Alexandre asked.

"Not at all. I think Park would have killed Delage no matter what. He has absolutely no scruples and he needed Delage out of the way for a few days. Park felt he was only an inch away from succeeding in his mission but that he would get locked out the coming Monday. So he just had to do something. Obviously, when he found out from Giselle that Delage was having dinner at Diapason it was a gift direct from the gods. Not only did he have a convenient way of committing the murder but he also had a good chance of making it look like an accident. Later he told us his original plan was to dump the body in front of Delage's front door. If he had done that it might well have been thought it really was food poisoning. But Delage obstinately remained conscious. Park knew Delage would eventually die but couldn't take the chance of leaving him somewhere where he could be found and tell his tale. Nor could he take the risk of driving around all night with a near-cadaver in the car. So the walk-in was ideal. And he had Giselle's key."

"What a grim act, locking a dying man in a refrigerator. Park must have no conscience at all. What's going to happen to him?" Alexandre asked.

"Actually, Jacques knows more about that part than I do."

Jacques beamed at being back on stage. "On the first go-around the director took the case out of the hands of the juge d'instruction. Park was a foreign intelligence officer after all, so it was technically an act of state, not a criminal matter. Our powers that be spoke to their powers that be. They denied everything, of course, except that

Park was one of their agents. They claimed that he had gone berserk while on an innocent mission and so it wasn't their responsibility. They actually encouraged us to take him to trial while halfheartedly attempting to cut a deal. You know, something like they wouldn't make a peep if we agreed his sentence would be no more than, say, five or ten years. When we turned them down they didn't seem to care all that much. We assumed they had just written Park off and were merely having a weak stab at minimizing the bad press. So the file went back to the juge d'instruction and Park'll go to trial stripped of any diplomatic privileges."

"Right," Capucine continued. "I don't think there's much doubt of a conviction and he'll get life with no possibility of parole."

"And the others?" Alexandre asked.

"Renault has brought both civil and criminal charges against Chapellier. Cases involving intellectual property are much more tricky than embezzlement because the court does not like to hazard a guess at the monetary value of the theft. It's pretty obvious, though, that in this case the value is huge. The juge d'instruction thinks he'll get a ten-year conviction. Maybe more. On top of that, the civil suit is for the value of the information that did get out. That's going to be one complicated lawsuit, but it certainly looks like Monsieur Chapellier will have to give over the better part of whatever salary he's able to make when he gets out of prison. He's a ruined man."

"And the two women?" Alexandre asked.

"Nothing will happen to Giselle. She got fired, of course, but no criminal charges will be brought against her. In her little pea brain, all she was doing was helping a restaurant spy who turned out not to be a restaurant spy after all. She's outraged that she was fired and is taking Labrousse to workers' court. He's absolutely livid."

"Poor man. But no more Giselle! *Quel dommage,*" Alexandre said. "And what about Delage's secretary?"

"Renault was quite decent with Clotilde. Obviously, they didn't want her around any longer, but they agreed not to press any charges if she resigned. She won't have any difficulty getting a job as secretary to the boss of another big company."

"So that's it. Case wrapped up. And brilliantly so!" Alexandre said. "We get to take a vacation. Marrakech, here we come! I haven't spent a whole night with you without the phone ringing and you rushing out in what seems like a month."

"Not so fast, my dear sweet letch. There's one loose end that still has to be tied up. Actually, that's going to be the most satisfying one of all."

Chapter 51

A sullenly taciturn maid in ancient carpet slippers and washed-out cleaning smock let Capucine in, led her to the sitting room, and left her to her own devices without a word. Capucine knew Guyon would make a point of keeping her waiting. She prowled. The kinetic sculpture was just as abrasive as it had been the last time, clicking away like a nest of irritatingly loud mechanical insects. Capucine walked around it impatiently, attentively. Once, twice, a third time around. Suddenly she stopped, extended her index finger, and lightly caressed a small, domed projection. At her gossamer touch the tiny knob retreated into the machine as if in outrage. The device made a loud chunk and fell silent, leaving the room ominously quiet.

Guyon burst in. "What on earth did you just do? It can't be stopped! It's not made to be stopped! How did you know how to do it?"

"Nothing could be easier. I just touched this little doohickey, right down there. See!" Capucine was delighted. "The damn thing just shut right up."

"How did you find that?! I've had the sculpture for years. I never noticed that lever."

"The symmetry was offensive. That little knob was sticking up in the wrong place. It made no sense for it to be there. It's the same reason I've come to take you to Quai des Orfèvres for questioning. You were sticking up in the middle of the case destroying its symmetry."

Guyon started violently. "But I understood you had arrested a Korean spy for the murder. You're crazy! You can't arrest me. Don't be silly." Guyon had backed away toward the sculpture, as if for protection. He shouted, "Leave me alone. Go away."

At the sound of the outburst, Momo and Isabelle, who had been waiting in the foyer, entered the room quietly. Isabelle went up to Guyon and held him gently by the forearm. "You'll have to come with us."

"Never! Get your hands off me. Get away!" Guyon shouted hysterically. He wrenched free and ran behind the sculpture. Isabelle followed slowly, making soothing noises. "Get away from me," Guyon screamed. He ran all the way around the back and out the other side, straight into Momo, who was waiting silently. In a single fluid motion Momo translated the élan of Guyon's rush into a rotation that crooked his arm, pinning it to his back and snapping a waiting handcuff on the wrist. Almost tenderly, Momo twisted the other arm around and squeezed the other cuff shut.

At the Quai, when he found himself in the room below the level of the Seine, Guyon ran completely amok, tearing against the handcuffs that bound him to the metal chair, opening deep cuts in his wrists. The handcuffs were removed, the wrists bandaged—"Probably needs stitches," the doctor tsked, "but the hell with it"—and his arms duct-taped to the chair. After a short pause Guyon renewed his efforts, jerking uncontrollably in the chair and spinning wildly on the floor when he fell over. Finally two stocky uniformed brigadiers managed to pick him up and forcibly hold him down in the chair, leaning over, bearing down on his shoulders, panting from their efforts.

Momo was delighted. "*Chauf!* This guy's the best. I'm going to go get my Polaroid. He's going on my wall."

The doctor whispered in Capucine's ear. "If you'd like, I can inject him with a cocktail of Valium and haloperidol. That'll calm him right down. He'll get sleepy and subdued and chatty. Of course, any statement he makes will not be receivable in court. But you know that."

"Oh, don't worry about that part of it, Doctor. Go ahead and give him the shot."

The injection took some doing. Guyon screamed so loudly that two brigadiers from the next room came in with worried looks. But within five minutes Guyon's head fell to his chest and he smiled a boyish little smile.

"Do you want to tell me about it? You know you won't get out of here until you do," Capucine cooed in her most maternal voice.

"I still don't know how you knew I was involved. I underestimated you."

"You didn't, really. It's just that our minds work in completely different ways. It's my failing as a detective, I suppose. When you look at a car you see all the rods and pistons and all those clanky technical things. When I look at a car I see an object, the sum of its parts. You're a master of rational analysis, something I need to get better at. But, thank God, I do very well drawing intuitive conclusions. That's what made that lever that stuck out just a bit too far on your sculpture so apparent. It destroyed the integrity of the whole. Do you understand?"

"So what was the protrusion that led you to me?"

"Oh, le président. Without you he never would have been part of the case."

"I'm not sure I understand," Guyon said softly. He was falling into a presleep languor.

"Tell me about your involvement first, and then I'll tell

you my side," Capucine said with the gentleness of a mother tucking in a small child.

"Not much to tell, really," Guyon slurred. "Typhon was my doing. It was I who sensed that this rocket fuel fluke had the capacity to put a new face on the automobile. I, and only I, realized its potential. It was a chance to rebuild the industry. Do you understand what that means? The whole foundation of the Western economy reinvigorated. A fresh new start for everything." He was beginning to get excited again. Capucine put her hand gently on his shoulder.

"From the very early stages I could see that it did not really interest Président Delage. He was after a global alliance. Renault had already joined forces with the Japanese. There was also a good hope of a link with those boneheaded Americans. I think he saw himself as the architect of the first really global automobile industry. He was a statesman, not an engineer. He saw triumph in negotiation, not in industry or technology." Guyon fell silent and seemed to lose interest.

"So what happened?"

"What? . . . Yes . . . He funded the project, of course. But he didn't have his heart in it. That was obvious. My fear was that once it got close to becoming a reality Delage might begin to think it could even be dangerous to his endless negotiations. I didn't know what he'd do. But the more I thought about it the more I became convinced he would find a way to keep Typhon in a closet forever. I was getting very worried. Very worried. Very worried." His voice had fallen to a whisper.

Capucine shook him. He jerked up with a start. "You don't understand at all, mademoiselle, do you? At Polytechnique a professor told us the fable of the pig and chicken who are behind our breakfast of ham and eggs. The chicken is merely involved; she only lays the eggs. But the pig is truly committed because he sacrifices his life. For our professor both those roles were viable. But it is the rooster who can have no place on the team. He merely struts around arrogantly, crowing and adding no value at all. Delage was that rooster. Don't you see?"

"I'll refrain from drawing the obvious conclusion. What happened next?"

"I approached them, of course."

"Who?"

"The KAMA, the Korean Association of Automobile Manufacturers, at the Detroit automobile show, of all places. Can you imagine! Their chairman was there. It was awful. They thought it was clever to serve sausages from stands at the meetings. They would wheel the stands right into the showrooms. Le hot dog! It's a sort of *choucroute garnie* on a long pastry roll. Must be some sort of Germanic influence. Impossible to eat because everything falls out of the bun onto the floor. Made me utterly sick, too." He came to a dead stop. It was painfully obvious that the doctor had been a little exuberant with his cocktail.

"Koreans?" she prodded.

"Yes . . . they were the most likely choice. They were desperate for something to leap-frog the competition. Their chairman went crazy with enthusiasm when I hinted about Typhon. He flew me to Seoul in his private jet. Wanted me to quit Renault and move to Korea immediately. I held out. I wanted to become the head of my own production company. With an important share of the equity. We had a long negotiation. They agreed, 'in principle.' But only 'in principle.' Only 'in principle.' "

"So then what happened?"

Guyon's features slowly reassembled themselves into a sharp, crafty look. "I began to suspect it was Typhon they wanted and not me." He shot Capucine a conspiratorial glance. "But I wasn't going to be their fool. I wasn't going to give them even a hint of the technology until I had a deal drawn up on paper. Things just went on and on. They promised and promised, but would sign nothing. Nothing. Nothing at . . . all."

"Guyon!" Capucine snapped sharply.

"Oh, yes," he said, lifting his head with a jerk. "Well, it became obvious they were just playing me. So I told the chairman of the KAMA that I wanted no part of it anymore."

Guyon paused. The crafty look vanished. His face relaxed. He looked younger. He became a small, injured boy. "And also, I realized that I had been greedy. I had wanted too much. It was all too dangerous. I wanted to be recognized as the hero I know I am, but if things didn't work out in Korea—and I had learned how dangerous the Koreans are—I would be seen as a traitor to my country. So," he beamed suddenly. "That's why I just told them the discussions were over. Voilà! Guyon *fini*." He burst into peals of laughter.

"That was when the troubles began. They said it was no longer my choice. They were going to assign an NIS agent to produce where I had failed them. You can't imagine their tone. Me, a failure! And they did! Some Korean began calling me at the office to tell me that he was an intelligence agent and had installed an apparatus—yes, that was his word—an apparatus to extract all my secret data right inside my own company. He would laugh. He would call again and again. He would tell me how well it was going and that he nearly had all the data he needed. Soon he would be going and I would be left alone. 'Thanks for all your help,' he said."

There was a long pause. Guyon stared at the floor, unblinking.

"So I had to do something. I knew what they were going to do. They were going to implement Typhon and blame me for the theft, so they would be protected from lawsuits. It was obvious.

"I got smart." Guyon looked pleased with himself.

"Yes, I handled the beginning badly, but I extracted myself brilliantly.

"When the Seoul R & D conference came up, I simply circulated the rumor that the catalyst had been perfected. But cleverly. I told a couple of blabbermouth press agents. In a matter of hours the rumor was all over the place. Brilliant. It was perfect. Once the rumor was launched I would be free to sic the authorities on those damned Koreans and, the best part, I would be free of any possible accusations." He looked up at Capucine for approval. "Isn't that brilliant?"

"Brilliant," Capucine said as if speaking to a small child. "And then what happened?"

"It was perfect. I told Delage about the rumor flying around in Seoul and he elected to take it to the highest levels of the government. My problems were over. Except . . . Except . . ."

"Yes," Capucine prompted him.

"I might have been just a little bit indiscreet. In my relief I hinted, no more than hinted, mind you, to one of my staff, that imbecile Vaillant—you know him, remember?—that I had solved a very sticky problem and that Président Delage was going to clamp down hard on the security for Typhon.

"Vaillant became overemotional and began asking me any number of questions. Too many questions. But it was perfectly correct for me to have spoken to him. There was absolutely nothing wrong in that. I was Vaillant's mentor. It was natural for me to share my emotions with him. No fault can be attached to me for that. Surely you can see that."

"Of course," Capucine said. "Anyone can see that."

Guyon smiled happily. "There. That's all there is to it."

"But when you learned that Président Delage had been killed, what did you think?"

"Oh, I knew without a shadow of a doubt that it had

been the Korean spy who had somehow killed him. You can't imagine how violent that man is. But so what? It wasn't me, was it? My involvement with those people had been purged. They could do what they wanted to. It had nothing to do with me anymore. Don't you think? I did quite well. I saved Typhon for *la gloire de la France*. Actually, I think I should get the Legion of Honor for my bravery. At the very least."

Capucine had a bad taste in her mouth that seeped through to the rest of her body. "But did you not feel any remorse that you had been instrumental in the death of Président Delage? After all, he had been your close colleague for a number of years."

Guyon shot upright with a start. "Remorse! Are you insane? Do you not see the enormity of his crime? Industry is about making things. Better and better things. He would have let the greatest development of the century languish because he wanted to create a paper empire. He was the nemesis of industry. Remorse! Indeed!"

As if guilty of their momentary lapse the drugs grabbed Guyon with renewed vigor and he fell asleep, his chin on his chest, snoring quietly through a contented smile.

Epilogue

It was almost a year later and smack in the middle of the handful of days at the end of August that sound the death knell of summer. The golden season had been officially over since the fifteenth, and Parisians were trickling back from the five weeks of annual vacation that they cling to so desperately both as an inalienable right and in the belief that that is what life is really meant to be. They showed off their tans, hinted knowingly at the unimaginable sexual, culinary, and cultural prowesses they had manifested over the summer, and prayed that fall, and the burden of responsibility that comes with it, would never arrive.

Alexandre and Labrousse were ensconced at the long table in the window of a shabby chic restaurant on the rue du Bourg Tibourg at the very edge of the Marais, the part where black-leathered-biker-gay yields with a surly sneer to slumming wannabe intellectuals from Saint-Germain who come to buy grossly overpriced tea at Mariage Frères. The restaurant had the apposite name of Le Verre Qui Fuit—"The Escaping Glass" or "The Leaking Glass" if you were feeling pessimistic. The walls were covered in yellowing cartoon murals satirizing some long-forgotten and incomprehensibly arcane literary rivalry. An un-Parisianly pneumatic girl polished glasses behind the deserted bar, smiling sweetly at a felicitous secret. At the very back of the restaurant a man with a blond goatee sat with a bottle of red wine making changes to a manuscript, bleating with rage each time he dramatically crossed out a word. At each ejaculation the barmaid shot him an anxious glance before returning to her private bliss.

Alexandre and Labrousse had not seen each other for over ten months and had agreed on a plan to drink a swath through the long hot afternoon and emerge at the far end faced with a deeply satiating meal, say a thick *pavé* of foie gras followed by a leg of lamb that had been slow braised for seven hours.

Their table overlooked the narrow street, all but deserted in the late afternoon. A remarkably thin and epicene young man in a pastel polo shirt and artfully crumpled linen trousers glided by on a venerable Dutch bicycle, resplendent in the sunshine, peering intently into the store windows. He glanced disdainfully at Labrousse and Alexandre and pedaled lazily on.

They had eschewed the three-star restaurants for their reunion. Even if well masked by rigidly disciplined faces, the staffs' adulation of the doyen of restaurant critics and the most celebrated of chefs would have ruined the tranquility of their reunion. At the Verre Qui Fuit no one had the slightest clue who they were other than that Alexandre look vaguely like some sort of man of letters and so was to be indulged.

"Is it as bad as they say?" Alexandre asked.

"New York? No. It's not bad at all. It's difficult to do it justice. It's very fast. One can never think. One has to rush around and do extraordinary things all the time. But in a way that is good." Labrousse paused. "In France we suffer from an excess of reality. We serve the god of authenticity. In New York the god is the exceptional, however unreal that may be. Their favorite word is 'extreme.' Everything is 'extreme.' Extreme sports. Extreme sex. Extreme socks. Extreme everything."

"And you wanted extreme?"

"Of course. All serious chefs want extreme. Haute cuisine has to be extreme. But in Paris I was forced to be conventionally extreme. Almost the only titillation my rigidly bourgeois clientele permitted itself in their rigidly conventional lives was my cooking. I was like a tiger pacing back and forth in a tiny cage of conventional living. Très bien. I could live with that. But the first time something genuinely shocking happened, my conventional clientele all abandoned me. I had no choice but to leave. I was driven out. Life would have been impossible after their defection."

"That can't be true. I heard that the wait for a reservation was over six months after the arrest was made."

"Of course it was, but who was trying to come? My patrons had abandoned me. I had only tourists! Americans. Japanese. They all came to gape and point at the table where it happened. They didn't even look at the food, so great was their desire to stare at the spot where they thought a famous man had died. If there had been a chalk outline of a cadaver on the floor, I could have doubled my prices. So I made my choice. If I had been condemned to cook for Americans I might as well cook for them in a place they would pay full attention to the food. The answer was obvious. Americans only take America seriously. So I packed my knives and a clean shirt and became yet another New York immigrant. And I had to be—at my age, if you please—humble again. You know what young chefs say about naming a restaurant? Better have it begin with an 'A' so people will see you first when they open the guides. You know, that's why so many three-star places begin with an A. Like Archestrate, Arpege, Apicius, Astrance. So I called my new place 'Aubade.' It's the perfect name. A song sung at dawn. My new dawn."

"And it really is better in New York?"

"Of course. These people have never eaten. It's all new for them. Here, in Paris, a man comes into a three-star restaurant and carries all the baggage of his heritage. His grandmother cooked. His mother cooked. His wife cooks. His mistress cooks. He has eaten in excellent restaurants ever since he was a small boy. He defines his culture in terms of food. He defines himself in terms of food. Then he eats my food and he has to overcome all that baggage while still remaining faithful to it. It's asking a lot of him.

"The French patron is knowledgeable, but he is cynical, too, and that's what makes him difficult. In America they know nothing. They eat foie gras for the first time when they are already rich adults. They have no childhood memories of it. Can you imagine what a joy it is to cook for people who have no prejudices at all? People who come to your table naked? People who like your food for what it is and not because it evokes something else? Bocuse says we must not try to make a carrot taste like what it is not; we must make it taste more like what it is. So be it, but in France we have become obsessed with making that carrot taste like what we remember it to taste like, unlike the Americans who come to the table wide-eyed, pure, open to anything, and ready for adventure."

"And you've freed yourself of the French heritage?"

"Of course. Now they speak Spanish in my kitchen, and"—Labrousse leaned confidentially across the table, putting his finger to his lips—"are actually far better chefs than most of the French. My new *chefs de rang* are Mexicans or Colombians who were so poor as children that McDonald's was their astral gourmet treat. But they do superb work. The prep chefs are the best I've ever seen. It's extreme!" He burst into loud laughter that verged on the edge of hysteria.

"And then there's the money, too. Do you know that when I was here I made less than what one of my waiters now makes. Can you imagine that! Less than a waiter! The owner of the best restaurant in Paris!"

"So you're happy."

"Happy! *Quelle idée!* Well, maybe sometimes I actually am. But I miss afternoons like this. Also, I'm a little afraid that if I drink too much one day I'll be tempted to open a restaurant in Las Vegas. That scares me. Or even have a TV show. They make me offers all the time. That scares me even more." He shook his head violently as if to dispel an evil spirit, stopped, and waved the girl behind the bar over. "Do you have any champagne?"

"*Evidemment*, Monsieur!" she said with a fetching smile. A rapid conversation ensued and a bottle of Krug was promised. When it came Labrousse rose, buttoned his jacket, and raised his glass to Alexandre. He was already a little tipsy. "I just heard this morning. *Mes hommages* to Madame le Commissaire."

"Yes, that." said Alexandre. "That's a bit of a mixed blessing, too. Capucine insisted on sitting for the commissaire's exam just after the case was closed. Her boss agreed even though she was officially two years too young. Of course, she passed brilliantly. She's now finishing up her training period in the Twentieth Arrondissement and will take charge of the Police Judiciaire branch there at the end of next month."

"And she's happy?"

"You know the Twentieth, it's one big malevolent ghetto. She's awash in violence. Brutality is the norm. Anyway, as she puts it, she was more concerned with becoming a real flic, which she unquestionably now is, than getting promoted to commissaire."

"You would think she would hate that. So unlike dear, sweet Capucine."

"My sense is she's cauterizing her spirit. She always said it was necessary for her to become more firmly attached to the world. There will be a next phase. She has blossomed, as they say, but the bloom is not yet resplendent."

"And what was the denouement of the story? The famous project. 'Typhon,' wasn't that what it was called? The mythical Greek giant sleeping under Mount Etna, who would be wakened to change the face of industry. What happened to him?"

"Still sleeping the sleep of the bloated, I gather. Capucine has family in the DGSE and collects rumors from them. When things got out of hand the whole project was transferred to the CNRS so it could be controlled by the government. It seems to have disappeared into the bowels of that labyrinthine organization. Capucine was told that the current CNRS view is that it's technically impossible. The chemicals seem to work all right, but they cannot be injected into the engine without the risk of a cataclysmic explosion, and the injection device envisaged by Renault simply will never work."

"And what happened to those appalling people who murdered one of my clients in my very restaurant?" Labrousse shuddered and poured himself another glass of champagne.

"Well, Delage's lawyer—remember, they caught him running off to Guadeloupe with his girlfriend in his boat—turned out to have nothing to do with the murder. But the minute the case went to court he sailed off to Antigua, where he still is, shuffling around in flip-flops with his woman, running a small yacht charter business. I can't make up my mind if he discovered fulfillment as an island bum or he was afraid they would arrest him for something even more nefarious.

"The Korean went to trial. Just at the time you left. His government turned his back on him and he went to court as an ordinary citizen. So now he's doing life without possibility of parole. He wouldn't have had parole in any case. He's already killed a man in prison."

"Good Lord! What an animal. So he was the real villain? Is he the one to blame for all this?"

"There's no question that the Korean injected the poison into Delage and then locked him in the walk-in to die. But I think he was just a tool. He can be no more blamed than a pit bull. The real murderer is Guyon, the executive. He was the prime mover. He hated his president because Delage did not share his vision. So he initiated the sequence of events without having the slightest idea where they would wind up. He felt he was nothing more than a victim of circumstance, but it all started with his goal of eliminating those who did not have his enthusiasm. He used the Korean agent as a tool in exactly the same way you use a knife in the kitchen. There's no question, he was the one ultimately responsible."

"But he was never convicted."

"Nor could he have been. There was no evidence at all. In fact, all he really did was plant a rumor about his own project. It was that rumor that triggered everything."

"And he's still on the job at Renault?"

Alexandre smiled and shook his head. "No, that would have been too much. He's in Seoul, working in some vague administrative capacity for their association of automobile manufacturers. Charitably, they took him on after the Renault debacle. It's one of these jobs with a very exalted title but devoid of content. Actually, it sounds pretty much like he's no more than some sort of consultant without a client. It's hard to imagine he's very happy. In any event, he'll never be able to work in French industry again. France is over for him."

Labrousse stared down at the table, making imaginary patterns on its spotless surface with his finger. After a few seconds his reverie broke and he caught the eye of the girl behind the bar. She queried with one barely raised eyebrow. He half nodded back. She appeared promptly with another bottle. Labrousse shook his head sadly. "Paris is over for me as well."